WASP SEASON

JENNIFER SCOULLAR

PILYARA PRESS

A catalogue record for this book is available from the National Library of Australia

Wasp Season
Version 1.0
ISBN: 978-1-925827-25-5

Cover art by Kellie Dennis at Book Cover By Design

Pilyara Press
Melbourne

To my parents, Doug and Alice Scoullar

Let us turn elsewhere, to the wasps and bees, who unquestionably come first in the laying up of heritage for their offspring.

— JEAN-HENRI FABRE

PROLOGUE

The fallen tree lay in a paddock behind Beth's house. A fierce mountain storm had uprooted it the previous autumn. Beth had tried to cut it up for firewood, but the giant gum tree and its broad hardwood trunk proved too much of a challenge for her small chainsaw. Eventually she'd hired a local handyman. Although he had yet to complete the task, Beth didn't mind too much. She knew that fallen timber was an asset in the natural scheme of things, providing a habitat for scores of insects.

She did not foresee that this might include European wasps.

One bright spring morning, high above Beth's house, a wasp queen was searching for a place to nest. Her big yellow body and jet black bands distinguished her from most other insects. Long black antennae, set high on her head, tasted the warm breeze. Iridescent wings beat impossibly fast as she surveyed Beth's garden.

She descended from a clear azure sky in lazy spirals to alight upon the fallen tree. When she was at rest, her wings folded lengthwise like leaves of a fan. Behind her narrow waist, a smooth, plump abdomen carried distinctive black V shapes, accompanied by rows of dots on either side. The tip of her abdomen hid a thin, pointed drill – her sting. The painful sting of the European wasp did not contain barbs like that of a honeybee. Therefore, she could strike her victims repeatedly.

This founding queen inspected her potential home with great care. She investigated every twig, fallen leaf and hollow. At last, with a satisfied tap of her antennae, the foundress made her decision. This was the place.

Of course, she wasn't the first one to discover the fallen tree. Centipedes and scorpions wriggled under it. Spiders crouched between its bark and trunk. A nest of tiny blind termites lived at one end, and a soft green carpet of lichens and moss grew over it, trapping raindrops and dew, hastening the tree's inevitable decay.

Many creatures used the rotting log as a nursery. Their eggs came in an array of fantastic shapes and shades. Tiny golden cocoons cradled the eggs of earthworms and leeches. Lizards buried pearl-like eggs in the rich humus. Wood-boring beetle eggs hatched into fat white grubs with bright orange heads, surrounded by all the food they could ever eat.

Some log dwellers actively protected their young. A mother centipede lay coiled protectively around her pale brood. A huntsman spider crouched over her flat white egg sac. The spiderlings would remain with their devoted mother for a month or more. An earwig guarded fifty eggs, diligently cleaning them of fungus while waiting for them to hatch.

A bush cockroach stayed by her hard egg case, which was almost ready to split and release her nymphs. She would rear them in an underground chamber, dutifully chewing wood into pulp to feed her babies.

None of these creatures, however, could equal the European wasp queen when it came to maternal devotion. She stood at the apex of waspine evolution, ready to single-handedly create a complex and remarkably caring society. She would feed and protect her young during their miraculous metamorphosis from helpless blind grubs to highly developed adults. They in turn would stay home to care for their mother and siblings.

With no natural predators in her adopted Australian home, the queen presented a ruthless and indomitable threat to the residents of the log and surrounding bushland. By the end of summer, her nest might number many thousands of individuals. This glorious future depended on the foundress choosing carefully and well during the coming months. A long and challenging road lay ahead of her.

CHAPTER ONE

A European wasp landed on Beth's kitchen windowsill.
She stopped washing dishes in the sink and studied the resting insect. It was bright and boldly coloured – striped like a tiger and really quite beautiful. Yes, the European wasp was an imported pest. Yes, it was a nuisance to picnickers and campers. However, as with all introduced species, the wasp itself was blameless, simply striving to survive in an alien world. Its presence was due to human interference in the natural scheme of things.

The wasp buzzed off the sill and disappeared into the garden.

As she gazed after it, another wasp flew into view. This one carried something in its strong jaws. Straight away, Beth recognised the wasp's prey – a fat emperor gum moth caterpillar. It struggled desperately, resplendent in emerald green coat and bright red standards.

Beth caught a horrified breath.

A vivid memory catapulted her back to childhood. She could see the ancient peppercorn trees standing firmly between the family's weatherboard house and the noise of the train line.

Adapting to a lack of gum trees, inner-city emperor gum moths laid their eggs on the peppercorn leaves. As a little girl, Beth had been intrigued by them. The bench seats of the old tramcar in her backyard were cluttered with jars containing sprigs of freshly picked pepper-corn, laden with eggs and hungry caterpillars at different stages of their life cycle. Nurturing them had inspired in Beth a lifelong rever-ence for the natural world.

The wasp lost hold of its struggling prey. With heart in mouth, Beth rushed outside to find the caterpillar lying on the path. But the determined wasp wasn't done yet. It dived down to renew the attack. Only after several angry swipes from Beth did it abandon its plump prize.

She turned her attention to rescuing the caterpillar. Rearing on fleshy hind legs, it brandished its mandibles to confront this new threat. Green blood seeped from where the wasp's powerful jaws had tried to crush its head. Beth carried the injured caterpillar to the edge of her garden, placed it on a young ironbark tree and wished it luck.

She wandered back through the fragrant garden. How glorious it was in springtime, crammed with flowers and a riot of colour. It framed the house, making it look like a picture postcard. Beth caught a fleeting glimpse of another wasp hovering among the scarlet blooms of a bottlebrush. The sight caused her an unexpected chill. Time to go inside and do some research.

Beth loved her home, a large and comfortable two-storey dwelling of cream weatherboards. Upon the walls, photographs of her children hung beside Tom Roberts prints and various landscape paintings that she'd found in second-hand shops. The floor was scuffed parquet, a blend of deep browns. Walls of forest green met high white skirting boards. The house had been built in the 1950s and although old-fash-ioned, was warm and welcoming and full of charm.

Beth had fallen in love with this house in the mountains several years ago. She and her husband, Mark, had purchased it as a country getaway, along with a few acres of paddocks and bushland. Beth named the property Benbullen, an indigenous word for *quiet high place*. She'd hoped it would provide Mark with some respite from the stress of his city accounting practice; help him to see that there was more to life than fat bonuses and corner offices and runaway ambition.

But it hadn't worked out that way. Beth could count on one hand the number of times they'd spent an entire weekend together at Benbullen. Mark was too caught up in the professional rat-race to be able to slow down and enjoy the peace. Even so, he'd been a good husband in the early years. They'd enjoyed a secure and loving marriage, punctuated by the birth of Sarah and then Rick, two years later.

Motherhood had come to Beth as an unexpected, blinding joy. Mark, on the other hand, experienced little of the happiness she felt. An ever-increasing workload meant he spent less and less time with his young family, and Beth watched with dismay as her husband became increasingly absorbed in his frantic climb up the career ladder. Inevitably they grew apart and Beth had moved permanently to Benbullen with the children.

Their breakup had been messy and painful, but it had not left Beth broken-hearted. Her marriage had been a lonely place for too long. She told herself that being single again at thirty-five wasn't the end of the world; that it gave her a chance to rediscover herself and what mattered in life. She'd begun by having her long red hair cut into a short, stylish bob. She lived in jeans and T-shirts instead of the fashionable clothes that Mark had loved her to wear; clothes that showed off her tall slender figure. Yes, there were times when she still felt lonely, but Beth liked who she was becoming. She could even say that she was happy again, at least happier than she'd been for a long time,

She wouldn't be happy if wasps took over her garden, though. Beth did a quick google of *European wasps* on her laptop and was disturbed by what she found. They could cause a lot of damage to the local habitat. She'd have to drive into town and buy a wasp trap. Beth tugged a comb through her hair and went out the back way, tired of dodging the bees swarming the rambling roses near the front door.

Full of purpose, she drove to her local hardware store. There were several brands of trap that all worked on the same principle – a chamber to fill with bait, and an entrance that wouldn't be an obvious escape route for the insects. Beth made her choice, bought some punnets of vegetable seedlings and drove straight home. When in town she usually stopped to do some shopping or have a coffee at the corner cafe. Not today. Today she felt oddly single-minded.

Back at home, Beth considered possible baits. They could apparently be sweet or savoury. Sugar, honey, or jam in a little water. Wine or orange juice left to ferment. Dog food straight from the can. She settled on honey-water, hung the trap on the lasiandra tree outside the kitchen window, then returned inside.

As she waited and watched, Beth let her thoughts wander. The family relied on rainwater tanks. Sometimes they bucketed bathwater onto the garden and into the stock troughs. She'd done so that very morning. The water troughs were a gathering place for throngs of shining dragonflies, darting to and fro on rainbow wings. But that morning, these aerial acrobats were joined by the odd tiger-striped wasp. Their presence deepened her sense of unease.

With one eye on her new trap, Beth finished washing the dishes in the kitchen sink. Not a wasp in sight. She felt a pang of disappointment. The ringing phone startled her. 'Hello, Mark. Yes, they'll be ready by five o'clock.'

Despite their two-year separation, for some reason neither she nor Mark had sought a divorce. However, that hadn't stopped Mark from moving on, and quickly. He no longer lived alone in their inner-city townhouse. His girlfriend Lena, short for Helena, and their new baby lived there too.

Mark's rebound family, as Beth called it, hadn't disrupted the friendly custody arrangements regarding their children – Sarah who was twelve and Rick who was ten. Mark was due to pick the kids up that evening for a regular weekend access visit.

Beth frowned. That morning Rick had said he didn't want to go.

When she'd asked him why, he muttered something about his dad having 'lost the plot'. What on earth did that mean? Sarah though, would be as delighted as ever – a real daddy's little girl, that one. In addition, baby Chance was a delightful novelty for her, and his mother, Lena, loved to spoil Sarah.

Lena had been Mark's personal assistant before the separation. Beth suspected that Lena's relationship with Mark overlapped her own at some point, but what did it matter now? At twenty-five, the girl was younger than Mark by more than a decade, and Beth found it hard to take her seriously. Although she was grateful that Lena always seemed to make her kids feel welcome.

Beth busied herself packing the children's things. It was the start of a long weekend, and they wouldn't be home until Monday night. She was looking forward to a few lazy days. Each time she passed through the kitchen, she glanced at the trap. Still no wasps.

When the kids tumbled in the front door after school, Beth had their bags packed and ready. Sarah searched through hers, then gave her mother a reproachful pout. 'You forgot Timmy.'

Timmy was Sarah's threadbare puppy dog pyjama case. Generations of children in the family had stuffed their pyjamas into Timmy's zippered tummy, Beth included. 'You said you were too old for Timmy.'

Sarah gave a little eye roll. 'He's not for me, Mum. He's for the baby. Timmy helps Chance go to sleep.'

Beth smiled and went upstairs to fetch the toy for Sarah. Such a sweet girl, always trying her best to keep the peace within her divided family. Beth found Timmy on Sarah's pillow. She stopped to look at a photo of Sarah and her pony that had been made into a poster. People said Sarah was the image of her mother, with her red hair, pale skin, and freckled nose. Her eyes too were like Beth's – serious, green eyes that observed the world from beneath her straight fringe.

Beth viewed Sarah's valiant attempts to keep everybody happy with a mixture of admiration and gentle amusement. The only person

Sarah had no patience with was her brother. Rick was small for his ten years, with blond, curly hair and melting brown eyes like his father's. Emotional and highly imaginative, Rick was inclined to get himself into trouble by speaking his mind no matter where he was. He remained a source of constant embarrassment to his polite sister.

Beth came downstairs to find Sarah stuffing more and more things into her bulging overnight bag: an extra top and pair of jeans, a bead kit for making jewellery, more books. Beth added Timmy to the pile.

Rick seemed to have overcome his reluctance to go to his father's. 'I'm hungry,' he announced, and followed his mother to the kitchen. 'What's that?' He pointed to the transparent plastic orb hanging outside the window.

At first, Rick was intrigued by the idea of the trap and watched it while Beth made a sandwich. However, no wasps quickly led to no interest.

Not so with Beth. She wanted to observe the first contact and continued to gaze at the trap long after Mark had picked up the children. Only the fading light drove her from the window.

CHAPTER TWO

Beth rose early the next day. She'd started teaching four mornings a week at Waverley Downs, a local equestrian school, and she enjoyed the work. The modest wage helped to buy the family some little extras: the latest *Brumby Mountain* book for Sarah, a computer game for Rick, a special bottle of wine to share with her friend, Karen.

That morning Beth took a group of young riders and worked with them on their own horses. They were a talented bunch. She loved watching them establish the elusive bond that developed with time between rider and mount.

After some parting advice to her pupils, Beth turned to leave. A voice hailed her. Noah. He managed Waverley Downs for the middle-aged owners, who left the day-to-day running of the place to him. She supposed that made Noah her boss. Not that you'd know it. His relaxed management style created an atmosphere of harmony and loyalty among everyone who worked there. And his dazzling horsemanship left Beth open-mouthed with admiration.

Noah was about her own age – a long, lean man with a face bronzed by wind and sun. He was also the first man that Beth had fancied since she'd broken up with Mark. She didn't expect anything to come of it. She kept her attraction well controlled, but it was there.

Noah grinned and gestured towards the stables. 'I want to show you something.' He pointed to a stall containing Tango, the school's new horse. Beth had seen the fat piebald mare being unloaded from a float earlier that morning.

She joined Noah, who was leaning on the stable door watching Tango munch some sweet lucerne hay. 'What do you think of our latest addition?' he asked.

'She's pretty, but she could lose a little weight.'

His clear blue eyes crinkled with pleasure. 'I don't think that will be a problem.' Noah opened the door and waved for her to follow him inside. He squatted beside the mare and Beth crouched beside him. 'Feel there. No, lower on her belly.' He took her hand and gently guided it. When Noah let go of her hand, Beth felt an unexpected twinge of disappointment. Tango's glossy black flank rippled beneath her fingers, and Beth distinctly felt a kick from the inside. Her eyes widened. 'You mean …?'

Noah put his cheek against the mare's flank. 'Hello little fella. How're you doing in there?' Beth couldn't stifle a smile. 'What?' he said to her in mock indignation. 'I always talk to them. They come out trusting me that way, knowing my voice.'

'What use is a pregnant mare to a riding school?' asked Beth, delighted to feel another strong kick.

'She was sold as a gypsy cob suitable for beginners,' said Noah. 'No mention of her being in foal. The owners bought her without consulting me.' He chuckled. 'I bet they won't do that again.'

'So you don't know when she's due?'

'She's waxing up.' Noah pointed to Tango's udder. A pale substance was oozing from each teat, forming what looked like little icicles. 'I'd say she'll drop within forty-eight hours.'

Beth felt a flush of excitement. She turned to see Noah watching her instead of Tango. Her flush deepened. He looked very handsome, with his sandy, sun-streaked hair and his mouth curled as if always on the edge of laughter. A complete contrast to Mark's brooding good looks.

Noah stood up, the strength of his thighs evident beneath his breeches. He reached out a hand and helped Beth to her feet. 'I can't wait for the birth,' she said. 'Is it okay to bring my kids along when the foal is born?'

Noah grinned again, filling the stall with warmth and good humour. 'I'll call you when it happens.'

Beth waved goodbye and headed for her car, thinking of the coming foal and thinking of Noah. She liked him, and he seemed to like her. For the first time, she wondered if he was interested in something more than friendship. Karen said that after being single for two years it was time for her to move on. Beth wasn't sure she was ready, but when she was, Noah was just the sort of man she'd choose.

Beth drove home dusty, tired and happy, intending to go for a ride herself after lunch. The long weekend stretched invitingly before her. But when she went into the kitchen, one glance out of the window glued her to the spot. Buzzing uncertainly within the confines of the small trap were four wasps. Circumnavigating the trap were half a dozen more. Beth watched the increasing panic of the trapped insects with decidedly mixed emotions. Hovering in confusion above the sweet liquid, one wasp dipped a little too low …

Beth was astonished at the energy with which the wasp began to swim. Her first instinct was to rush out and rescue it, as she did with butterflies and beetles that fell into the birdbaths dotted around her garden. But she couldn't do that, could she? The whole point of the exercise was to kill the wasps. She'd deliberately set the trap for that very purpose. All she could do was watch as the powerful insect swam and swam, hoping to gain some foothold on the sides. But the walls were smooth and curved, designed to give no purchase to tiny, hooked feet.

A second, then a third wasp hit the water. One managed by sheer wing power to lift free of the surface tension. Momentarily, Beth felt thrilled that it was safe. But of course it was doomed. After several minutes of fruitless, frantic buzzing within the trap, each insect, due to a combination of battered wings and exhaustion, dropped into the water.

Beth could no longer watch. She made herself a coffee and left the kitchen. The wasps were just doing their job, she thought sadly; collecting food for their queen and larvae. Curiosity compelled her to take a book about insects off her shelf. She owned a decent collection of field guides. They helped her to identify the myriad birds, small mammals and invertebrates that lived at Benbullen. She wondered if European wasps organised their nests like honeybees.

Vespula germanica, she read. *Each nest is founded by a mated female who rears the first generation of all-female brood by herself. These become workers and take over the task of nest building and collecting food for the young. The queen then confines herself to egg-laying. Colony defence and the day-to-day perils of foraging often result in the death of these worker wasps.*

Beth was genuinely inspired by this self-sacrifice and devotion to duty. She imagined the wasps setting out each day, some never to return, a bit like bomber pilots during a war. But then her mind returned to the ruthless attack she'd witnessed on the emperor gum moth caterpillar. Few native insects would be a match for these powerful alien marauders. The thought helped her to justify the trap, but she still avoided looking at it. Instead, she went for a ride, leaving the helpless wasps to continue their futile swim into oblivion.

CHAPTER THREE

Weekends without the children always seemed to last longer. Beth found herself slipping into a kind of slow motion. She rose late on Sunday morning. What a luxury, just suiting herself. Without the need to cook meals and ferry the children here and there, time held no sway over her. She took her breakfast out to the verandah and lazily planned her day.

The honey on Beth's toast attracted a wasp. Her hand brushed against it as she reached for the second slice. Startled, she jumped to her feet and swatted at the insect. After several ineffective attempts to drive the intruder away, Beth conceded defeat and retreated inside. She checked the trap. A dozen dead wasps floated in the water. Now they were dead, she was pleased. Her ambivalence of the previous afternoon had evaporated.

The clear sky and brisk morning air promised a glorious October day. Beth donned old clothes and set about planting the new seedlings in the vegetable garden. When she stood up to stretch, her gaze fell on her home's ivy-covered walls. Picturesque though it was, she'd have to have the ivy removed. It had flowered profusely last autumn, and the dozens of young ivy plants sprouting from her paths could also be colonising the nearby bush gullies. Ivy was potentially a significant environmental weed. Still, it would be a pity, especially in January, when its cool green mantle no longer insulated the house from the fierce summer sun.

Rambling roses trailed up the ivy, using it like a trellis to scale the weatherboards. Beth stopped to admire the bright beauty of their blooms and noticed something odd. At first glance they seemed to be swarming with bees, busy collecting nectar from the abundant crop of vivid pink flowers. But a closer inspection revealed that the insects were, in fact, European wasps. Not a single bee remained.

Beth was incredulous. During the course of one short week the invaders had utterly displaced the legion of honeybees. A wasp buzzed in her direction and she sprinted for the safety of the house. She couldn't help herself, although she knew it posed no real threat. Foraging wasps were innocuous, preoccupied creatures, much more inclined to fly away than fight. Only when their nest was threatened would they display the group aggression they were infamous for – attacking intruders and stinging en masse.

The incident left Beth thoroughly unnerved, and she resolved to increase her trapping rate. Of course the only permanent way to control the wasps was to destroy the nest. But where was it? A quick inspection of her home's exposed timber eaves revealed nothing. She was reduced to eliminating the insects one by one.

She found a webpage that gave simple instructions for making traps. Using plastic bottles salvaged from the recycle bin, Beth commenced construction. First, she sliced the top off each bottle just below where the neck narrowed. Then she inverted the top, inserting it into the opening to form a funnel entrance which fitted snugly against the sides. A little glue to finish and she had homemade traps along the lines of the commercially manufactured one.

Beth continued her production line until she ran out of bottles. Now she had seven traps and decided to conduct an experiment using a variety of baits. A little tub of pineapple pieces past its use-by date, bubbling with natural fermentation at the back of the fridge. Orange juice in another, cola in one, tuna in another. She taped the new traps to the lasiandra tree beside the first, and soon observed wasps hovering about. Within minutes, the tuna had trapped several of them.

Beth noted the individual success rates of the various baits. Time slipped away.

The sound of the phone startled her. With a stab of irritation, she paused in her observations to answer it. Karen's cheerful voice greeted her. She glanced at the clock, surprised to see it was so late.

'Hi,' she answered absent-mindedly, her mind still on the little drama playing outside her kitchen window. 'Come over. I'm not doing anything.'

Karen was Beth's best friend ever since school. The pair had steadfastly supported each other through life's ups and downs. Beth was there when Karen and her children escaped a marriage plagued by domestic violence – another kind of trap, Beth thought. Likewise, Karen provided company and childminding when Beth's own marriage was reeling. She'd even moved from town so she could be closer. Now happily remarried to Paul, they were a living example of how well a stepfamily could work with a lot love and compromise all round.

Half an hour later Karen rolled up the tree-lined drive in her battered old Land Rover. She was slim and vivacious, with wild blonde hair pulled back in a messy ponytail. Although the same age as Beth, Karen always seemed like a younger sister. Karen smoked, drank too much, drove too fast and wore her heart on her sleeve. Cautious Beth envied her friend her brimming enthusiasm for life.

'What are you trying to do here?' asked Karen as they poured themselves a coffee. Outside the kitchen window, the array of traps reflected the rays of the late afternoon sun. A light breeze made them jostle together like some bizarre wind chime.

Time to secure them more firmly, Beth noted to herself. The movement could deter her prey. 'I have a European wasp problem,' she said. 'I'm trying out different traps.'

'Goodness, you have been busy,' laughed Karen. 'It looks like a wasp smorgasbord out there. When you do something, you sure don't do it by halves, do you?'

It had been a warm day, but spring evenings cooled quickly, so the two friends decided to eat inside. They put some foil-wrapped salmon fillets in the oven, and while Beth tossed together a salad, Karen opened the bottle of wine she always brought along on such occasions. Through the open window they could hear the dusk chorus of cicadas tuning up. Before long, it would rise to a deafening crescendo.

As usual, Karen inquired about her friend's non-existent love life, and for once Beth stopped short of a full-blown denial. 'It's about time.' Karen poured them both a drink. 'Tell me *everything*.'

'There's not much to tell. His name's Noah and he manages the riding school. He's a wonderful horseman.'

Karen gave her a knowing smile. 'Does Noah have any other good qualities?'

'Well yes. He's sweet and funny and kind ...'

'And good-looking?'

'And good-looking,' said Beth.

'And single?'

'Of *course* he's single. What do you take me for? Anyway, I think he likes me too. I can't be sure, it's just a feeling.'

Karen was delighted. 'Ask him out.'

Beth rolled her eyes.

'Why not?' asked Karen. 'That's how I got Paul.'

'Yes, but that's you.'

'True. Ask him for a favour, then. Say it's important. Men love feeling important.' Karen looked thoughtful. 'You say he's a horseman.'

'He certainly is. One of the best I've seen.'

'Okay, tell him your horses desperately need exercising and you can't ride them both at once.'

This was true. Beth had bought Caesar for Mark to ride, but he'd never been interested. 'I'll think about it,' Beth promised.

The topic of conversation moved to their children. Beth told Karen about Rick's increasing reluctance to visit his father on weekends.

Karen frowned. 'There must be some reason for a sudden turn-around like that. What do you think it is?' Beth didn't know, but resolved to take the matter up with Rick on his return. She'd always enjoyed a close, easy communication with her son, and it bothered her that he was shutting her out.

After dinner they opened another bottle of wine, argued about politics, listened to music, and generally enjoyed themselves until a knock at the door announced Paul's arrival. He always dutifully collected Karen on these occasions, aware the two friends often had the odd wine or three. Beth was grateful for Paul's attention to Karen's needs. She felt an unexpected prickle of envy. It would be nice to have somebody like that in her own life.

Karen hugged her. 'I'll pick up the Land Rover in the morning.'

Beth said goodbye and went upstairs. Perhaps she'd watch the late movie. Tonight, it was an Alfred Hitchcock thriller, *The Birds*. She fell asleep before the horror began.

When Beth woke the next morning she sat up, bleary-eyed, unsure for a moment what day it was. Of course – Monday, last day of the long weekend. She sank back on her pillow and let her mind wander. She smiled as she remembered the previous evening – Karen was always great company.

Later, standing in the kitchen with her morning coffee, Beth glanced at the new traps. The wasps that had spent the night in them weren't dead. They wandered sticky, cold and exhausted around their prison. Two had even crawled out of the opening, only to find that their damaged wings would not fly them home. They set about trying to clean themselves in a weary, useless fashion. She felt a gush of pity. This slow, creeping death was crueller than drowning the wasps in the liquid lures.

Beth's thoughts turned to the European wasp queen, safe in the nest somewhere. Was she aware that some of her workers had not returned? Did she worry about the welfare of her growing larval brood? Was she grateful for the self-sacrifice of her daughters? Beth wondered why the worker wasps struggled so hard to ensure the survival of the queen's offspring, their sisters, when they themselves did not reproduce?

The sudden barking of her dogs alerted Beth to someone's arrival. She peered out the window, then glanced at the clock – only ten o'clock. The children weren't due home until that afternoon.

Mark strode through the front door without knocking. He was an attractive man, tall and well built. He had dark, wavy hair, even features and he carried himself with a commanding air of self-confidence. However, Beth had long since grown immune to his appeal.

Rick marched in wearing a wooden expression. Even patient Sarah seemed put out.

'Is something wrong?' asked Beth. 'You're all back so early.' She looked around at the debris from the night before, annoyed that Mark had arrived before she'd had a chance to tidy up.

'The baby has some sort of a bug,' said Mark. 'Lena's been up all night with him. She's exhausted, so she asked me to bring the kids home.'

'I didn't hear Lena say that,' piped Sarah, her voice high with indignation. 'She told me that she wanted us to stay. I was helping her. She said I was a big help.'

Sarah adored her baby brother and prided herself on being a perfect big sister. Lena sometimes complained lightheartedly that she never got to see Chance on access weekends. Sarah was too busy looking after her little living doll.

'No, Lena said you were just getting in the way,' snapped her father. Sarah grabbed her overnight bag and flounced from the room, as only a self-righteous twelve-year-old girl can.

Beth rinsed out her coffee cup, surprised by Mark's words. Sarah was a highly capable, sensible child, and Lena adored her. Beth couldn't imagine that Lena would ever refer to Sarah as *being in the way*. Still, after a sleepless night, Beth supposed that even the good-natured Lena could get a bit grumpy.

'No worries. I'd just like you to ring first next time to make sure I'm home,' said Beth.

'Why? You never go anywhere.'

He looked at the full ashtray and unwashed dishes with an expression of distaste, silently requesting an explanation. Beth glared at him and repeated her request for a phone call next time. Mark called out goodbye to Sarah and gave his son a playful punch on the arm before leaving.

Rick headed for the kitchen and Beth went after Sarah, concerned her feelings had been hurt. She found her daughter sulking on her bed, playing with Spooky, their white Persian cat.

'What's up, kid?' Beth asked.

Turning her tear-stained face towards her mother, Sarah blurted out that it wasn't Lena who'd wanted them to go home early. 'It was Dad. Chance wasn't even sick. Dad was just in a bad mood. I know he sometimes yells at Rick, but he never usually yells at me. This time he was even mean to Lena.'

Beth comforted her daughter and tried to distract her by suggesting that they go and bake something. Sarah brightened and trotted downstairs to take the old yellow *Margaret Fulton Cookbook* down from the shelf. She was happy to see her daughter's mood lift, but remained annoyed at Mark's insensitivity.

Beth was proud that, as co-parents, they'd always managed to put their differences aside for the children's sake. Up until now Mark had been an attentive father, and she'd had little to complain about. He was generous with child support and reliable with access arrangements. Beth's personal interactions with him remained politely cold. He, in turn, showed scant interest in her life. This suited Beth perfectly. It worried her that Mark seemed to be unilaterally changing their arrangement.

Rick had cheered up at the prospect of cake. Beth didn't have the heart to tackle him about his father and risk upsetting him. That conversation could wait. For the rest of the afternoon she and the kids settled back into their comfortable family routine. Sarah baked muffins and Rick ate muffins. They argued over the computer, had dinner and watched television until bedtime.

Beth had forgotten the wasps.

CHAPTER FOUR

The dapple grey mare thundered towards the striped bars of the jump. Her body quivered and her ears snapped forward as Beth used her heels to indicate the precise moment for the mare to rise. Easily, gracefully, she cleared the obstacle with a stylish kick of her heels and flick of her tail. Beth circled the horse at a collected canter, finally coming to a halt beside a dark-haired girl standing in the centre of the riding arena.

The girl kissed the mare on the nose, eyes shining with excitement and pride.

'Why doesn't she jump like that for me?'

Beth dismounted, smiled in an encouraging way and gave the young rider a leg-up.

'It's all in the hands and seat. You have a beautiful mare here with loads of potential. In time you'll learn to work together as partners. Right now, you both need more practice. So let's go.'

For the next hour Beth devoted herself to her enthusiastic pupil. What a privilege to watch the girl and mare progress so quickly. At some point during the lesson, Noah appeared by the railing. Beth didn't know how long he'd been watching, leaning with lazy nonchalance against an arena post, chewing on a piece of sourgrass. He gave her a wave and Karen's advice came back in a rush. Could she ask him to help exercise her horses? Could she summon up the nerve?

Noah ducked under the rail and strolled over with a loose, long-limbed stride. 'Well done,' he told the student. 'I think you're ready for that C Grade jumping comp at Berwick next week.' She squealed with excitement and led her mare off towards the wash bays.

Noah turned to Beth. 'You've done an amazing job. It's hard to believe she's the same nervous girl who started here three months ago.'

He was still talking, but Beth wasn't listening – too distracted to be flattered. How could she invite Noah to her house in a way that wouldn't sound contrived?

'Beth?' He touched her arm. 'I asked about your horses?'

'Oh.' This was too perfect. 'Well, the kids have a palomino pony called Skittles, and I mainly ride Shannon, a black Anglo Arabian mare. She's lovely, but rather highly strung. Then there's Caesar, my chestnut Warmblood – 16.2 hands high and a real handful.' Beth ran her tongue over dry lips. 'The trouble is ...' She could almost hear Karen urging her on. 'The trouble is I don't have enough time to work them both.'

Noah responded without hesitation. 'Can I help?'

Beth felt heat rising, flooding her cheeks with warmth – she who was usually so cool and collected. The strength of the reaction took her by surprise. She silently counted to five, unwilling to rush her reply. 'That would be great.' She could hear the slight stammer in her voice.

Noah pressed the point. 'How about tomorrow? I have Saturday off.'

She nodded, feeling like a breathless girl of eighteen. Her instincts had been right. This was a mutual attraction. Whatever was she getting herself into?

Beth began the short drive home, feeling happier than she could remember. Purple swamphens foraged with their chicks in long grass by the side of the road. Tango and her three-week-old colt raced along the fence beside the car, bucking and kicking with the sun on their backs. Late spring, with its burgeoning new life, was Beth's favourite time of the year.

She turned onto the winding forest road, and the beauty of her surroundings struck her afresh. How she loved living here in the mountains, with a clear blue sky peeping through the canopy of gum tree crowns. The road left the trees and emerged into a patchwork quilt of red ploughed paddocks and green pastures. Contented cows grazed in daisy-studded fields. A wedge-tailed eagle soared in solitary circles over the ridge to her left. White ibis foraged in flocks along the river valley to her right, and scattered wattle blossom gave the whole world a sun-kissed effect. Beth whistled a tune as she neared the entrance to her tree-lined driveway. Life didn't get much better.

There was only one shadow on her horizon. It was Friday afternoon, and Mark was due to pick up the children after dinner. Beth wasn't looking forward to dealing with Rick, who would be back from school by the time she got home. The access weekends were now a decidedly sore point, and Beth felt guilty pressing him to go. She hated seeing him sulky and depressed, but she also knew it was important for him to see his father. Beth remembered her resolve to talk to her son and get to the bottom of his changed feelings. She had neglected to do so.

Beth found Rick and Sarah arguing in the kitchen. Rick seemed in a reasonably good mood. His dad had promised to take him bowling. Perhaps some fun time spent together would ease the tension between them. For some reason Sarah hadn't been invited and was making her protests loud and clear.

'What about me?' she wailed.

Rick grinned at his sister in triumph and poked out his tongue.

'Stop it, Rick,' scolded Beth. 'Go upstairs and check that you're all packed.'

Beth took Sarah's hand and sat her down at the kitchen table. 'Honey, it sounds like your dad has planned a boys' day out,' she said in a soothing voice. 'Ask him to take *you* somewhere special time next time, just the two of you. The Melbourne Aquarium perhaps, or the Zoo?'

Sarah's freckled brow creased in an uncharacteristic frown.

Beth tried again. 'Or you could do something with Lena. What about that new movie you want to see? They have special sessions at the Dendy where people can take babies.'

Sarah made a face and rolled her eyes.

'I don't understand,' said Beth. 'I thought you loved spending time with Lena.'

'Not anymore. Lately, all she does is bitch about dad.'

'Really?' Beth traced a knot of wood in the tabletop with her finger. She shouldn't ask, she knew that, but couldn't help herself. 'What sort of things does Lena say?'

Sarah heaved a great sigh. 'She says Dad's always on at her about spending money. You know, shopping and maxing out her credit cards. Lena complains a *lot*. Calls him a stingy bore and a penny-pinching miser. She's become a real whinger.'

Beth stared at Sarah, disbelieving. It was totally inappropriate for Lena to badmouth Mark in front of his daughter. She had no right to involve Sarah in her private relationship problems. Children deserved to be protected from adult issues, not put squarely in the middle of them. Not that Lena's complaints made any sense. The Mark that Beth knew was generous, even careless with his money. When they were together, she'd been the one to pull in the purse strings when needed. Had he really changed so much?

It was Sarah's turn to stare. 'Mum, are you okay? Your mouth is open.'

Beth swept up her puzzled daughter in a great hug. 'I'm fine, darling. Now go and make sure you're all packed.

Mark arrived early. He walked through the front door and straight into the kitchen. Beth fought against a surge of irritation and almost challenged him. But he seemed in a conciliatory mood and she didn't want to start an argument. It was important for this weekend to go well. She hoped it would put Rick and his father back on track.

Beth made coffee, and they chatted idly in the kitchen while the kids fetched last-minute additions to their bags.

Mark glanced out the window and saw the traps. 'What's all this?'

'I have a wasp problem.'

'Get an exterminator.'

'It's not that simple,' said Beth. 'I can't find the nest.'

He flashed her his most charming smile. 'I'll find it for you.'

Beth stiffened and the sip of sweet coffee suddenly tasted sour. So Mark still thought he could solve all her problems. 'Why exactly do you think you could find the nest when I can't?'

Old feelings of resentment took hold, and she was reminded of why she'd left him.

'Keep your shirt on,' he laughed. 'Or then again ... maybe not.' Without warning, Mark moved close and attempted a clumsy kiss. One hand fondled her left breast. Beth pushed him away and stepped sideways. Too shocked for words, she fled from the kitchen.

When Beth returned with the children, Mark behaved like nothing out of the ordinary had happened. She bundled them all out the door as quickly as she could, watching the car drive away with a creeping sense of unease.

What on earth was going on with Mark? Over the past two years he'd never shown the slightest physical interest in her. At the beginning Beth had even been a little hurt by how easily and completely he'd been able to cut himself off. But at least it had kept things simple. She didn't need this sort of a complication in her life. Hopefully it was an isolated incident; an aberration brought on by some temporary difficulty with Lena.

A walk might settle her thoughts. Outside, the beauty of the approaching evening helped distract her from her worries. The rollicking laughter of the local kookaburras made Beth smile. They always seemed to know something about her that was worth laughing at. Dragonflies darted here and there, catching and reflecting the late rays of the sun on rainbow wings. An eastern spinebill, handsome in chestnut and white plumage, hovered hummingbird-like to feed from a flower. The sky remained a brilliant blue, only fading where it met the mountains.

Beth headed across the lawn to the path that led down to the stables. Beyond the stable, two horses and a pony grazed in a paddock, flanked by a gully of gum trees. They raised their heads at Beth's approach and, one by one, came over to the fence. Caesar led the way, prancing and tossing his copper-coloured mane, showing off like the glamour boy he was. How would Noah handle him tomorrow? The headstrong gelding was bound to test out any new rider.

Shannon strolled over more sedately, giving a friendly whinny and flicking at flies with her shining black tail. Last came Skittles, their palomino pony who, Beth noted, could do with losing some weight.

As she affectionately rubbed their faces, a flash of black and yellow beneath the stable eaves caught her eye. She went to investigate and found a series of neat clay cylinders nestled in a cavity between the flashing and stable wall. A wasp was packing a mouthful of mud onto a partially finished cell. At first Beth mistook the insect for a European wasp. Had she solved the mystery of the nest location? But on second glance she realised this was an entirely different insect.

Beth had discovered a nest of native mud daubers, also known as potter wasps. Despite a superficial resemblance to its European cousin, this wasp had a finer body structure and possessed an impossibly thin waist. Beth felt a little envious. Hard to believe such a fragile reed could support the wasp's plump abdomen. With its curled antennae, narrow waist, and delicate legs, the insect resembled a tiny, costumed ballet dancer.

Beth moved closer. The wasp made a loud contented, buzzing sound as she applied the mud pellet to the nest. How fascinating. The insect flew off to collect more mud, returning again and again until the little pot was nearly finished. Intrigued by the wasp's industry, Beth forgot the time.

It was almost too dark to see when the wasp returned with something besides mud in her jaws. Gripped firmly between her powerful mandibles was a large black house spider. The motionless spider was stuffed unceremoniously into the top of the clay cylinder. Beth was both spellbound and horrified.

Conceding that it was too dark to continue her observations, she headed for the house. She knew that some wasps paralysed living prey to provide food for their young. It was like something from a Gothic horror tale; the victim, buried alive, unable to move or scream, devoured alive by the wasp's voracious, slug-like infant. Beth shuddered. Could she rescue the spider? Reason told her that she could not. It would remain helplessly paralysed by venom from the wasp's sting, whether inside or outside of the grim nursery.

Beth's revulsion was tempered by a grudging respect. After all, the mother potter wasp was simply trying to protect and provide for her babies; labouring alone to construct and provision those stout mud walls. Paralysed spiders were an ingenious solution to a lack of refrigeration, as the food remained fresh. Immobilised prey could neither escape from nor damage their tomb.

In a weird way, Beth found herself identifying with the mother wasp. Would she do as much for her own children? Would she kill for them? Squirming out of the silly moral dilemma she'd somehow placed herself in, Beth headed indoors for a long, relaxing bath.

CHAPTER FIVE

Beth awoke to rays of morning light streaming through the window. Her mind cleared the fog of sleep, allowing yesterday's uncommon events to crowd in. Noah's eager offer of help, Mark's unwelcome advances. It was almost funny. After two years of living like a nun, she'd suddenly drawn the attention of two men at once.

Mark's clumsy pass had so unsettled her that she'd briefly thought about cancelling her ride with Noah after lunch. But no. What happened wasn't Noah's fault, and she might never gather the courage to ask him again. Beth stretched and jumped out of bed, determined to stay in a positive mood.

Such early sunshine heralded another perfect day. She dressed quickly and headed downstairs for breakfast. As she made toast, she saw that her traps, piled high with dead wasps, needed emptying again.

Despite the apparent success of these traps, the wasps remained a nuisance. Beth loved to eat out on the verandah, but their constant pestering had caused her to forgo this simple pleasure. Unwilling to fend off the pesky scavengers, she settled for breakfast in the sunroom.

Bay windows overlooked the garden where a troop of fairy-wrens was feeding. The jenny wrens' plain brown plumage was in dull contrast to the dazzling blue of a single male who lorded it over his harem. The tiny birds fluttered to and fro, pecking at the freshly mulched beds to disturb insects. Beth glanced around, relieved to see Spooky lying asleep in a sunny patch of the floor. The wrens presented an easy target for such an accomplished killer.

The bright morning beckoned. She would head down to the stable and tidy up a bit; make sure that her tack was organised, and the saddles were clean. How long since she'd ridden out with a companion? Far too long. What a pleasure it would be.

Upon reaching the stable, the first thing Beth did was to check how the potter wasp's work was progressing. She arrived in time to see another unfortunate spider being shoved unceremoniously into the top of a seventh chamber. The queen sealed it with a mud plug and then spent several minutes running over the nest, inspecting each cylinder in turn. A final tap of her antennae and she seemed satisfied. With the job complete, the mother wasp flew away, never to return. She'd done all she would do for her young.

Beth gazed up at the little row of red clay pots, intrigued to see that the queen's technique had improved from the first to the last. She imagined their dark interiors. Within each cell lay a single egg, together with its allotted prey. They needed to be separated, as the voracious larvae would eat each other just as happily as they would their helpless spider victims.

A shudder trailed up Beth's spine. Sigourney Weaver and the *Alien* movies had nothing on this little drama.

Last night she'd spent hours researching potter wasps. According to the Australian Museum website, each species worked to a unique design blueprint. Some built nests resembling wrinkled brains. Others built mud jugs with tiny spouts. Beth inspected the remaining stable eaves, looking for signs of more potter wasp activity. What she found surprised her even more than her discovery of the previous afternoon.

On the opposite side of the stable hung another partially completed nest. This one was grey and seemed to be made of paper.

Honeycomb-shaped cells were visible underneath the structure, which hung suspended from a stout stem. Was this the European wasp nest? The arrival of its tenant soon dashed that hope. The wasp that landed bore no resemblance to its larger European cousin.

It was of medium size, slim and hairless with a narrow waist and short antennae. Orange bands encircled its dark brown body, and its narrow wings stuck out at an angle. Beth recognised the insect – a native paper wasp queen.

The nest posed a potential hazard because these wasps could sting, but Beth decided it was too far from the house to present any real danger. She would warn the kids to stay away, then enjoy watching nature at work, pleased that native wasps were holding their own against the foreign invaders.

The wasp stuck a pellet of chewed pulp onto an unfinished cell, moulding it into shape with her mandibles. Unlike the potter wasps, this was no sinister horror tale unfolding. The paper wasp queen was truly social, devoted to her children, striving to rear the first generation of brood all by herself. If she succeeded, they would live as an extended family of a few dozen workers, cooperating to raise the young. Beth felt quite protective towards the fledgling colony.

Such an exciting find. She took some photos. A major drawback of single life was that at times like these there was no one with whom to share the news. She didn't even have her children home. They weren't particularly interested in insects. They would have listened politely and then turned to each other, giggling. Yet it would still have been nice to have someone to tell.

The dogs began to bark in their run. Beth checked her phone. How could it be two o'clock already? She rushed about, tidying brushes, stacking feed buckets and hiding a torn rug behind a chaff bin. No time to sweep.

Beth looked up the hill towards the house, squinting into the sun and using a hand to shield her eyes. Noah was coming down the path. She gave him a wave.

Caesar whinnied and trotted to the fence, curious to meet the visitor. Beth rubbed his ears, slipped on a halter and opened the gate. 'Come on, mate,' she whispered. 'Let's have some fun.'

'He's a beauty.' Noah stroked Caesar's nose, visibly impressed. The horse, sensing admiration, arched his golden neck and sent out a trumpeting neigh.

'This is Caesar.' Beth handed the leading rein to Noah. 'He's yours for the day. I'll be riding that black mare.' Shannon was pawing at the rails, concerned that she'd be left behind.

They set about grooming the horses. 'This place is beautiful,' said Noah, looking around at the paddocks and gum tree gullies. 'Is that a creek down there?' He pointed to a line of trees at the bottom of the hill.

'Dingo Creek,' said Beth. 'If you sit on the bank and stay very still, you can sometimes see a platypus. And there are wombats and wallabies, even lyrebirds in the gullies. Benbullen really is a small slice of heaven.'

'You'll get no argument from me.' Noah took the bridle that Beth handed him and expertly guided the bit between Caesar's teeth. 'Since I'm currently living in a one-bedroom bungalow in a backyard at Bingham.' He grinned, sheepishly. 'Newly divorced. She got the house.'

'That's tough,' said Beth as she tightened Shannon's girth. It also explained why an attractive man like Noah was single.

'The worst thing is there's no garden,' he said. 'The truckie who owns the land has concreted over the yard. It's no place for bees, that's for sure. I've had to farm out my hives more than an hour away.'

Beth's ears pricked up. 'You keep bees?'

'Probably half the reason my ex booted me out. She didn't share my passion, especially after she was stung a few times. I never could convince her how important bugs are; that if they die out, so do we.'

Beth was delighted at this turn in the conversation. 'Did you see that documentary on the ABC about insect extinctions? *Insectageddon* they called it. All about the collapse of the world's insect populations.'

The two of them chatted about the joys of bees and gardens while they finished saddling up. Then they mounted and took the track that led to a ford in the creek. Beyond lay Wombat State Forest, lying on the southern slopes of the Great Dividing Range. It was a vast tract of undisturbed bushland, although its majestic mountain ash forests had been logged in the late 1800s. The only sign that remained of the once thriving timber industry was a rusting steam donkey at the confluence of Jackass Creek and the mighty Wombat River. Its steam-powered winch had dragged giant logs from the forest for transportation by bullock teams to the mills downstream.

Caesar leaped about, spooking and snatching at the reins, testing out his rider just as Beth had predicted. Noah sat his saddle easily, clearly enjoying the dance. They came to a wide, grassy trail along the riverbank. 'Race you!' said Beth.

Noah's smile was as broad as the river itself. The horses sprang into a gallop, filled with the joy of swift running. Beth gave Shannon her head and took the lead. She loved the wind in her face, the sensation of controlled power beneath her, the wild freedom of it. Beth's heart seemed to beat in time with her mare's as they tore down the track.

Caesar, who never could tolerate second place, pounded close behind, gaining ground. He drew level, and with an astonishing burst of speed, flew past Shannon. Beth laughed out loud and reined in her mare. Caesar seemed satisfied with his win. He slowed to a canter, then to a trot, before he and Noah circled and returned to Beth. The horses stood nose to nose, blowing hard, their satin coats damp with sweat.

'Congratulations.' Beth gulped down air as the rush of adrenaline began to wane. 'But Shannon and I demand a rematch next time.' The words had come out without thinking.

'Next time?' Noah stroked Caesar's neck and eyed her with amusement. 'Does that mean I can come again?'

'I suppose it does.' Beth smiled and tucked a stray lock of hair beneath her helmet. 'Come on. I'll show you the waterfall.'

It was late afternoon before they forded Dingo Creek and trotted their tired horses back to the stable. Lonely Skittles whinnied a welcome. Beth and Noah dismounted in companionable silence, hosing down their mounts and turning them out with a generous pile of hay each.

Beth collapsed onto a canvas chair under the stable eaves. 'That,' she announced, 'was the best ride I've had in years.'

Noah leaned against the wall, looking thoughtful. 'This place is amazing, Beth. A gorgeous garden, beautiful horses and the forest right on your doorstep. You weren't kidding when you said Benbullen was a small slice of heaven.'

Beth closed her eyes, basking in the moment as a light breeze cooled her brow. Noah was right. At that moment she felt like the luckiest woman in the world. A touch on her shoulder caused Beth to look up.

'Have you seen this?' Noah pointed to the paper wasp nest. 'Such a clever design. I've never had a good look at one before.'

Beth scrambled to her feet, eager as a child to show him more. Her earlier wish had been richly granted. Not only did she have someone to tell, that someone seemed equally fascinated by the native wasps. 'You're as weird as me,' Beth said, happily. 'Come up to the house for a cold drink before you go.'

Noah sat at the breakfast bar in the kitchen with a glass of lemonade, long legs folded awkwardly, looking out of place. Beth had never seen him inside a house before. It didn't suit him.

She sat down opposite. 'I was thinking about your beehives. If you want them closer, why not bring them here? I don't use insecticides and my garden has plenty of flowers.'

Noah pointed to the traps outside the window. 'Your garden also has plenty of European wasps. They're a major threat to honeybees.'

Beth frowned at the half-filled traps.

Noah drained his glass and rose to leave. 'Best advice I can give you is to find their nest and destroy it, before you have a truckload of trouble on your hands.'

CHAPTER SIX

~

The European wasp queen had laboured long and hard to build her nest in the cavity beneath the fallen tree. Years ago, when the stringybark gum stood lofty and strong, the hollow had been a kookaburra nursery. Before that, it belonged to a pair of boobook owls. Before them, a colony of tiny bats. Before them, sugar gliders and possums and parrots. Perched high above the ground, it had provided its tenants with a century of protection.

Now the hollow lay almost entirely buried. It was a roomy space, half a metre square, accessible only to tiny creatures, and the foundress was putting it to good use once more. Painstakingly, she cleared an entrance by moving aside small barriers: twigs and grass and little clods of mountain clay. She piled a screen of gumleaves around the hole to camouflage it from the outside world.

While a queen bee built with wax produced by her own body, this queen's construction material lay all around her. She stripped fibres from the timber lining the cavity and chewed them thoroughly. Then she moulded the paste into a short stem and attached it to a gnarled knot of wood protruding from the roof of the hollow. A cell gradually took shape. While a queen bee's comb lay horizontal, this queen's cell grew vertically and opened downwards. Her babies would grow in a topsy-turvy world, suspended upside down from the roof of their cramped, hexagonal paper cradles.

Some invisible design blueprint lay in the mind of the foundress, and at the end of that day, her first few cells hung near completion. Exhausted and hungry, she paused to examine her work. Outside the nest, a warm spring afternoon was melding into a cool evening, yet within the protective shelter of her hollow, the temperature barely changed.

The weary wasp had one more vital task to complete before she rested. Backing into each unfinished cell, she deposited a sticky, milky-white egg. Finally content, she positioned herself on a handy ledge and slept.

The nocturnal inhabitants of the underground world emerged to go about their nightly business. Suspended ominously above them hung the embryonic nest, with the quiet form of the queen on guard. They had no way of knowing that most of them would soon fall victim to this formidable new menace.

Over the coming days the foundress kept up a breathtaking pace, working from dawn to dusk. She was a sun-loving creature, who revelled in the lengthening light and the warming temperatures. On grey days, she confined herself to her nest, but when it was sunny she made regular forays to feed on nectar from the flowers crowding Beth's untidy garden beds. The queen quietly took her place beside butterflies and bees at the sweetest blooms, replenishing her energy for the task ahead. They had nothing to fear from her yet. Trips to the birdbaths on the lawn quenched her thirst and allowed her to collect water for her papier-mâché creations. In between these outings, she continued building.

Her homemade paper was surprisingly strong. Wasps had

mastered the art of papermaking long before Beth's ancestors were recognisably human. While cave tribes laboriously scratched primitive symbols into rock faces, wasps were already manufacturing their durable paper homes. It is likely that early people learned the art of papermaking from such wasps.

At about the same time as the foundress completed her first shelf of cells, she started to build an envelope around them. This began as a parasol-shaped ceiling. It would eventually balloon around the entire nest, protecting her growing brood and making the nest easier to guard.

She maintained a miraculous rule of symmetry, ensuring that each new cell intersected its neighbour at precisely one hundred and twenty degrees. The hexagonal shape of the cells provided the greatest possible amount of space with the least possible amount of construction material. Each of the six walls also acted as a wall for an adjoining cell. No space was wasted between them at any point. The foundress was an architect par excellence.

The hexagonal symmetry of wasp and bee cells had intrigued mathematicians, biologists, and philosophers for centuries, defying scientific explanation. Aristotle, Pliny, Kepler and Darwin all wrote treatises on the subject. Early critics of Darwin's theory of evolution argued that only God could endow insects with the power to construct such perfectly efficient shapes. The simple truth was that the young queen, ignorant of both God and science, achieved this astonishing feat again and again in the hidden silence beneath Beth's fallen tree.

A week or so after nest construction commenced, the queen's behaviour changed. Her building rate slowed, and she spent more time checking and rechecking her brood cells. She made more frequent trips to gorge herself at Beth's nectar-bearing flowers in preparation for the next stage. For her first egg was about to hatch. Its transformation into a larva was barely perceptible, but on the queen's umpteenth cell check, she found that the egg now had a mouth and could move. In other cells, more eggs were hatching. In the world of wasps, adults were mainly vegetarians, but their babies required a hearty meat diet. With hungry mouths to feed, the foundress went hunting.

It was midmorning when she emerged from the nest, intent on making her first kill. It didn't take long. She flew to a nearby flowerbed as she'd done daily for the past few weeks. But for once she ignored the sweet, crimson bottlebrush blooms hanging heavy on the callistemon bushes. She flew past the jasmine's creamy flowers with their intoxicating fragrance. She ducked around the crabapple tree, splendid in its spring blossom mantle.

Behind the apple tree, on a sprawling daisy bush, the foundress spotted movement. She was about to demonstrate why wasps were some of the most fearsome predators to be found anywhere in the animal kingdom.

Her target was a pale green caterpillar of the emerald moth, commonly known as a looper or inchworm. Thin and cylindrical, it progressed along a leaf by stretching out its front half and then bringing up the rear in one action.

She approached her prey downwind. The caterpillar, sensing danger, rose on its hind legs and froze, mimicking a plant stem. But the queen wasn't fooled. Swiftly she pounced, seizing her victim by its neck and crushing its head with her powerful mandibles.

It took all of the inexperienced queen's strength to subdue the thrashing caterpillar. European wasps only used their stings for defence, not for hunting. The queen would learn to pick on smaller targets as she honed her skills.

Next came the tricky task of carrying her booty home. She considered carving off a portion and returning later to retrieve the rest, but her fear of thieves was too strong. After many failed attempts, she managed to manoeuvre the caterpillar evenly beneath her body and make the short, laboured flight to the nest. Her babies had their first meal of meat.

The queen soon became an efficient killer and Beth's garden provided an abundance of prey. Nevertheless, this was a taxing and lonely time. Her eggs were hatching quickly, and the survival of the nest depended entirely on her ability to both survive and provide.

While her young ate and grew, the queen kept on building. Occasionally she rested or took time out to groom herself. She polished her antennae between tiny spurs on her head. She cleaned her eyes with her forelegs. She cleaned her forelegs with her mandibles, just as Beth's cat, Spooky, licked his paws and washed his face after dinner. To clean her abdomen and delicate wings, the queen rubbed them against fine brushes on the inside of her hind legs. She even groomed the open tip of her abdomen and its exposed sting.

Her firstborn was growing quickly. In its first few days, the hatchling was held in place by little more than mucous, and appeared to be in imminent danger of falling out of bed. But as she grew sleek and fat, the pressure of her body against the soft paper walls held her fast.

After a few more days the hatchling was big enough to extend her head a few millimetres over the edge of her cradle. This slight movement developed into a simple communication between mother and daughter. The queen, complete with a pellet of food, paused at the nursery cell and signalled her presence by rapidly tapping the paper wall.

The resulting vibration produced a brief buzz, clearly audible to the other inhabitants of the hollow below. An earwig paused in its food gathering and a startled king cricket hopped for cover. A lumbering wood cockroach cocked its head to the side in puzzlement. The increasing hum of the nest was still a novelty in this previously quiet space.

The infant wasp responded to her mother's tapping by stretching her body and bringing her mouth clear of the cell. After two moults she was now a fat grub, usually cream in colour, but currently rendered green by the blood of her mother's favourite caterpillar prey. The baby's brown head capsule bore neither eyes nor antennae. Her powerful jaws seemed out of proportion to the size of her head, and she possessed the beginnings of a spinneret, with which she would soon weave a cocoon.

As her firstborn ate, the queen attended to her other youngsters. She was a devoted mother, frequently visiting each nursery cell and finding little time to rest. These first young were destined to be workers. As grown wasps they would be smaller than their mother, and although all female, they would never mate. But before they reached adulthood, they would undergo an astonishing transformation – metamorphosis. During this bizarre pupal stage, almost all larval tissue was broken down and reassembled into an adult form. Only the nervous system and part of the gut remained unchanged.

While her babies grew safely within their nest, the foundress hunted for hours each day, ranging far and wide. She always returned home without hesitation, sure of her way. After all, she'd lived at Benbullen for most of her life. She knew and loved the bountiful garden, just as Beth did. And like Beth, she'd chosen it as the place to make a home for her family. They had a lot in common.

CHAPTER SEVEN

It was a hot Sunday afternoon in early summer. The flush of flowers at Benbullen had begun to wane, though late spring rains meant the pastures remained lush and green. The garden took on an attractive, unkempt appearance as Beth's sporadic pruning failed to match its rampant growth.

The children were at Mark's house and Noah was visiting his parents in Ballarat. Beth didn't relish spending the whole weekend alone, so she'd invited Karen and Paul over for lunch, along with eleven-year-old Rebecca and nine-year-old Simon.

They all lined up to watch as Rebecca tried to ride Skittles over several small jumps. A combination of heat and laziness made the pony less than keen. With much whooping and flapping of arms and legs, Rebecca rode towards a pole resting on some bricks. Skittles dutifully trotted to the obstacle, ducked around it and began to graze. Rebecca squealed with disappointment.

'Try again,' said Paul. 'Don't give up.'

'That's right, be firm.' Beth gently chased Skittles to get him moving again. 'Show him who's boss.'

'That's the problem,' wailed Bec. 'I think he already knows.'

Simon scowled and trailed a stick along the ground. 'This is boring. Can I go inside and play video games?' His mother nodded and the boy ran off.

Karen caught Beth's eye. 'Let's go back too. I could use a cold drink. Paul will keep an eye on Bec, won't you honey?'

The two friends walked up the path to the house. Beth knew what was coming. She'd been rather circumspect on the subject of Mark lately and Karen's curiosity was aroused. Beth was in for an interrogation. Secretly, she was pleased. Over the past few weeks Mark's behaviour had grown increasingly erratic. The child support payments that usually appeared like clockwork in Beth's bank account each month had not arrived. She was starting to regret that their arrangement hadn't been formalised with a court order. Her lawyer had urged her to do so at the time of separation, but Beth had trusted Mark. Back then, it seemed inconceivable that he might abandon his financial responsibilities towards his family. Now she wasn't so sure.

Equally worrying were the sexual innuendos and physical advances that had recently accompanied Mark's visits. And then there were the phone calls. Beth suspected these disturbing calls were made after he'd been drinking – Mark sharing fractured, rose-coloured reminiscences about their married life. Beth did her best to curtail these one-sided conversations. He seemed emotionally needy during them, and this too was unlike the Mark she knew. One of his flaws had always been his cool, almost cold, self-sufficiency. Beth resented that he was displaying this new side of himself when she had neither the desire nor the right to respond.

In addition, the situation with the children's access visits continued to deteriorate. Mark seemed indifferent and prone to make promises he failed to keep. With few exceptions, the kids returned with complaints about their father.

It had started when Mark cancelled an access weekend. This was a first. The excuse was his need to work overtime. Beth had felt a stab of concern as she detected a degree of pain in his voice. Overtime was a plausible excuse, but Beth didn't buy it. Until recently Mark had always viewed the time spent with his children as sacrosanct.

To her surprise, the kids had greeted the news of their cancelled weekend with enthusiasm. 'Cool!' Rick had said. 'Can Simon come over to play Zelda?'

Sarah was equally unconcerned.

'I have a project to finish for school anyway. I can never get anything done at Dad's. There are too many rows.'

Although pleased at her daughter's studiousness, Beth had also been puzzled. A few short months ago the kids would have been disappointed to miss a weekend with their father. Beth sometimes felt a little jealous of their close bond, especially whenever it seemed they'd rather be at his house than with her. However, she also admired and respected Mark's ability to salvage his relationship with his children from the wreck of their marriage. Inexplicably, he now seemed to be sabotaging his earlier good work.

As they reached the house, Beth found herself looking forward to the coming inquisition. It would be good to unburden herself.

They sat at the kitchen table. 'Spill!' was all Karen needed to say.

Beth gave a wry smile and confessed all – her financial worries, the change in her children's attitude towards their father and Mark's unwelcome advances. Outside the window, wasps were piling up in her traps. Karen listened attentively, asking only the odd question here and there to flesh out a thought.

Beth's mouth went dry. She sighed and licked her lips. 'One of the reasons I invited you guys over here today was so that someone would be here when Mark drops off the children. I'm tired of fending him off.' Beth heard the element of apprehension in her voice and was ashamed.

Karen remained silent for some time, digesting her friend's words. 'I'm glad you told me,' she said at last. 'Beth, I've known Mark for almost as long as you have, and this behaviour definitely isn't like him. Sounds like he's become a little unhinged. I'm very glad that Paul and I are here.'

'So am I,' admitted Beth. It felt good to finally give voice to her fears. For too long they had lurked, shadowy and indistinct. Now they began to take form.

'And Noah?' asked Karen. 'Is that still going well? When do I get to meet him?'

An excited Rebecca burst into the kitchen. 'We did it! Skittles and I jumped the jump – twice!'

Karen hugged her. 'That's wonderful, darling.'

A smiling Paul followed Rebecca into the kitchen. 'We'll make an Olympic horsewoman out of her yet,' he said, proudly.

Beth and Karen busied themselves making sandwiches, while Paul poured them all a drink and went off to battle Simon on the Play-Station.

At four o'clock Mark arrived with the children. Rick ran to find Simon, while Sarah and Bec went down to the stable. Mark showed little inclination to leave, instead joining the women on the verandah.

Karen, who hadn't seen Mark for months, was observing him curiously. Beth tried to see Mark through her friend's eyes. Would Karen notice the subtle change in him? Physically he'd lost weight. His usually immaculate hair was longer and a little tousled. It gave a debonair touch to his undeniably handsome features.

Mark helped himself to a can of beer, then leant on the verandah rail, spinning his car keys idly in one hand. Beth listened as he and Karen made small talk. When the conversation came around to Lena, he visibly stiffened.

'Are you and Helena having problems?' Karen inquired boldly. She was always one to overstep the boundaries, but to Beth's amazement Mark answered with startling openness.

'You know how it is, Karen. Every relationship has its ups and downs.' He sighed, sadly. 'If you must know, Lena and I aren't seeing eye to eye on a lot of things right now. It's hard when your partner doesn't understand you.'

He met Beth's surprised eyes with a steady, searching look. A play for sympathy was the last thing she'd expected from the self-possessed Mark.

Paul came from round the side of the house. 'G'day Mark. Long time no see.'

Mark acknowledged him with a nod. Paul seemed to sense the tension in the air and an awkward silence followed. 'I'll just go and check on the girls then, shall I?' He directed his question to no one in particular.

'Hang on, Paul,' said Mark. 'I'll come with you.'

Paul missed the subtle shake of Beth's head. The two men set off down the path to the stable, shielding their eyes with their hands from the glare of the afternoon sun.

Karen caught Beth's eye. 'You're not wrong. Something is definitely up with that one.'

Beth smiled wanly and nodded. Part of her was relieved that Karen had noticed a change in Mark. Yet part of her also hoped that her friend might have reassured her, told her it was all in her imagination. Validation made her anxiety harder to deny.

Beth wondered how the children's weekend had gone and resolved to do her own fair share of interrogating later that evening. Sipping her wine, she watched the two men head down the hill. Mark swigged beer as he walked. Suddenly he began swatting at his face, waving his arms and ducking his head. He jumped violently to the side and dropped his can.

'Wasps,' murmured Beth beneath her breath.

Mark bent to retrieve the can, while frothy, amber fluid drained away between rocks edging the track. As he picked it up, a wasp emerged from the opening and buzzed loudly in his direction. Mark cried out and dropped the can again.

Paul grinned. 'Hey man, you're not afraid of a little bitty bee?'

Mark swore. 'It wasn't a bee.' He'd been stung by wasps when he was small and had never lost his childhood fear of stinging insects. More than that, he loathed them. One reason he enjoyed city life was because of the relative absence of crawling, biting bugs. Mark took a final look around and, seeing no more wasps, he continued down the path.

The can lay at the edge of the gravel path, the last of its contents ebbing out onto the baking earth. Another wasp descended from the clear sky to sip at the spilt liquid. Soon more sisters joined her, savouring the fermented fluid as it lay in little pools on the hard ground. Some entered the discarded can where, hidden from view, they replenished themselves in peace.

Mark and Paul found the two girls taking turns on Skittles. Sarah rushed over to her father.

'Dad, want to see me jump? Mum's been teaching me.'

'Not now, love. Maybe next time.'

Sarah turned away, a flush of disappointment tingeing her cheek.

'Beth needs to get an exterminator in,' Mark told Paul, still on edge over the wasp incident.

'Have you seen those traps outside the kitchen?' said Paul. 'They seem to be doing the job.'

Mark snorted scornfully. 'They won't really solve the problem though, will they? Just a bandaid measure. Beth needs to get rid of the nest. She never did know how to be thorough.'

Paul looked uncomfortable. 'Beth looks well, eh?' he said, trying to change the subject. 'Country life suits her.'

'She looks great.' Mark fixed his gaze on Paul. 'Do you know what she's up to these days? If she's seeing anyone?'

Paul's frown showed he did not approve of the direction this conversation was taking. 'I wouldn't know, mate.' He left Mark standing in the shade of the stable and went into the paddock to retrieve Rebecca.

Late afternoon sunshine filtered through the gumleaves, lending a mottled glow to the peaceful scene. Paul said goodbye and headed back up the path towards the house. As Mark turned to follow, a flash of yellow and black startled him. A wasp flew past his head, then up and underneath the stable eaves.

Beth waited in the kitchen, impatient for Mark to leave. She was overwhelmed by her confession to Karen, suffocated and threatened by Mark's presence in her home, and constrained from talking to her children until the visitors were gone. In spite of Karen's assurance that something was wrong with Mark, Beth also felt a little silly. Had she been guilty of an overreaction?

Gazing out the window, deep in thought, she saw a wasp enter one of her traps. It hovered, seemingly suspended in midair, uncertain and confused within the confines of its clear plastic prison. Beth felt a sudden surge of sympathy for the insect. Did it feel foolish? Did it realise and rue the split-second decision that would inevitably destroy it?

Karen called Beth away from the trap. 'I can't find Bec's riding helmet. Can you help me look?'

Oh. Beth's heart sank. That meant Karen and Paul were leaving.

'Don't worry,' whispered Karen, catching sight of Beth's glum face. 'We won't go until Mark does.'

Beth shot her a grateful smile.

Mark came in, gave Beth a quick peck on the cheek and took off down the drive. Although happy about his rapid exit, Beth wished he'd taken the time to go upstairs to Rick. It wasn't like Mark to forget to say goodbye to his son.

Even so, Beth felt a rush of relief – a sudden lightness now that Mark was gone, like she was free of something. These days she became tense and flustered when he was around. She couldn't concentrate. That's probably why she'd forgotten to confront him about the child support money, or rather the lack of it. Never mind. It would be easier to do it over the phone. But that call could wait. The day had demanded enough of her already.

'See you soon.' Karen gave her friend a heartfelt hug at the front door. 'Ring me anytime, day or night. Promise?'

That evening, Beth cooked a simple meal of chicken and chips, the children's favourite. 'Your chips are the best, Mum,' announced Rick after finishing two servings.

He always said that, but it still brought Beth a flash of pleasure to know that she'd made him happy. Rick burped loudly, much to his sister's disgust, and left the table.

Sarah scowled at him. 'Mum, you said we have to take our plates to the kitchen.'

Rick turned and heaved a mighty sigh. 'I don't have time for that. My homework is due tomorrow.' Then he disappeared into the family room.

Since when did her head-in-the-clouds boy care about homework? But Beth didn't have the energy to enforce the rules. She took Rick's plate to the kitchen herself, provoking an understandable glare of outrage from Sarah.

Time to placate her daughter. 'I have the new *Horse Deals* magazine in my bag. You go look at it and let me clear up tonight.' Sarah's frown vanished.

After Beth packed the dishwasher, she peeked into the family room. Well, fancy that – Rick really was doing homework. She observed him for a few moments. His sensitive face was intent on the task, his tongue protruding ever so slightly between his teeth as it always did when he was concentrating. She wondered as she often did how he would look as a man. It was hard to imagine. Rick glanced up to see her watching him.

'You look like you're doing a good job,' said Beth. 'Need any help?'

'I'm just printing out a story for English.'

'Can I see?'

He hesitated. 'You'll think it's silly.'

'I won't, I promise. You know I love to read your stories.'

With a shrug, Rick handed over two sheets of paper. He gave her a quick, unexpected kiss and ran off. Beth took the essay into the lounge room and settled into her favourite chair. She loved to read her children's writing, always marvelling at how imaginative they were. This time was no exception.

Rick wrote of her wasps. It was a sweet little story about a wasp named Sabrina, who went out one day and became caught in a trap. She was very clever though, and escaped, saving her friends as well. They all flew home to the nest where their queen mother, Zenandra, was waiting for them. There was even a little maxim at the end of the tale. It read, 'If someone offers you something that looks too good to be true, be careful. It might not be as good as it looks.'

Beth finished reading and sat for a long time, deep in thought. Then she went to find Rick, who was building a model plane in his room. 'This is great.' She brandished the pages. 'How did you choose the names?'

'I looked them up in that old baby name book. Sarah helped me. Zenandra is Persian for *queen* and Sabrina is Latin for *princess*.'

'What gave you the idea for the story?'

'I was watching the traps outside the kitchen window. A wasp went in but got out again, and then some others followed. It was cool.'

Beth was intrigued. She had not observed such a thing herself. She also had not realised that the insects had so captured Rick's interest.

'I love the little moral at the end,' she said. 'It reminds me of one of Aesop's fables.'

Rick's face fell. He almost looked guilty. 'Dad made me think of that.'

Something in his voice gave Beth a chill.

'How do you mean?'

'Dad said not to tell you. That you'll just get upset.'

'Don't be silly, Rick. You sound a little upset yourself, and I need to know what's wrong.'

Rick looked away and was silent. Beth waited expectantly, knowing her son could not deny her anything for long. At last he spoke.

'Dad wants Sarah and me to go to live with him. He says we could go to a better school and have better holidays and stuff.'

Beth felt sick. A giant knot formed in her stomach and began to tighten. This idea had never been canvassed. It caught her completely off guard. She tried to calm her pounding heart.

But she couldn't fool Rick, her little emotional barometer. He gave her a quick hug. 'Don't worry, I said no. Dad's just trying to bribe us. He's offering all this good stuff, but I don't think it would be as good as he says. It made me think of the wasp. It thought it would be good in the trap, but then it wanted to get out.'

Beth gave silent thanks to the clever little wasp. 'What did your sister say?'

'Not much. I think Sarah might kind of want to go. She misses Dad. He's not paying her much attention lately.'

Beth forced a smile, kissed her son, and left the room in a state of shock. She went downstairs and slipped out the back door. Pacing the verandah. Thoughts racing a million miles a minute. The night, inky black with no moon, matched her mood.

An assortment of moths and beetles were battering themselves against the kitchen window, drawn inexorably to the light they would never reach. Beth could stand the senseless waste of life no longer. She hurried inside and yanked down the blind. Every muscle in her body felt like a coiled spring. She took a deep, shuddering breath, knowing sleep would not come that night. Who was she kidding? Sleep might never come again.

CHAPTER EIGHT

T hree weeks earlier

~

As Zenandra laboured alone to establish the nest, Sabrina, her first-born, was preparing to spin a cocoon. Thanks to her mother's dedicated care, she'd grown long and fat as a wasp grub should. She'd shed her skin five times and had stopped feeding, refusing her mother's offerings. Time to clean up her cradle.

It wasn't a hard job to discard the few scraps of skin and uneaten food. In the three weeks since her birth, Sabrina had never fouled her bed. These wastes showed as a dark spot through the creamy, translucent skin of her abdomen.

Once her cell was pristine, she started to weave fine strands of silk produced through her spinneret. Instinct guided her to attach these silken threads to various points on the cell wall, forming a loose, anchoring framework.

While Sabrina quietly spun, her mother paused to watch. Zenandra's lonely existence was near its end. Soon the hive would be filled with helpful companions. Zenandra moved on, impatient for the future.

Sabrina kept on spinning, hour after hour. Night came and still she spun. By morning, the waspling hung wrapped in an ellipsoid of the softest silk. With her work almost done, Sabrina defecated for the first time, excreting a sticky black pellet, encased within a delicate membrane, into the end of the cocoon.

Sabrina's final task was to weave a white cap over the opening of her cell, neatly sealing herself into bed. The freshly spun cocoon gleamed softly in the faint light coming from the nest entrance. Secure in her silken shroud, metamorphosis began. To Sabrina's observant mother, this seemed to be nothing more than a resting period, but in fact it was a time of extreme change.

The waspling's larval tissue broke down and remodelled itself into her adult form – an alien process, with no counterpart among the higher animals.

Nine days after Sabrina spun her cocoon, the transformation was complete. She used her mandibles to laboriously cut away the cap that sealed her cradle. Stiff and unsure, she pulled herself out onto the edge of the comb. No longer a wormlike, cell-bound baby, neither was she as large and beautiful as her mother. Her wings were weak and uncoordinated. Instinctively she tested them, making a faint but distinct buzzing sound.

Zenandra felt the strange vibration and, after rushing to investigate, discovered the birth of her daughter. With great excitement she inspected the new addition, touching her all over with her antennae. Sabrina responded with faint movements of her head and renewed attempts to use her hardening wings.

For the next few days she did little but buzz and preen and beg mouthfuls of food from her mother. All around her, more adult sisters were emerging. Soon, Zenandra would be relieved of her house-keeping duties. She would have an army of helpful companions. The European wasp population was set to explode.

Meanwhile, under the stable eaves, the potter wasp larvae were also growing – in little clay pots and without the protection of a proud parent. Their mother had provided for them before she left though, and her babies hatched to find a store of paralysed spider prey ready and waiting. A living larder.

The first of these wasplings hatched from her egg into complete darkness. She latched onto one of her helpless spiders with saw-like teeth, feeding carefully around her victim's vital parts to keep it alive and fresh for longer. Fat and gonads were a favourite first meal. Eventually, the tortured spiders succumbed to the relief of death, but by then the larva had eaten her fill. She spun a protective cocoon, just as her cousins had in the nearby nest of the European wasp. Yet unlike Zenandra's babies, she had no anxious mother to tend her when she emerged. As she began, so would she remain – a lonely predator.

With metamorphosis complete, the newly minted potter wasp prepared to leave the dark confines of her clay pot. When her mother had sealed off her cell, she'd made a mud plug with a convex inner surface. The larva had detected this difference and turned towards it when spinning her cocoon. Now, she already faced in the right direction for her eventual escape.

She used saliva to soften the cap of her cell so that she could gnaw her way out. Working steadily, using her sturdy mandibles as cutting instruments, she finally broke free of her macabre nursery.

The beautiful young potter wasp perched on the nest edge, dazzling in colour and perfection of shape. Even before her wings were hardened for flight, she would try to sting if touched. Beginning life entirely alone required a keen instinct for self-preservation. Apart from her brief nuptial flight, she could expect no interaction with others of her kind. Inherited instinct guided her, but that instinct could be modified by individual judgement and experience. She entered the world as a precise and capable adult, both intelligent and inventive.

Within the other little clay pots, her siblings had not fared so well. Mother wasp had provisioned six more chambers and laid an egg in each. Unaware that a treacherous guest had crept into the nest while she was off hunting, she sealed the completed cells, thus also sealing the fate of her unfortunate offspring. For in the gloom, amongst the paralysed spiders, hid a diminutive parasitic wasp known as a wowbug. It had found the nest by climbing up the stable wall to investigate promising sheltered sites, like those situated beneath the eaves.

The wowbug female seldom flew, although her wings were well developed. With a little luck she'd never need them. Having found a suitable host, she would remain in the potter's nest for the remainder of her short life.

At barely one millimetre in length, she appeared inconsequential and harmless enough. Yet she was set to wreak havoc. Safely sealed within a cell, she fed on both the defenceless spiders and the developing waspling. Time and time again, she pierced their skin and imbibed the exuded blood. This did not prove immediately fatal to the larva or the spiders. The wowbug patiently waited in the dark cavity until the sickly, anaemic potter grub pupated. She then chewed a hole in the cocoon and, once inside, laid dozens of eggs on the body of the pupa. These hatched almost immediately into a mass of minute, hungry grubs that consumed the helpless waspling entirely. They became cannibals if food ran out. In under two weeks the horde spun vestigial cocoons and emerged as adults.

Male wowbugs were blind, flightless and spent their brief lives in frenzied mating behaviour. These degenerate drones were so aggressive that they often engaged in fights to the death among the debris of spider legs and desiccated wasp pupae. Even a dead male wowbug, or part of one, was fiercely pounced upon and savagely hurled about by his brothers.

This new generation of wowbugs chewed through the carefully constructed mud walls separating the cells. They repeated their life cycle until the remaining six nest chambers lay barren and wasted.

The single surviving potter wasp clambered uncertainly about, testing her wings, tasting the breeze. Soon she'd be strong enough to fly, to seek out nectar-bearing flowers and satisfy her hunger. Then she must find a mate and go on to select her own nest site. Although likely to remain close to her birthplace, she would never reuse an existing nest. The chance of deadly parasitic infestation was too great.

A second potter wasp nest nearby had also fallen victim to attack. This time the culprit was not a wasp, but an enormous fly. Earlier in the season, a bee fly had been attracted by the buzzing sound of a potter wasp as she constructed and provisioned her nest.

The female bee fly had a stout, orange body with no waist between thorax and abdomen. She bore a superficial resemblance to a large bee, hence her name. However, there the similarity ended. She had the slender, smooth legs of a fly. Long, mottled wings extended flat from her body as she perched on the stable roof, and wide compound eyes keenly observed the industrious wasp. The bee fly had a labour-saving plan in mind. This cuckoo of the insect world waited until the mother wasp left to collect clay, then darted in to lay eggs on the surface of the partially completed nest. These hatched into tiny, eel-like maggots.

The newly hatched grubs made a concerted assault on the nest walls, gaining entry to the chambers through tiny fissures in the masonry or unsealed openings. Once safely inside they entered a brief period of suspended animation, unnoticed by the growing wasps. As soon as the wasplings began to spin their cocoons, the maggots came to life, attaching themselves to the bodies of the fat larvae. The baby bee flies consumed the living pupae and metamorphose in the safety of their victims' cocoons. At the same time as the first young potter wasp successfully emerged, the neighbouring nest gave birth instead to bee flies.

In spite of her industry, the mother potter wasp achieved a low survival rate for her offspring. The complex nest represented a huge parental effort. Unfortunately, it also presented an obvious target for enemies. How much better protected were Zenandra's babies, guarded by their formidable family. The survival of the solitary potter wasp's offspring was, by comparison, very much a matter of chance.

Zenandra's social way of life afforded her family many more advantages. The queen would soon be free to devote herself to egg-laying alone, while her daughters performed all domestic duties. Another advantage was the restriction on males. They were only produced when needed, and their short lifespans ensured the colony did not have to support them for long. Zenandra was founding an efficient and impressive dynasty. Her adopted country, free of even the few predators she would face in her native land, was proving to be a promised land indeed.

CHAPTER NINE

Monday morning. The phone call woke Mark. He glanced at the wall clock, mind befuddled by sleep. Still an hour before his alarm was set to go off. Who would ring him at this time? Sunshine streamed through the slim-line blinds at the bedroom window. The strength of the rays at such an early hour warned of a coming scorcher. While Lena slept on, Mark sat up and reached for his phone.

Chance was cradled in the crook of his mother's arm. The baby lay quietly, although the call had woken him too. His wide blue eyes watched Mark as he answered the phone.

'Hello. Beth?' He decided to take the call in his home office. Content beside his mother's breast, Chance made no cry as his father pulled on shorts and left the bedroom.

Mark closed the door of the office after him, unsure of what the call was about, but pleased nonetheless that Beth had reached out to him.

'Since when do you want the children to live with you?' said Beth, her voice cracking with emotion.

'So, they told you.'

'Of course they told me. You had no right to ask them not to. Why didn't you talk to me first?'

Her frantic tone belied the reasonable nature of her question. Mark imagined her sleepless night, checking and rechecking the clock, trying to judge the earliest time she could ring him.

'Well?' asked Beth, raising her voice. 'For pity's sake, say something!' Her shrill demands rendered Mark mute as his pleasure at her phone call leaked away. He felt backed against a wall, not only by Beth, but by life itself. His response to pressure these days was to retreat into sullen silence.

Beth hung on the phone, all anger and desperation. Mark stayed silent and her heart beat faster. He was stonewalling her. How could she reach him?

Beth took a few deep breaths and tried to rein in her emotions. She was woefully out of practice when it came to dealing with Mark, but staying calm had to help. 'Let's meet to discuss this,' she said, lowering her voice, speaking more slowly. 'No, not at my place.' She had visions of dancing about, avoiding Mark's advances.

'Lunch in town then,' he said. 'Later this week. How about Friday?'

Her heart sank. Today was Monday. How could she live until Friday with this pit of anxiety deep in her stomach? Curbing her impatience, Beth agreed to the date and time. She needed Mark onside now, as she never had before, even if that meant being trapped in an emotional limbo for days.

Mark finished the call, his mind abuzz. He considered going back to bed, but didn't want to deal with Lena and the baby. He grabbed a quick coffee instead, then showered and dressed.

Mark worked at Blue Sky Financial Services, an award-winning company of chartered accountants, renowned for innovation and dynamic business planning. He was on the verge of becoming a senior partner, the youngest person ever to reach that position. When he'd proudly told his mother, Vanessa, she'd merely sniffed and said, 'You always were lucky.' That had hurt. Scrambling up to the dizzy heights of the corporate ladder had nothing to do with luck. Working ten-hour days, six days a week – that's what it took. 'Work–life balance is for pansies,' he used to say. Now he wasn't so sure.

Mark's thoughts turned to the coming day. He'd drive his red Ford Mustang coupe through the snarls of commuter traffic to his city office. He'd park in his reserved space, before taking the elevator to the twenty-second floor. His pretty personal assistant would greet him with smiles, fluttering lashes and reminders of his daily appointment schedule. Mark frowned. He no longer looked forward to such days.

For months now, he'd seemed to be operating on autopilot. The truly frightening thing was that nobody else had noticed. Increasingly, he felt like a dispassionate and objective observer of his own life. This disconnection was accompanied by a crushing loneliness.

Lena provided him with little comfort. Since the birth of Chance, she was preoccupied with the baby, her girlfriends and shopping. Mark felt like little more than a money-making machine, important to Lena in that he afforded her a certain lifestyle. The cost of that life-style was soaring. Lena's credit card debt continued to mount. It had been the subject of several bitter arguments lately.

Mark's thoughts drifted to Beth and the worry lines on his face softened. During their marriage, he'd been the spendthrift. He recalled Beth's gentle, exasperated chides about keeping expenses down. He pictured her, tight-lipped and serious, doing the monthly budget at the kitchen table, flicking strands of flame-red hair behind her ear – a look of intense concentration on her beautiful face. A shock of painful comprehension hit him; a shock so intense that it caused him to drop his car keys. He was still in love with Beth. How had he not realised it before? A wave of missing her made him weak.

Slipping back into the bedroom, he grabbed his briefcase. Lena was half awake. He went to kiss her goodbye, but stopped when he met his baby's calm gaze. For a moment he felt a connection to the child. Then Chance turned to nuzzle Lena's naked breast. She snuggled him close and helped him find her soft, rosy nipple. The baby sucked contentedly, his eyes closed. Mark felt a familiar stab of jealousy, followed by shame. Irrationally, he felt rejected by them both. He turned and left the room. Friday couldn't come quickly enough.

Lena heard the front door slam and blinked back tears. She was keenly aware that Mark had left without kissing her goodbye. It seemed these days that he never gave her any attention, except to criticise.

She took comfort in the sweet, heavy warmth of her nursing infant. It never ceased to amaze her how intensely her emotions were now entangled with this child.

Still, motherhood did not entirely compensate her for the growing distance from Mark. Why couldn't they both share this newfound joy? The more she lost herself in maternal bliss, the more Mark turned away. Lena's mood lightened a little as she planned her day. She'd arranged lunch with friends. That would help deal with the loneliness. Then perhaps a little retail therapy.

The early morning phone call with Mark had left Beth paralysed. The threat of his sudden custody grab loomed over her like a giant spider preparing to strike. Instinct urged her to defend herself, but how?

She woke the children and tried to focus on the routine tasks of a school morning – making lunches, checking timetables and preparing uniforms. By eight o'clock she'd bustled the kids out the front door to the bus stop.

Beth brewed herself a coffee, thoughts swarming in her head. Like kaleidoscope images, scenarios no sooner popped into view than they disappeared again, replaced by some equally undesirable permutation. The kids would want to live with their dad. They wouldn't. One would, one wouldn't. They would be embroiled in a bitter custody battle. They would hate her if she did this or that. They would hate her no matter what she did. They would hate their father. She would hate their father. The possibilities were endless and the uncertainties mind-boggling. Her meeting with Mark was not until Friday. How would she get through the next few days with her sanity intact?

There was one thing Beth was certain of though. She'd have to stop seeing Noah. Their romance had been moving forward, albeit slowly, ever since that magical ride together in the forest a month ago. She and Noah had enjoyed some more rides and some lunches at the local pub, always on weekends when the kids were with Mark. They'd swapped stories about their lives. They'd shared a first tentative kiss. Not much more than that, for Beth had deliberately held her passion in check. Motherhood weighed heavily on her. She wanted to be absolutely sure before beginning a serious relationship; before introducing a new man into her children's lives. Noah never pushed, but neither did he back away. By word and deed he'd proved that he would wait until she was ready.

Beth loved him for it. She loved him for his thoughtfulness, his compassion and his gentle sense of humour. She loved him for putting up nesting boxes for birds and bats in the gullies, and for taking photographs of beetles and butterflies. Noah was her perfect match, and tears welled in Beth's eyes at the thought of losing him.

She knuckled them away. What choice did she have? There must be no shadow of impropriety to taint her custody claim. Mark could offer a high income, a stable home and a stay-at-home partner who the children already knew and liked. How might his lawyer twist things if Beth's relationship with Noah was discovered? She couldn't afford to find out, so there was no sense putting it off. Beth let out a long, shuddering sigh and rang his number.

'Hey there, beautiful,' said Noah. 'I was about to call. How would you like to come to the International Horse Trials at Werribee with me? We could stay overnight and come home Sunday.'

Beth gulped back tears, dizzy with disappointment. Here was an invitation to more than an equestrian event; an invitation she may well have accepted, if only ... Beth found herself weaving slightly, unsteady on her feet.

She took the phone along with her coffee cup into the lounge room and sat down. Her voice faltered as she began. 'Noah, something dreadful has happened.' Beth laid out the stark, unedited truth, determined for Noah to understand that this breakup was not what she wanted.

He argued against it with a passion, making her care for him all the more. Yet she remained unbending in her resolve. 'No, I can't say when I'll be free again … No, I won't meet up so we can talk … Yes, it will be hard seeing each other at the riding school. That's why I've decided to resign.'

Beth ended the most painful phone call of her life. She poured her cold coffee down the sink and went outside. How dare the day be so bright and beautiful. Whistling the dogs, she walked down to the stables. A ride might help relieve her misery. The beer can Mark had dropped yesterday still lay beside the path. She stooped to retrieve it. The can was already warm to the touch. The first stinking hot day of summer was here. A bold willy wagtail, resplendent in black and white plumage, followed them. It hopped from stone, to fence, to ground, wagging his upright tail and chattering cheekily at the dogs.

Dell, her graceful Scotch collie, placed her muzzle in Beth's hand, gazing up with concerned, amber eyes. She recognised that something was wrong, and was too worried about her mistress to bother with the impudent bird. Not so the terrier pup, Scrap, who was yapping at the wagtail in a state of high excitement. The bold little bird seemed unaware of the danger. It blithely whistled a song, *'Sweet pretty creature, sweet pretty creature.'* Scrap pounced after it, growling. Beth picked the pup up and carried him the rest of the way.

The horses were dozing in the shade of a bush gully, twitching their smooth summer coats, tails swishing at the flies. Beth stopped to check that the automatic water trough was operating. A leaking valve had created a damp patch of soil beneath the inlet pipe, and a variety of insects were taking advantage of it. European wasps and honeybees stood side by side, drinking from the wet earth. Beth watched a potter wasp, intent upon gathering her load of clay. The industrious insect forced her head down into the moist soil, at the same time raising her body into a nearly vertical position. While she worked, she gave vent to her feelings in a loud, satisfied hum. Finally, she ceased singing and rose with a large lump of mud held proudly in her jaws. Intrigued, Beth followed her to the stable.

On arriving at her chosen nest site, the wasp positioned the soft mud with her mouth, mandibles and feet, extending a half-finished chamber. Beth inspected the roof and found more nests under construction. The eaves were abuzz with busy potter wasps.

Beth wandered around the back of the building, where the now completed paper wasp nest was alive with activity. The young queen had successfully raised her first generation – no easy feat for any single mother – and Beth admired her for it. Cautiously, so as not to arouse the ire of the irritable insects, Beth moved closer.

The nest consisted of a single comb of hexagonal cells, contained in a paper cup that hung from a central stem. It looked rather like an inverted umbrella. From beneath, Beth could see up into the nest. The shallow peripheral cells at first appeared to be empty. However, when her eyes adjusted to the deep shade, she could distinguish minute white eggs within. These eggs were cemented to the cell wall. Deeper central cells contained larvae. Two cells had white caps, and already contained pupae, whose silken cocoons lined and closed the chambers' entrances. Three or four adult wasps guarded the nest. An impressive set-up, although it would never equal the far larger and more sophisticated nest of a European wasp queen.

Out of the corner of her eye, Beth spotted movement. A huge, hairy fly zoomed past and perched at the tip of an overhanging branch. It was powerfully built, with a short, sharp proboscis, a long thin abdomen and enormous eyes. Its face bore an ugly beard. The fly looked dangerous and very much the bad guy. Beth recalled seeing something like it in one of her field guides, but she couldn't remember its name.

A paper wasp approached the nest with a pellet of fibre in her jaws. The fly suddenly darted in and grappled with the wasp in mid-flight. Avoiding her desperate attempts to sting, it held on tight with long spiny legs and stabbed its proboscis into the victim before flying off with its prize.

Now Beth recognised the murderous insect – an assassin fly. It killed by injecting venom and enzymes to paralyse and liquify its prey. Beth's mouth went dry. The paper wasp nest was young, consisting of maybe a dozen individuals. This opportunistic predator presented a real threat to its survival.

After a few minutes the assassin fly discarded the desiccated husk of the wasp and returned to its vantage point overlooking the nest. Its large, compound eyes observed the colony as it patiently awaited its next opportunity to strike.

Beth set her jaw, crept closer and swatted the fly hard with a well-timed whack. The force of the blow hurled it into the fork of the tree. Before it could recover, she squashed the stunned insect with the heel of her hand. It made quite a mess. Beth wiped the remains of her kill on the bark of the tree.

She felt a curious sense of elation. The ugly marauder would trouble the nest no more. Beth cast a final, protective glance at the stable eaves before going for her ride. She didn't know that the European wasps posed a far greater threat to the paper wasps than the solitary, native hunter that she'd just destroyed.

CHAPTER TEN

It was finally Friday. Mark took more care than usual when dressing that morning. He hummed to himself under the shower, his mood brighter than it had been for weeks. Lena was having breakfast in the sunroom. The open windows revealed an expanse of floor-length glass. The sunroom was situated on the northern side of the house, and the air conditioner was already working overtime. Mark contemplated the size of the next electricity bill and wished that, just sometimes, Lena could pull the curtains to keep the room cool.

As he did so often lately, Mark contrasted her behaviour with Beth's. On hot days Beth would close the windows and drapes to keep out the heat. Woe betide anyone who left a door open. She said that air conditioners were not only costly to run, but they contributed to climate change. How irritated he'd been by her behaviour back then. Now he saw it as sensible and caring. Why couldn't Lena be more like that?

Mark finished his shower and joined his girlfriend for breakfast. He looked around for the baby and didn't see him. Chance must still be asleep on the king-size waterbed in the main bedroom. Mark had always wanted a waterbed, but Beth had been dead against it. Now that he had one, he felt as if he was sleeping on a giant bowl of jelly.

Lena insisted on keeping it though, because she said the movement helped the baby sleep. It seemed Chance never slept in his cot anymore. Sometimes Mark felt it would be better to move into the spare room.

Lena wore a pink satin dressing gown over matching briefs. Mark had not seen the particular ensemble before. He wondered how much it had cost him. The gown fell open to reveal her full breasts. Always large, they looked particularly luscious since she'd been nursing. Her body was evenly tanned, testimony to lengthy sessions at the local solarium. Her stomach, no longer flat like a girl's, was instead enticingly plump. Her long, shapely legs were delicately crossed. Mark's gaze travelled up to the silken pink triangle of her panties. If anything, Lena was even more beautiful since giving birth – her body softer, more yielding.

Mark felt a familiar tug of arousal. He crossed the room and pulled her to him without warning, his mouth urgently seeking hers, his hands finding the tender mounds of her breasts. Lena stiffened and pulled away. Mark's desire vanished and he and withdrew to the kitchen.

Lena's eyes followed Mark uncertainly as he left the room. She hadn't meant to reject him. His sudden ardour had taken her by surprise, that was all. He'd shown so little physical interest in her lately, and when he did, it was ill-timed. Lena didn't mind too much. Her libido was low since giving birth to Chance. She'd even gone so far as to mention it to her doctor.

'Don't worry,' he'd said. 'A low sex drive is common in new mothers.' His advice had reassured her.

Yet Lena did miss Mark's attention and companionship, if not the sex. She followed him into the kitchen, rubbing against him and smiling as he made coffee. But he was no longer interested. Mark had retreated to somewhere she could not follow, and Lena didn't know how to summon him back. Gulping down his coffee, Mark left with a perfunctory goodbye.

Lena felt resentment rise in her like indigestion. What she needed was to get her mind off things for a while. She waited for Mark to leave, then went to the bedroom to fetch Chance. The sleepy baby smiled, melting her heart as always.

Lena kissed his soft cheek. 'Come on sweetie, time for a bath. You have a big day ahead of you.'

Today Chance was going to childcare for the very first time. It would do him good to socialise with other babies, and she trusted Bright Beginnings to provide the best possible care. After all, it was the most exclusive creche in Toorak. Meanwhile, Lena and her friends had arranged a day out: brunch at Le Republique, a spa at the Como Hotel, some shopping on Chapel Street. Finally, they planned on slumming it – playing poker machines at a venue two suburbs away. If that schedule didn't cheer her up, nothing would.

Lunchtime. Mark arrived at the restaurant early, but Beth was already there. It seemed that she'd also taken extra care dressing that morning, choosing a cool, deep green linen suit that matched her eyes. Her hair was pinned back, in deference to the heat of the day, perhaps. But he remembered that Beth also thought that it made her look stern. She was wrong. It merely accentuated the sweep of her milky white neck, such a contrast to Lena's artificial glow.

Mark saw the worry behind Beth's forced smile. It made him feel important, even powerful. Truth be known, his suggestion for the children to live with him had been ill-conceived from the start. He'd regretted it almost as soon as the offer was out. His motivation at the time had been purely to annoy Lena. Mark had cautioned the children not to tell their mother so it would be easier for him to quietly back out of the proposal. The effect of the news on Beth, however, had been an unexpected bonus.

She watched Mark cross the room to her table, looking suave in a grey silk shirt and tie. Beth suddenly felt unsophisticated and gauche.

She'd waited all week for this moment, but now she was unexpectedly nervous. They'd not met in such a way since long before their separation. Mark put on his most charming smile and smoothed his lapel. His body language made it seem more like a date than a meeting to discuss the future of their children.

Mark sat down. She broke eye contact when the menus arrived, and he took it upon himself to order drinks. 'No wine,' said Beth, contradicting him. She poured herself a glass of water from the bottle on the table. Her hand shook ever so slightly, a fact that did not escape Mark's attention. Time to take control. 'I couldn't believe it when Rick said you wanted him and Sarah to live with you.'

'Why? You don't have a monopoly on loving them.'

'No, of course not ...' His dismissive self-righteousness infuriated her. 'But you never said that the current plan didn't suit. Whatever happened to talking to me?'

'I've tried to talk to you.' He leant forward and gave her a knowing smile. 'I think someone's been avoiding me. Am I right?'

What on earth? She silently examined their past few encounters. Beth couldn't recall Mark trying to *talk* to her about anything. She took a sip of water and composed herself. He was confusing her, making her second-guess herself. She had to get back on the front foot.

'The kids are settled with arrangements the way they are,' said Beth firmly. 'You can see them pretty much whenever you want, as it is. What about that weekend you missed last month? How can you possibly say you want more time with them when you're cancelling access visits?'

Mark's eyes were fixed on Beth with a gaze intense enough to make her squirm. She seemed to have his full attention. So why did she feel like he wasn't listening to a word she was saying?

'Let's talk after we've eaten.' Mark signalled the waiter, who arrived to take their order. 'We'll have the seafood risotto.' Then to Beth, 'It's very good here.'

He sounded so cool, so nonchalant, as if this meeting was merely a pleasant social occasion. It was maddening. 'What's wrong with you?'

Beth's raised voice betrayed her frustration. 'We're here to discuss the children, not have a lovely lunch. Let me make my position completely clear. I will not consent to any change in our current custody arrangements.' She was almost shouting now. The couple at the next table glanced over at them.

'Calm down.' Mark looked so smug, she wanted to slap him. 'Perhaps we should let Rick and Sarah decide.'

'They *have* decided. The children do not want to live with you full-time. They told me that, both of them.'

'Is that so?'

It wasn't so. Beth had spoken to Rick, but she didn't know what Sarah wanted. She hadn't even broached the subject with her daughter. The lie left her feeling a little desperate.

Mark shrugged. 'Then we might need to let the courts sort it out.' Beth was close to tears. He was studying her, taking in her rising distress with a kind of dispassionate curiosity. She couldn't fund a protracted Family Court proceeding, and he knew it.

'Please, Mark,' she said, her voice breaking. 'Please don't do this.'

Mark's expression softened. He reached for her hand and she let him take it. Had she got through to him? Was he going to back off?

Mark took a deep breath. 'I could change my mind, if …' He seemed stuck for words.

A wave of hope washed over her. 'Yes?'

'If we could spend more time together. I miss you, Beth, so very much.' He ran a finger across her open palm.

She pulled her hand away, neatly folded her napkin and stood up. With as much dignity as she could muster, Beth turned on her heel and walked away.

CHAPTER ELEVEN

Seven summers ago, when Beth's fallen tree still towered above the landscape, a cicada had lain eggs on a branch in its leafy crown. Using sharp serrations on her ovipositor, she cut a slit in the surface of the bark and deposited a dozen tiny, pale eggs. By repeating this process over the next few days, she concealed hundreds more throughout the gum tree. With her life's work complete, she quietly died. Yet her death marked the completion of an extraordinary and successful journey. Her young were about to embark on a similar adventure.

Eight weeks later, nymphs no bigger than fleas hatched from the cicada's eggs. These tiny paratroopers launched themselves skyward and floated silently to earth, their fall cushioned by the soft leaf litter. Instinct drove them to dig into the ground using specially adapted forelegs, and within minutes the nymphs were safely concealed.

So began years of secret, subterranean development. Each baby cicada sought out a juicy tree root and dug an adjacent burrow. There it could feed on sweet, sticky sap in relative safety. In perpetual darkness and isolation, each nymph grew, periodically moulting and enlarging its cell.

But even underground they faced dangers. Depending on the location of their tunnels, some dried out or drowned. Others starved when their tree root died or became diseased. Some had their bodies infected by mould or were parasitised by beetle larvae. However, the majority survived their years of solitary confinement until they were fully grown.

These nymphs did not undergo the same dramatic metamorphosis as Zenandra's wasplings. From the very first they were tiny, wingless copies of their mother. During their long years underground, they gradually grew buds on the outside of their bodies – buds that burst into wings after their last moult.

Now the ungainly brown babies began the gruelling task of digging up and out of their cramped homes of roots and clay. After days of work, their escape tunnels were nearly complete. Some unfortunate nymphs emerged into the cavity containing Zenandra's nest. The doomed insects blundered about until their movements attracted the attention of the workers on guard above. The wasps pounced on the clumsy juveniles. Tough shells gave some protection, but not for long. The cunning wasps attacked the cicadas' soft bodies through chinks in their plated armour, slicing living tissue into pieces with razor-sharp mandibles. Before the nymphs were even dead, their meat was being carried into the nest to feed the growing hordes of hungry wasplings.

Other nymphs were more fortunate. Those who successfully completed their escape tunnels stopped digging just short of the surface. A soft summer rain was falling, causing them to retreat temporarily to their underground chambers. There they waited for the invisible signal that would compel them to emerge.

The next night was hot, still and clear. Time for the patient nymphs to begin their exodus. Climbing to the tops of their burrows, they broke through the thin earth plug and into the open air. The night already reverberated to the chorus of a multitude of their kin.

Unrequited longing for the companionship of their kind spurred the lonely nymphs forward.

Accustomed to total darkness, even the soft light of a new crescent moon was enough to temporarily blind them. Slowly their eyes adjusted, and with faltering steps, each instinctively sought a vertical surface. Some climbed up the bark of Beth's fallen tree – a dangerous place to be, come morning. Most scaled nearby gum tree trunks, thereby gaining additional height and safety.

Having chosen a suitable perch beneath a branch, a nymph began its change into a winged adult. To any casual observer, nothing much seemed to happen at first. Yet underneath its ugly brown casing, the juvenile was pumping air through its breathing holes, or spiracles. The build-up of pressure eventually split its outer shell. Slowly but surely, a brilliant green head and thorax appeared, in dramatic contrast to the original drab, muddy skin.

By midnight the cicada was transformed. It hung from its discarded case, crumpled wings unfurling under the pressure of blood being driven through a network of branching veins. Its new, delicate legs were quite different from the broad, shovel-like feet of its nymphhood. Its dazzling emerald colouring faded during the remaining hours of darkness. By dawn it was a dull green, its wings having hardened and lost their bright aqua opacity.

Owls and small, insectivorous bats had taken several emerging cicadas during the night, but most survived to witness their first sunrise. And one by one they embarked on their inaugural flight to freedom, together with all the perils freedom brings.

The throbbing, cadenced song of the males was irresistible to the opposite sex. Females alighted on cicada trees, drawn by the deafening serenade of their suitors. At an appropriate moment the males softened their calls, crept up to the females and mated. Each female took the opportunity to mate several times over the next day or so. She then commenced to lay her eggs, her final task before death.

Many cicadas fell victim to predators over the next few days. Birds ate their fill. Huge huntsman spiders scurried over the tree trunks, so excited by the profusion of prey that they exposed themselves even in daylight. But spiders and cicadas alike faced an even more formidable predator – wasps.

Oddly enough, the giant spiders had no strategies to repel hunting wasps. They ran about in blind terror, or cowered, trembling under the wasp's cold scrutiny. Over millions of years, wasps had become skilled at spider hunting. The spiders, on the other hand, had developed inferiority complexes when it came to dealing with their hereditary killers. Why did the spiders always play the victim? They were well-armed and much larger than their attackers. Yet for some reason the wasps held the psychological advantage.

The cicadas also faced killer wasps, although Zenandra's children sought easier prey. In the eroded patches along the edge of Beth's neglected lawn lay several irregular mounds of earth. The holes adjacent to the grooved piles of dirt had convinced Beth that these were the nests of bull ants. She'd given her children strict instructions not to venture barefoot onto the grass. But had she been more observant, she would have found these to be the nests of wasps, not ants.

One still, humid summer evening, a large, yellow and black wasp alighted on a patch of earth beneath Beth's apple tree. She'd emerged from her birth burrow and mated only one day before. Now her urge to nest and to complete her own life cycle was overwhelming. Somehow, she knew she must hurry, for she would live for only thirty days.

The wasp chose a patch of ground that was devoid of vegetation; well-drained and with friable soil. She tunnelled downwards, working all through the warm night, shovelling soil from the burrow mouth and scattering it behind her. Periodically she backed up to heap soil at the entrance. This she left as a surrounding rim, as did many ants. The resemblance to a bull ant nest would afford her babies some protection.

Her forelegs constantly raked back the displaced earth, and the *click-click* sound of her mandibles biting into the clay caused a passing cricket to cock its head.

By the time she was finished, she'd dug a tunnel half a metre deep.

All around her, the air vibrated to the loud, rhythmic song of a host of cicadas. The wasp paused to listen. She would find no shortage of victims in the morning, for she was a queen cicada killer wasp. Shortly after sunrise, having paused neither to rest nor feed, she went hunting.

The queen's flight was rapid and determined as she approached a nearby gum tree likely to harbour her quarry. Circling the tree trunk, she spiralled upwards through its limbs and branches. It wasn't long before she found what she was looking for. A large cicada sat motionless beneath a leaf. The wasp darted back and forth in front of her target, positioning her sting downward and forward, picking her mark.

Without warning, she slammed into her victim, thrusting her sting neatly between shell segments and paralysing it. To perform this feat, the queen needed an intimate knowledge of the cicada's anatomy. Her specialisation was so precise that she would take no other prey.

The insect uttered a loud, distressed squawk and buzzed shrilly for a moment, but it soon ceased to struggle. The attacker and her victim dropped to the ground with a thud that produced a last rattling protest from the stupefied cicada.

The queen threw the cicada onto its back so it would glide along more easily. Using her wings for assistance, she dragged her prey through grass and over sticks with surprising speed. It was hard work. The cicada weighed six times more than she did. At last she reached her freshly dug burrow. The cicada, in a state of deep paralysis, was now packed unceremoniously – upside down and headfirst – into an underground mud chamber.

The queen laid a single egg on the helpless insect.

Two more cicadas soon joined the first. Hungry and tired, the queen returned to the precise spots where she'd captured her prey, feeding on the sweet sap oozing from holes in the bark made by her unlucky cicada victims. She then returned to close the mud chamber, packing earth against each victim's abdomen and wing tips, before going on to provision more cells.

Two days later the first egg hatched, growing rapidly in comparison with Zenandra's babies. Cicada killers lived a fast-forward life, timed to match their prey's brief existence above ground. After a week of feeding, the grub spun a cocoon. In another week she emerged as an adult, programmed to repeat her mother's predatory cycle. During the course of the summer, her kind posed a clear and present danger to the cicadas of Beth's garden.

Meanwhile, the nearby nest of the European wasps continued to expand. Sufficient adult daughters had now been born to allow Zenandra to remain at home and concentrate on egg-laying duties.

It was a sunny summer morning when Sabrina embarked on her first foraging flight for the day. She might make twenty such trips before sundown. When she'd first ventured from the nest on her inaugural flight, she'd stayed close by her home, memorising its location by observing conspicuous landmarks. She dipped and circled, noting an unusually shaped branch here and a prominent gatepost there. Soon she felt confident to fully explore Beth's garden.

She discovered the sweetest flowers and the nearest water. She found the plants that bore the most succulent caterpillars and she investigated potential sources of fibre. A weather-beaten wicker chair on the verandah provided Sabrina with her favourite supply of pulp, preferring it to the pile of cardboard boxes discarded behind the stable.

She gathered construction material by walking slowly backwards while rasping off strips with her mandibles. This made a soft *click-click* sound, clearly audible from several feet away. She then rolled the strip into a ball, took it in her mouth and flew back home.

On entering the nest, she looked for a willing sister to receive her pellet of pulp. Sabrina preferred to spend her time on the wing. However, since there were no takers, she decided to do the job herself. Sabrina was the definition of a multitasker.

She applied the pulp to an unfinished cell, regurgitating water from her crop to make the material more malleable. She used her mandibles as an artisan uses tools, delicately smoothing and shaping the fibres, working them over and over, never faltering in her design despite working in almost total darkness. When she'd finished, she groomed herself, cleaning away any adhering particles to maintain her immaculate appearance. As she took a well-earned rest, a fat grub reached for her, asking for food. Sabrina made up her mind to go hunting.

Although not displaying the highly specialised behaviour of ants, a rough division of labour had emerged among the wasps in the colony. Each individual was capable of performing all required tasks, but they did develop personal preferences. Sabrina was a career-woman wasp. Caring for the babies held no appeal for her. She liked to hunt, but first she required a decent feed.

As she left the nest, a curious grey fantail considered making a meal of her, before changing his mind and fluttering off. He'd already had one painful encounter with a similar wasp. Everyone in the garden knew of the formidable sting of Sabrina and her kind. She flew on, quite fearless.

Spiralling skywards, she confirmed her bearings and then flew to Beth's house. She made a beeline, or in this case a waspline, for the traps outside the kitchen window. Under the dappled shade of a purple lasiandra tree hung an orb containing an easy meal. A hole led to the central chamber where a dozen dead wasps floated in the sweet liquid lure. Sabrina alighted on the outside of the trap, and trotted up and in.

Once inside, she progressed with great care, clinging to the side and tap, tap, tapping her antennae ahead of her as she approached the food. Expertly maintaining her foothold, she imbibed the delicious honey-water. All around bobbed drowned corpses, some of them her sisters.

Upon first venturing into the orb, the dead wasps had frightened her, signalling danger. And after drinking her fill she'd found herself trapped. But it didn't take long for the clever little wasp to find her way out. Several other captive wasps – ones that had yet to succumb to their sticky fate – saw her leave. Following her example, they too made a successful escape. Since that first day, Sabrina often fed at the trap. Having satisfied her hunger, she made a practised departure.

The warmth of the sun and the energy provided by her sugary meal gave Sabrina a new bounce to her buzz. She set off in the direction of the big stock tank. Sabrina and her sisters were opportunistic hunters, quick to capitalise on any food sources found within their territory. Her ability to adapt to new circumstances gave her a huge advantage over native wasps such as the cicada killers, which were constrained by specific prey preferences and hunting behaviours. Sabrina had recently discovered a young paper wasp nest in the pump house beside the tank. Today she would turn cannibal. Wasps, or to be more precise their babies, were on the menu.

Sabrina wasted no time when she arrived at the prey nest, callously breaking open the cocoon cap on a pupal cell. A few agitated paper wasp workers buzzed around the marauder, unsure of what to do. Not having evolved with the threat of European wasps, the colony seemed to lack any defence response. Sabrina dragged out the fat pupa within, grasped it firmly with her legs and mandibles, and flew off to deliver it to her little sisters. When she arrived home her nest-mates took and distributed the meat, thus freeing her for another trip.

Over the next few days Sabrina repeated this procedure until there were no more pupae or larvae left. In the end the paper wasps abandoned their plundered nest. Their middle-aged queen had no energy to begin again. A single European wasp had destroyed her one chance of producing a new generation.

While Sabrina loved hunting, others had their own favourite day jobs. Some liked to build. Some liked playing nursemaid. On hot days many younger workers enjoyed collecting water. They needed it for papermaking and used their gut as a storage tank, but it was also fun to cool off.

No matter what task a worker chose, it was always for the good of the colony. Zenandra was well served by her capable daughters whose numbers continued to grow.

CHAPTER TWELVE

Mark returned to his office, hollowed out and confused by Beth's abrupt departure at lunch. He'd desperately wanted to stay and spend time with her. He'd barely been able to restrain himself from giving chase when she left. It made no sense. Lunch had been her idea in the first place, yet they hadn't resolved a thing. Even in the brief time they'd been together, he could tell there was still something between them. Was that it? Had Beth been overwhelmed by rekindled feelings? He wasn't sure, couldn't tell, but the possibility sent a delicious warmth through his whole body.

He was sure of one thing, however. The custody question gave him leverage. He'd use that leverage if that's what it took to get closer to Beth. For at a gut level, Mark realised an important truth – he needed a true connection.

For years he'd been too busy to devote time to his relationships, with the exception of Rick and Sarah. Old friends from school and university, good mates from the cricket club – he'd let them all slide. When was the last time he'd had a night out with anybody other than Lena? Work colleagues didn't count. They weren't friends. They were professional rivals, who'd cut his throat if it meant a step up the career ladder. He had to admit that recently he'd been the same. Who could blame him, raised as he was to regard wealth and privilege as the secrets to happiness? 'They open every door, fulfil every dream,' was his mother's constant mantra as he grew up.

And to all external appearances he was living that dream – a beautiful young girlfriend, a prestigious professional position, an expensive wardrobe, overseas travel, two luxury cars, and a magnificent home. So why did he feel a deep and growing dissatisfaction with his life?

Beth had been shocked by his mother's views, dismissing them as shallow and wrong. 'You don't really believe that, do you?' she'd asked him. And he didn't, not with Beth there to ground him. She'd had a way of making him appreciate the small things. But as he commenced his meteoric rise up the ranks at Blue Sky, even Beth's wisdom couldn't temper his ambition. That was why their marriage had failed. Work had become all-consuming.

By contrast, Lena didn't seem to mind if he spent all his time at the office. She loved their lavish lifestyle and was starstruck by his achievements. It had been flattering at first. But Lena's attention was focused on baby Chance now, and she no longer had time for Mark. So what was the point of all this endless striving for success; where would it lead? To loneliness and despair, that's where.

There was one way to bring meaning back into his life, and the answer resonated so powerfully that it made his ears ring. Reunite with Beth. The one person who'd been truly there for him during his years of ambitious career building. The only woman who'd ever loved him. He needed her by his side again.

Beth embodied all the qualities that were missing from his life – love, commitment, self-sacrifice, and last but not least, a vital and joyful appreciation of the world. These aspects of her personality were suddenly irresistible when compared to Lena's shallowness and his own barren existence. He was certain that sheer physical proximity to Beth would somehow revive his own dwindling life force.

Restless and unable to concentrate, Mark left the office at three o'clock that afternoon. This raised a few eyebrows. He was usually the last to leave. He had no particular desire to see Lena but, unable to come up with a more attractive destination, he headed for home. As he pulled into the driveway, he saw that Lena's silver Audi was not in the garage. Good. He could use some time alone to think.

Mark contemplated ringing Beth. No, give her time to rue her behaviour. Undoubtedly she already regretted her rudeness and would soon phone to apologise. Mark brewed an extra strong coffee and sat down to watch the cricket.

His mood grew darker as the afternoon wore on. By six o'clock his team had lost, Beth hadn't rung and Lena still wasn't home. He was calling Lena on her mobile when he heard the key in the door. She struggled inside with a crying baby in the capsule and half a dozen shopping bags.

Lena seemed taken aback to see him. Small wonder. He rarely arrived home before eight o'clock. Neither of them enjoyed cooking (the most commonly used appliance in their sparkling stainless steel kitchen was the microwave oven), so they would generally order a takeaway meal and perhaps spend the evening watching Netflix.

Mark had always assumed that Lena whiled away her days at home, caring for Chance and waiting for him. For some reason, the idea of her having somewhere else to be irritated him. 'Where were you?' he asked, his tone belligerent.

Lena stood open-mouthed, lost for words. How could she tell him that she'd been playing poker machines at a hotel and had stayed on long after her girlfriends went home? Firstly, she hadn't discussed her decision to enrol Chance at the childcare centre with Mark. It hadn't seemed to be an issue that might concern him. Secondly, she'd lost far more money than she'd intended to, unwisely chasing her losses. Recently they'd had some rather heated arguments about her spending. She could well imagine Mark's anger if he knew about her afternoon of gambling.

Lena mumbled something about shopping, before disappearing into the nursery with Chance. Well, it was true. She had gone shopping – twice. Once with her friends, and then again after she'd collected Chance from the creche – her way of cheering herself up after the disaster at the poker machines. Those darn things must be rigged.

As the damage escalated, she'd started dropping one hundred dollars a spin, playing as many lines as she could to maximise her chances of winning. That strategy had not worked. Still, what did it matter? Mark was loaded, wasn't he? To be honest, that had always been a large part of his charm. He'd certainly spun her head with expensive gifts and extravagant holidays while they were dating.

Lena hadn't been raised in a rich family. That was an understatement – they'd been dirt poor. So perhaps she'd been too easily impressed by Mark's wealth. However, never having much money meant she'd never learned how to look after it. *Easy come, easy go* was her philosophy. No, she did not regret her afternoon at the pokies. It was the first time since the birth of her son that she'd enjoyed any extended time to herself. She adored Chance, but it was hard being stuck home alone with a baby. It would be different if she had her mother nearby for some practical support, but she lived in Sydney and could only come for the occasional weekend.

'What about Mark's mother?' Mum had asked her after one of her brief visits. 'Can't she help?'

Lena had just laughed. Vanessa hadn't been thrilled at becoming a grandmother the first time around. She was even less enthusiastic about Chance, dismissing Lena as no more than a phase her misguided son was going through, saying it right to her face. That still hurt. These past six months at home with Chance had been such a lonely time. Surely she deserved her day out.

As Lena settled herself in the chair to breastfeed Chance, Mark came into the room. Without a word, he emptied Lena's shopping bags onto the change table. 'So that's what you've been doing all day; dragging our baby around a shopping mall.' He glanced at the price tags attached to the scattered items of clothing and swore.

Lena stared at him sullenly while Chance suckled, eyes closed. Mark spotted her handbag beside the chair, grabbed it roughly and extracted her purse. He removed her store cards and credit cards, then fetched a pair of scissors. Cutting each piece of plastic in two, he hurled the pieces to the floor. Lena held her tongue, relieved that he hadn't discovered the whole truth. She gazed at the ruined credit cards, resentment bubbling up in her throat like bile. No matter. There were plenty more where they came from.

Mark poured himself a scotch from the bar in his office. He rarely needed a drink to calm his nerves. Tonight was an exception. There had been a lot of exceptions lately.

Half an hour later he sought Lena out to apologise. He shouldn't have been so rough on her. It wasn't her fault. She didn't understand how to live within a budget, he knew that. To be honest, he'd chosen her more for her figure than her head for figures.

Lena thanked him for the apology, promised to curtail her spending and then held up one of the new dresses against her body. 'Don't you just love it?' She swayed her hips.

There was a time when he would have joined in her enthusiasm, declared her irresistible and taken her to bed. Not today. Instead Mark studied Lena dispassionately. There was something so vacuous, so childish in her expression as she admired herself in the mirror. He tried not to compare her with Beth and failed.

CHAPTER THIRTEEN

It was Saturday morning, the day after the disastrous meeting with Mark. Beth woke to find Rick snuggled beside her. Since the separation, any upset always saw him creeping quietly into Beth's bed. It happened less frequently now, but occasionally he still craved the security of his mother's warm body.

Beth stroked strands of pale hair from Rick's eyes, causing him to stir and smile in his sleep. An intense surge of privilege overwhelmed her, bringing with it the sting of tears. This simple pleasure of everyday mornings with her children could become a thing of the past if Mark had his way.

Why had she walked out on him like that? What a fool. Did she expect to change Mark's mind by antagonising him? She had to repair the damage done, and as quickly as possible.

Easing out of bed so as not to disturb her sleeping child, Beth showered and dressed, all the while considering her next move. She went downstairs and slipped out of the front door. A walk in the garden might help her to think more clearly. Although barely seven o'clock, it was already hot and humid outside. The sky loomed oppressive and grey.

There'd been a termite swarm overnight. The morning air was still thick with them. Some struggled weakly on the windscreen of Beth's car, waterlogged and plastered to the dewy glass. Some crawled over the concrete porch, piles of their discarded, silver wings fluttering despite the apparent stillness of the air. Others clogged the untidy spider webs that festooned the outside lights under the verandah roof. It seemed a curious contradiction. Insects that had evolved in complete darkness were, for one wild moment of their lives, irresistibly drawn to the light.

Flycatchers, fantails, and dragonflies targeted those still in flight, feasting on their succulent, nut-brown bodies. Beth frowned. Swarming termites always made her feel vulnerable. Where did they all disappear to? Once upon a time, she'd been suspicious that they vanished into the woodwork of her home. What about that cartoon where a single termite ate every stick of timber in sight?

A little research had eased her concerns. The cartoon termite was based on an insect known as a powderpost termite, capable of living in very dry wood with no connection to the ground. It could indeed reduce wooden furniture to powder as its name suggested. By contrast, the termites swarming in Beth's garden lived in the damp, decaying wood of the forest floor. They would not damage the sound timber frame of her home. Yet a small part of her still worried when they appeared in such vast numbers.

She was also saddened by the carnage. Fully ninety-nine percent of these royal termites perished. Their bodies lay all around. Beth screwed up her face and went back inside. She had more important things to think about than termites.

Sarah was oiling her saddle in the kitchen. Old newspapers covered the table, which was strewn with greasy rags and tins of leather dressing. She was supposed to clean tack out on the verandah. Sarah looked up as her mother came in, no doubt expecting a lecture. Instead Beth hugged her daughter's shoulders and pulled up a chair.

'Where's Rick?' asked Sarah, looking pleased with herself.

'Still asleep.'

Here was an opportunity to sound out her daughter in Rick's absence. 'I want to talk to you about your dad.'

Sarah's smug face fell.

'He asked you to live with him, didn't he?' Silence. 'You're not in any trouble. I know he asked you not to tell me. But honey, I really need to know what you're thinking.' Sarah polished her saddle harder, looking cornered. Beth gently took the rag from her hand.

'I don't know what to think, Mum. I love you and Dad. How do you expect me to choose? I shouldn't have to make a decision like that.'

Out of the mouths of babes. Sarah was right. Children needed protection and guidance, not to be put in the middle of a domestic dispute. It was their parents' responsibility to take control and offer leadership – provide them with safety and a sense that the world was predictable. Beth felt like a failure. It wouldn't happen again. From now on she would make the decisions – in the best interests of her children, of course – and that meant they should stay with her.

Beth stood up, kissed her daughter and admired the sheen on her saddle. Rick came downstairs, rubbing sleep from his eyes and yawning. He hugged his mother tight and then inspected her face.

'Are you okay, Mum?

'I'm fine,' she said. 'Why did you think that I wouldn't be?'

'I had a nightmare. It was about you, Mum. It was the worst nightmare in the world.'

Rick often used superlatives to describe his bad dreams, so Beth wasn't too concerned.

'Go on.' She smoothed his hair. 'Tell me about it.'

'So, there was this giant wasp and it was trying to get you. You were running, but it could fly super fast with these great big wings. I tried to help, but then this other wasp grabbed me and flew up into the air. I looked down and saw that the giant wasp had you and was sucking your blood. You were screaming and screaming … Then I woke up.'

'Gross.' Sarah made a face.

Beth turned Rick's chin towards her and kissed his cheek. Bizarrely, she couldn't help reflecting that the wasp would not suck her blood. It would instead crush her head in its mandibles and feed her flesh to its giant wasplings. She shook her head to clear it. There goes that imagination again, she told herself. Working overtime. She was as bad as Rick.

'It was just a dream, darling. A very scary, but very silly dream. You know nothing like that could ever really happen.' She ruffled his hair. 'Come on, let's have pancakes for breakfast.'

'Yay,' said Rick, and the children ran into the kitchen. Beth mixed up the batter, poured a portion into the hot pan and glanced out the window at her array of traps. They needed emptying again. No, on second thought, she would take them down entirely. Native wasps and bees were turning up among the casualties and that was unforgivable. She was wasting her time, anyway. The European queen would be laying eggs faster than Beth could kill the workers. For the millionth time she wondered where the nest might be.

'Mum!' Rick pointed to the smoking pan.

'Whoops!' Beth had forgotten to flip the pancake. Sheepishly she threw it into the compost bucket and started again. Get a grip. Forget about the wasps. Her preoccupation with them was bordering on obsession, and it was clearly disturbing Rick.

After breakfast Beth rang Mark from the privacy of her bedroom. A plan was brewing in the back of her brain. Mark seemed keen enough to talk, and she took this as a good sign. Perhaps it would be easier to mend fences than she'd imagined.

'Sorry I left so suddenly on Friday, Mark. You took me by surprise, that's all.' Beth wanted to say more. She wanted to say that any hope for them had long since died. That it was ridiculous to think otherwise. She wanted to say how wrong it was for him to even hold her hand. Instead she bit her tongue.

'It's okay,' said Mark. 'I understand why you did it.'

Beth let go of a breath. It was unusual for Mark to be so conciliatory. Encouraged, she enquired about the holidays and his plans for the children. It beggared belief that Christmas was coming up and they hadn't arranged anything yet.

Mark was frustratingly vague. 'I don't know,' he said. 'I suppose we'll go to Mum's.'

Beth gathered her courage. 'How about you, Lena and little Chance come to Benbullen for Christmas lunch? Then, if you like, you can take the kids back with you for a few days.'

To Beth's surprise and delight Mark agreed to the proposal on the spot, without consulting his girlfriend. Beth felt her spirits lift. A family lunch would be a wonderful Christmas present for the children. And if everything went according to plan, it might also help scuttle Mark's scheme to gain custody.

The barking dogs announced a visitor. Beth glanced out the window and saw Ted Beaumont's truck. Ted was Beth's sometime handyman. She had called him earlier that week, insisting that he finish cutting up the fallen tree. He'd started the job last autumn, but being a supremely unreliable handyman, he'd never finished it. After some nagging, Beth had convinced him to return.

With bushfire season just around the corner, she couldn't risk having so much dead timber lying about. Windblown embers could quickly take hold in dry wood and move a fire front dangerously close to the house. Beth nodded at Ted through the window and waved him on.

CHAPTER FOURTEEN

Ted drove past the house and through the open gate. He parked his truck beside the fallen tree and cast an experienced eye over it. He'd forgotten how big the log was. Its sheer size staggered him all over again. What a giant the tree would have been in its heyday. It was impressive even in death.

Ted got to work, the roar of his chainsaw deafeningly loud. As noise tore through the silence, a flock of gang-gang cockatoos rose above the treetops, bright red crests raised in alarm as they uttered their haunting warning cries.

Little skink lizards ran for cover. A sleek copperhead snake slithered away. Ted almost stepped on the venomous reptile hidden in long grass at his feet. Fortunately for them both, the snake preferred retreat to confrontation. Notwithstanding its deadly reputation, Ted was by far the more dangerous of the two. He would surely have killed the snake had he seen it, despite its protected status.

～

Zenandra's nest lay at one end of the fallen tree. The queen had been laying yet another egg in a cell when the vibrations began. The chainsaw bit into the log with tremendous violence, and the effect on the delicately balanced nest structure was akin to that of an earthquake.

Ted sawed the timber into large rounds, then used the log splitter to cut lengths for the firebox of Beth's wood heater. It was hard work. By midday he'd run out of fuel for the chainsaw, and realised that he'd forgotten to bring spare jerry cans of petrol. Perhaps he could burn the log out instead. So much easier. He started a fire near the middle of the tree and fed the flames with bark and sticks until it took hold.

Sabrina joined the guard wasps outside the nest. They swarmed about the entrance hole, crowding the smoky air –their buzzing loud and angry. Some flew reconnaissance, swiftly identifying Ted as a potential enemy and ready to mount an attack if he came too near.

Soon a new danger threatened. As the fire crept closer, the temperature inside the nest quickly climbed. In response, a convoy of wasps flew to the old birdbath beneath the apple tree on the edge of Beth's garden. Its shallow base was the perfect shape for them to land safely.

Before long, a thick ring of European wasps surrounded it, gathering water and ferrying the droplets back home in an ingenious waspine bucket brigade.

The efficiency of this operation would have put many a human disaster response to shame. Returning workers distributed their load throughout the nest, while others fanned their wings. The combination of moisture and breeze cooled the nest using the same principle as the evaporative air conditioner on Beth's roof.

The comparison didn't end there. The multilayered paper envelopes surrounding the nest worked a lot like the insulation bats in the ceiling and walls of Beth's house. Zenandra's home had nine complete envelopes wrapped around it, with another under construction. Air pockets interspersed between the layers helped maintain a constant temperature inside. Under normal conditions it fluctuated by less than three degrees, day or night, whatever the weather.

But these were not normal conditions. As the fire approached, some wasps chewed ventilation holes in the protective envelopes. Their frantically fanning sisters appeared at these gaps, increasing airflow and helping to cool the nest. Yet despite these mighty efforts, the wasps could not defeat the heat forever.

Ted had underestimated how long it would take to burn the fallen tree. After two hours, the blaze had barely consumed a quarter of the log. He took a few steps backwards, shielding his face from the flames. Time to call it a day. He would put the fire out for safety's sake, and finish off the job tomorrow with the chainsaw.

Ted walked back to his truck, planning to fetch water to douse the flames. In doing so, he passed dangerously close to the nest. The wasps, whipped into a frenzy by the heat and smoke, launched their attack.

They streamed after Ted, bold and antagonistic. A wasp stung his arm. Others landed on his sweat-soaked shirt and stung his back.

The sting of the European wasp is more painful than that of the honeybee. But it was the sight and sound of the swarm that terrified him more than the pain of their stings. Ted almost opened his mouth to scream, but managed to control himself. He knew what could happen to a man with wasps in his mouth.

Ted sprinted for the safety of his truck, parked just a dozen strides away. The sudden movement served to further infuriate his attackers. Wasps produce alarm pheromones, chemical signals that mark intruders and attract other wasps to the sting sites. Zenandra's daughters swarmed after him.

Ted reached the truck, scrambled in and wound up his window. Some of the insects had entered the cabin with him, hitching a ride on his back. Inches from his face, a thousand wasps dive-bombed the windscreen, looking like a scene from a horror movie. He stared into their wide, furious eyes. They could see him but not reach him, and they thronged outside the cabin, beside themselves with frustration.

Ted was grey with fear. A river of fire coursed through his left buttock and he could strangle his scream no longer. He let out an ear-splitting cry that set the dogs barking up at the house. Ted wriggled and slapped at himself in a vain attempt to dislodge his tormentors, but he was hopelessly restricted behind the steering wheel. Gritting his teeth against the pain, he started the truck and drove erratically back through the gate.

The enraged wasps trailed after Ted for a short distance before returning home. Zenandra waited and watched at the nest entrance. She had not joined in the assault. Her wings were frayed and worn from the friction of inserting her body into thousands of paper cells. Her abdomen was heavy with the weight of egg-laden ovaries. The queen's flying days were over, but she still buzzed a little at the memory of her lost aerial life.

The rising heat made her retreat into the dimness of the nest. Hundreds of white-capped brood cells hung from the roof, containing pupae on the point of emergence. Pride swelled Zenandra's tiny insect heart. She moved to join her daughters, fanning her battered old wings in time with theirs.

The successful attack on Ted had proved enormously taxing for the colony. As the weary warrior wasps returned, they had no time to rest. The violent vibrations had stopped, but the temperature kept on mounting. Every wasp was needed for a desperate, last-ditch attempt to cool the nest.

Ted burst through Beth's front door, yelling for help. 'I've been attacked by a mob of bloody wasps!'

Beth rushed in from the kitchen to find Ted moaning and swatting at his back with a sofa cushion. She slapped the few remaining insects off his back, dispatching them on the carpet with her heel.

Rick and Sarah came to see what all the noise was about and stood at the doorway. Shaking and whimpering, Ted took off his shirt to reveal a dozen raised, throbbing welts on his back and shoulders.

Beth sat the hysterical man down and told Sarah to wrap a pack of frozen peas in a tea towel. She then applied it to the sting sites to reduce the pain and swelling. Ted began to calm down. Beth's thoughts, however, were not with Ted. She felt a thrill of excitement as he told his story. By accident her handyman had discovered the location of the European wasp nest.

'The fire's still going,' he said. 'You'll have to rig up a hose to douse it. Sorry luv, but there's no way I'm going back over there.'

Beth made some comforting noises and said that of course she didn't expect him to go back. He seemed consoled. After a cold drink and some more sympathy he rose to leave. Ted put on his shirt, pulling the rough fabric gingerly over his body.

'You're not allergic to wasp stings are you?' asked Beth. Less than ten percent of people were, but it was important to know.

Ted shook his head. Good. That meant he'd probably suffer no more than some localised swelling, and a few days of soreness and itching. An allergic reaction to a sting was a much more serious matter. It could cause inflammation and pain all over the body. It could precipitate an asthma-like condition that made breathing difficult, even impossible. In severe cases, one sting could stop the heart from beating.

Beth's fascination with the European wasps had caused her to research everything she could about them. They possessed a potent venom – a mixture of toxins, enzymes, and proteins, including serotonin and histamine. The greatest risk was a sting in the mouth or throat. Such an attack could result in complete blockage of the airways.

Ted rose stiffly and turned to Beth with a grim expression on his leathery face. 'You've got to get rid of them wasps. Now. Today. I know a bloke who'll do it. I'll get him to give you a ring. And tell them kids of yours to stay right away – the dogs too. I'm warning you luv, those wasps are deadly.'

After Ted left, Beth told Sarah and Rick to stay inside and then she went to take a look at the nest for herself. The sky was an ominous, leaden grey, growing darker every second. The termites had vanished, and the eerie cries of black cockatoos sounded round the hills. Their dark shadows, rippling across the ground, made Beth look up. The cockatoos were right overhead – huge birds with a distinctive, laboured flight that made Rick call them the manta rays of the air. Black birds against a black sky. The flock vanished behind a forested peak, though their mournful calls still echoed. Otherwise the world was strangely silent and still.

Black cockatoos were a portent of rain. Summer storms in the mountains could be violent, and it seemed the wise creatures of the bush had all sought shelter. Not even a fly buzzed by. The world was holding its breath.

Beth approached the fallen tree, noting wryly that only a third had been cut up for firewood. A column of smoke rose from the middle of the trunk. She shook her head and frowned. Ted wasn't supposed to burn off at all. Fire restrictions forbade it. She'd asked him to dump the offcuts in a gully to decay naturally.

Beth still couldn't see the nest. She crept closer, and closer still. Aah, there it was. A dozen European wasps buzzed around a small hole in the ground that was almost completely hidden by leaves and branches. Smoke from the approaching fire drifted over the insects, driving them back inside. Their underground bunker offered a degree of safety for now, but the log was fully alight. With the flames progressing relentlessly, in the end Zenandra's home would be reduced to ash.

Beth squeezed her eyes shut and scrubbed her hands over her face.

She'd been wanting to destroy the nest for months. If she left the fire to burn, that task would be accomplished quite simply. Problem solved.

So why did she feel so torn? Beth imagined the rising panic of the insects underground, as they faced the destruction of their home; the death of their queen and brood. She shivered a little, despite the heat.

Beth suddenly made up her mind to put out the fire. After all, it presented a bushfire risk. She was thinking of a way to extend the hose from the water tank when a large droplet of water splashed onto the back of her hand, then another. Seconds later the skies opened, releasing a torrent of rain. Beth ran for the house, glad that the decision was out of her hands. She would deal with the nest some other time.

CHAPTER FIFTEEN

~

Inside the nest, a combination of heat and exhaustion had taken its toll on Zenandra's daughters. Hundreds of older wasps lay collapsed and dying among their fanning sisters. Others, desperately thirsty, drank the droplets of water scattered throughout the nest chambers, sabotaging the cooling system.

A tired Sabrina greeted her mother and then went to inspect the larvae. Rising heat caused them to extend their bodies out of their cells as far as possible, waving their head capsules to take advantage of any breeze created by the buzzing adults. Sabrina hurried to reassure the frightened babies, tapping them with her antennae, and communicating with soft *click-click* sounds.

Zenandra was failing, struggling to keep her wings in motion. But just as she thought her spiracles would burst, she detected a new vibration. Not violent and earth-shattering as before. This was a soft murmur. The queen's spirit soared – rain.

Gradually the air cooled and the choking smoke cleared. Thirsty wasps sucked at moisture seeping in around the entrance to the hollow. Larvae relaxed back into their brood cells. Workers began to clear away the corpses of casualties. Their bodies would soon be fed to the growing wasplings. Even in death they nourished their sisters. Sabrina, worn out by her labours, fell into a well-deserved sleep. Zenandra also needed to sleep. But first she would lay just one more egg …

The European wasps weren't the only local social insects to be grateful for the storm. At the other end of the log, a colony of termites also welcomed the rain.

They were the only insects to remain cohabitants of the log with the wasps. The other denizens had long since been devoured by its voracious new tenants. The clever termites however, sealed safely within their tunnels, lived lives undisturbed by the danger on the doorstep. Their nest was the point of departure for the winged reproductives that had swarmed the previous night.

Termites were thin-skinned, soft-bodied, defenceless creatures. Totally blind, they fed on decayed wood and other plant material. They belonged to a more primitive insect family than the wasps. Yet like the wasps, their societies were numerous and highly successful.

There were two significant differences between their respective social structures. In the termite world, a full-time king and queen shared royal duties. Unlike the wasps, males and females were present within all termite forms at all times. Secondly, their babies did not undergo the miraculous metamorphosis of the wasplings. Termite hatchlings were complete, though underdeveloped, replicas of their parents.

The hatchlings could grow into workers, soldiers or reproductives, depending on the needs of the colony at that particular time. This flexibility contributed to their success as a species, with each minute worker living and learning for up to three years and helping to raise several thousand offspring.

The termites led secretive lives, moving to new food sources through secure subterranean passages. Their soft, fleshy bodies offered scant protection against predators or the open air that could fatally desiccate them within minutes. They shunned the outside world, instead seeking the comfort and security of their dark underground cities. Yet when certain conditions prevailed, a select group of winged reproductives within the nest reversed their normal behaviour and were irresistibly drawn to the surface.

Last night had been such a night. Factors of temperature, humidity, and light had all converged to create perfect conditions for a swarm. Worker termites had slaved all of the previous day, preparing exits from the colony that was usually kept so tightly sealed.

As night fell and the full moon rose above the clouds, the young royals had swarmed out through carefully concealed openings. Somehow they synchronised their emergence with other termite nests. The combined swarm consisted of hundreds of thousands of individuals. Such vast numbers increased the odds that at least some pairs would survive the dangers that beset them on their nuptial flight and go on to successfully establish the next generation.

Stay-at-home termites, even the soldiers, were blind, unpigmented, and thin-skinned. By contrast, the reproductives had thicker, darker exoskeletons, allowing them to endure light and dryer air. Even so, they only swarmed on humid evenings. Unlike their nestbound brothers and sisters, they possessed wings and eyes. But their flight was weak and fluttering, and unless aided by air currents, none travelled too far from their birthplace. Upon landing, they discarded their wings, having no further use for them. The insects crawled around on the ground until they chanced to meet a member of the opposite sex.

The female raised the tip of her abdomen provocatively and emitted an attractive scent. The besotted male then fell in line behind her, and together they searched for a nest site. Having lost their wings, they reverted to their proper termite senses. No longer attracted by light, they were now sensibly repelled by it.

Agreeing upon a rotting tree stump as a suitable home, they prepared an underground chamber and sealed themselves securely within. Only then did they consummate their union. The fortunate male was not doomed to an early death, as were the drones of wasps and bees. Instead he would reign for years, side by side with his queen, over a vast and complex insect society that had changed little over millions of years.

Meanwhile, back at their birth nest, the swarm exits were swiftly sealed.

Although blind, the termites possessed sensitive antennae, along with sensory pores and hairs all over their bodies. When they detected the vibration of Ted's chainsaw, soldiers struck their heads against the roof and floor of their tunnels to communicate the alarm.

It was critical to the well-being of such thin-skinned creatures to maintain humidity at close to saturation point. But unlike the European wasps, these native termites had evolved in a fire-prone landscape for millions of years, and their nest contained a built-in fire escape. As the heat and noise rose, the insects retreated, carrying their eggs to deeper, cooler nest chambers further underground. Here they sheltered, insulated by the earth, until rain moistened the upper chambers. Only then did they venture upwards and return to lives of dark normality.

CHAPTER SIXTEEN

Christmas morning. Never before had Beth experienced such intense pleasure in the delight of her children. The looming custody dispute imbued each happy exclamation and glad smile with special poignancy.

Things she once took for granted about the festive season had taken on a heightened significance. Decorating the tree, playing carols, wrapping presents. Final checks on Christmas Eve. The shining anticipation in her children's eyes. Beth tried to hold onto and savour each precious moment. Such an uncertain future stretched before her, and she appreciated, perhaps for the first time, the brevity of childhood.

Rick and Sarah had roused Beth at dawn, spreading goodies from their Santa sacks over her bed, both talking at once. Afterwards, they went downstairs to open the presents under the tree.

'Not all of them,' said Beth. 'We have to save some for when your father comes.'

'Which presents can I have now, Mum?' Rick put a gift to his ear and shook it.

'That one, and that one … and the one wrapped in purple paper at the back. Nan and Gramps sent it all the way from France. We'll Zoom with them after breakfast.'

Beth's parents lived in Lyon. She hadn't yet confided in them about her difficulties with Mark. Her mother, in particular, was a terrible worrier and Beth wanted to spare her. Anyway, after today the problem might well be solved.

As she watched the children rip open their presents, a sudden rush of tears stung her eyes. She didn't know if they were tears of pleasure or pain.

Sarah glanced at her mother and saw the glistening drops on her cheek. A cloud of concern crossed the girl's face. Beth wiped her eyes and smiled at Sarah, whose worry seemed to evaporate. She rushed over, swinging an ornate bridle in her hand.

'It's beautiful, Mum. Look, the browband is royal blue to match my new saddlecloth.'

Not to be outdone, Rick produced a toy laser gun and began to shoot his sister. Extricating herself from the excited pair, Beth gathered up the torn wrapping paper, planning her day as she went.

Mark and Lena were coming for lunch. Although this was a daunting prospect for Beth, Rick and Sarah were thrilled. What children wouldn't love having their parents together for Christmas? But their joy was merely a happy side effect. The main purpose of today was for Beth to convince Lena that the children should stay exactly where they were. The Family Court would never award Mark custody if his partner wasn't on board.

Beth had all her persuasive arguments ready. First, she'd appeal to Lena, mother to mother, and ask her how *she'd* feel about being separated from Chance. Then Beth would throw in some practical considerations: the extra expense, the lack of privacy and the additional stress that full-time stepchildren would place on Lena's relationship with Mark.

It wouldn't be easy to build a bridge. Beth's attitude to Lena up to this point had been cool, even cold. Well, what could the girl expect? Lena wasn't solely responsible for the demise of Beth's marriage, but she'd willingly given it a decent kick downhill. Beth tried to compose herself. Enough with the negativity. To recruit Lena as an ally, she needed to put on a positive face.

Beth busied herself in the kitchen. Soon the house was filled with the tantalising aroma of roasting turkey and steaming pudding. Once the cooking was under control, Beth called Sarah and they went down to the stable to give the horses their Christmas carrots and apples.

Walking back, they'd almost reached the front porch when Beth heard a rustle in the bushes and saw a swift flash of dark toffee-coloured scales. She put a cautionary hand on her daughter's arm.

A two metre eastern brown snake emerged from the garden and made a beeline for their fluffy white cat, Spooky, who was sunning himself on the doorstep. The foolish cat gazed curiously at the approaching predator, seemingly unaware of the danger.

Beth picked up a plastic plant pot, and with a deft toss landed it close enough to Spooky to startle him into retreat. The snake, however, was not of such a timid disposition. It coiled the full length of its flawless, musclebound body in concentric rings upon the porch.

Snakes were usually shy creatures. So shy, that Beth had rarely seen one before at Benbullen. This reptile was apparently an exception. Beth and the snake regarded each other from a safe distance. They appeared to have reached an impasse.

Beth warned Sarah to move back. Eastern browns were the world's second most venomous land snake, after the inland taipan. The reptile raised its head, which was small and barely distinct from its sinuous body. Its orange-flecked belly was coloured a rich creamy yellow, and its skin was textured like expensive silk. It was, without a doubt, magnificent.

Beth found herself thinking of the snake as female. It seemed distinctly elegant and feminine. And its eyes – twin golden globes – were mesmerising. Snakes were notorious for their spellbinding stare. Intellectually, Beth knew this was because they did not blink. A transparent scale protected their fixed eyelid. Yet she'd never seen such a hypnotic gaze in the pet snakes she'd encountered. Their eyes held nothing of this wild creature's magnetic fire.

Was that why Spooky had remained motionless on the porch? Had he been held captive by the reptile's stare. Beth felt a little paralysed herself.

'What are you going to do?' asked Sarah as the bold snake showed no inclination to move.

Good question. Beth tossed another plant pot. The snake raised its body off the ground in an S shape, forked tongue darting in and out between thin lips. Then it flowed into the little garden by the front door and disappeared into the tangle of ferns and cornflowers.

Beth found herself in a quandary. She couldn't take her eyes off the garden for fear the creature would slip away unnoticed to somewhere else close to the house. For the moment, at least, she knew where it was.

'We can't leave it by the front door,' said Sarah. 'What about when Dad comes?'

She was right, of course. 'Take Spooky and the dogs inside via the back door, then go get your brother,' said Beth. 'And can you bring me my phone? It's in the kitchen.'

Sarah returned with an excited Rick in tow and a book about snakes under one arm. Beth instructed the children to put on gloves and collect rakes and brooms from the shed. So armed, they stood guard on either side of the garden while Beth made a frantic phone call to her neighbour. He was an excellent bushman and would know what to do. He didn't answer. The shire ranger's number also rang out, as did the local snake catcher's. Fighting a rising feeling of panic, Beth rang Noah, but his phone was turned off. She tried a few neighbours further down the road, but nobody could help. It was, after all, Christmas Day.

Beth felt increasingly horrified by the advice she was receiving, even though she knew it was well-meant.

'Sorry, we're not home or Doug would come straight round. Why not use a whipper-snipper? That'll chop it up pretty good,' and, 'We're on our way to my brother's place, but I wish I was there with my shot-gun,' and, 'Take an axe, break its back, then chop the bastard's head off.'

Beth couldn't believe what she was hearing. Snakes were protected under the Wildlife Act. It was illegal to kill or harm them, and Beth didn't want to. But how to move it from beside the front door?

She checked the time on her phone. Good grief, after eleven already and Mark was due at one o'clock. She gave what she hoped was a reassuring smile to the children who were bravely holding their positions, and considered her options. One thing was certain – the snake couldn't stay where it was. It had to go. Beth looked at a garden spade leaning against the wall of the house, considering the awful possibility that she might have to kill the snake after all.

Sarah followed her mother's gaze and her eyes widened in horror. 'You can't, Mum. Not on Christmas!'

Beth sighed, remembering the snake's proud, bright eyes, so full of life. With a sinking feeling she realised there was only one thing she could do. She must catch it herself.

How hard could it be, anyway? She didn't have a proper catching pole, but Beth had seen people on television succeed without one. She went through the technique in her mind. Take one snake. Immobilise by pressing a stick onto its neck and then quickly grasp it directly behind the head. Drop it into a handy canvas drawstring bag. Take it to a wildlife park where the snake can be exhibited for the education of the public, milked for antivenene or released back into the wild.

She explained her idea to the children.

'Cool,' said Rick. 'Can I keep it?'

Sarah looked unconvinced by the plan. 'Are you sure you can do this, Mum?'

'Of course,' she said, with a confidence she did not feel. 'You two stay here while I get ready.' Beth dashed into the house and put on thick trousers, a jumper, gumboots, and impervious (she hoped) leather gloves. Then she ventured into the patch of garden. Right! First, catch your snake.

Her attempt was accompanied by cheerful remarks from Rick, who was armed with the book of facts about snakes. 'Did you know that they can rear up as high as your waist to deliver a fatal bite?' he said, as she parted the ferns with an old axe handle. 'It says here that nearly all Australian snakes are highly venomous,' and, 'I thought I saw the snake near your leg just before. I forgot to tell you,' and, 'If the snake doesn't get you, I think that spider might.'

'Be quiet, Rick,' hissed Beth. 'You're not helping.' She didn't need Rick to tell her how dangerous the snake was.

Methodically she prodded the ground in an effort to locate her quarry. After ten nervous minutes Beth spotted the telltale gleam of amber scales. Pushing aside the foliage, she discovered the snake weaving its head to and fro in a vain attempt to escape through the narrow slats of a ventilator grill set in the wall of the house. The creature was in a state of panic, yet even with the threat of Beth looming large, its every instinct was still to flee. Beth took a bottomless breath, pressed the axe handle into the nape of its neck and made a grab ... gotcha!

Rick jumped up and down, cheering. Beth had the snake gripped firmly behind the head. This indignity was the final straw for the frightened reptile. With its neck craned at an impossible angle, it delivered a desperate sideways attack.

Beth watched as the snake clamped its jaws onto the edge of her gloved hand. Two things saved her from a fatal envenomation. The awkward angle of the bite and the fact that eastern browns had short fangs relative to their size; fangs that penetrated the thick exterior of the glove, but didn't reach all the way through. With a remarkable sense of calm Beth watched streams of opaque venom run down the tough leather. She gently manoeuvred her fingers closer to the reptile's head, increasing her control.

Beth admired her prize in disbelief. When the snake wrapped its powerful body around her arm, it felt like an honour.

At their mother's invitation, the children approached to stroke the snake.

'It's beautiful,' said Sarah. 'The skin feels so soft.'

'Not slimy at all,' agreed Rick. 'Are you sure I can't keep it?'

Beth was equally enchanted. A few flakes of what looked like tissue paper clung to its body. So, the snake had recently shed its skin. That explained its dazzling colours and brilliant eyes. The new skin was like a coat of clear celluloid, highlighting the vivid hues beneath.

Delightful as this unusual wildlife encounter was, Beth couldn't hang onto the snake forever.

'What happens now?' asked Sarah, reading her mother's mind.

'We'll keep it somewhere safe and out of the way until after lunch. Now, where to put it?'

'A chaff bag?' suggested Rick.

'No, it might bite through that.'

'How about your old leather duffle bag?' said Sarah.

'Good idea. Go get it,' said Beth, growing increasingly nervous. The angry snake whipped its tail from side to side. It was likely to attack upon release.

Sarah returned with the battered overnight bag and opened it wide. Beth cast an appraising eye over it and decided it would have to do. She looked back at the snake, mesmerised once more by the golden liquidity of its gaze. Part of her wished the moment would never end.

Heart hammering, Beth prepared to relinquish her prisoner. She lowered the snake into the darkness of the bag with a trembling hand. Steady now. One, two, three! In one swift motion, she let go and slammed the bag shut. Seconds later, the case was zipped and secure.

'Hurray!' Sarah hugged her mother, who was feeling a little weak at the knees.

Rick gave her a congratulatory shake of the hand and knelt down beside the bag, eyes bright with excitement. 'That's the coolest thing I've ever seen.'

He tried to pick up the bag and could barely lift it. Then Sarah had a go. The snake was heavier than they expected. Beth hefted it out of the sun and onto the shady porch.

She was considering her next move when an ear-splitting electronic shriek came from the house. All the colour drained from her face as she recognised the sound of a smoke detect0r. 'The dinner!' she howled.

Sarah rushed inside to investigate. Moments later, she called out. 'It's all burnt. Everything's ruined.'

As Beth absorbed this disastrous information, Mark's red sports car turned into the driveway. The piercing smoke alarm screamed on, a bizarre soundtrack to catastrophe.

Sarah came to the door. 'Mum, didn't you hear me? Dinner's burnt and the dogs have eaten the ham. What will we do when Dad arrives?'

Beth shook her head miserably and pointed down the driveway. Sarah's mouth dropped open as her father's car pulled up on the gravel at the front of the house.

CHAPTER SEVENTEEN

Rick ran over to Mark's car in a state of high excitement. 'Guess what, guess what? Mum's got a huge, poisonous snake in that bag and she's burnt Christmas lunch.'

Sarah, glaring at her brother, looked close to tears.

Beth turned her back, steeled herself and went inside. In the kitchen, she was confronted by a terrible scene. Dell was contentedly chewing on the remains of the leg of ham. The plum pudding that Beth had made with such care had long since boiled dry and lay like a large, wrinkled prune in the base of a blackened saucepan. She couldn't bear to look in the oven to discover the fate of the turkey and vegetables.

Beth opened the window and the sliding door. All the while, the infernal shrieking of the smoke detector blared on. Fetching a broom from the laundry, she used its handle to silence the alarm. Then she shoved the dogs into their run before venturing onto the front porch, where she found Mark curiously poking the duffel bag with his foot.

Lena stood at the bottom of the verandah steps wearing a white halter-neck top that exposed her midriff. Cut-off designer jeans barely covered her underpants. Lena's evenly tanned legs were bare, except for a pair of strappy, leopard print high-heeled sandals. A ridiculous outfit for a day in the country.

Sarah was sitting in the car beside Chance, who was asleep in his baby capsule. Rick was gleefully relating the events of the morning to his father, adding a few colourful embellishments along the way.

Beth gritted her teeth and gathered her wits, determined to salvage the situation. 'Why don't you all come inside?' she said with forced gaiety.

'What on earth were you thinking?' asked Mark in amazement, when Rick finished his story. 'You and the kids could have been killed.'

Lena ventured up the porch steps and stared nervously at the duffel bag. 'Is there really a snake in there?' she asked in a small voice.

'Yes,' answered Beth brightly. 'But don't worry, it's quite safe. I mean, you're quite safe while it's in there. I'll put it away, shall I? Then you can get little Chance out of that hot car.'

As her guests looked on in dismayed silence, Beth picked up the bag, from which came an occasional thump. With an effort, she turned towards the door.

'Inside?' Mark shook his head. 'You must be joking. What will you do then? Invite it for Christmas dinner?'

The children giggled and Beth glared at him.

'I'll put it in the shed and work out what to do with it later. The main thing is to get the kids out of this heat.'

'Chop its bloody head off. That's what I'd do with it,' said Mark.

Beth pretended not to hear him. Mark scowled, but held his peace. His attempt to assist Beth with the bag was politely but firmly refused, so he busied himself helping Rick and Sarah bring the presents inside. Lena took the baby capsule from the car and stepped warily into the hallway.

Meanwhile, Beth hauled the bag around to the back of the house. She had no intention of putting it in the shed, which became unbearably hot during the middle of the day. Concerned for the welfare of the already stressed reptile, she dragged it up the steps to the back door and stashed it in the cool laundry. Then she shut the door and joined her guests in the lounge room.

Beth found the children happily examining a pile of colourfully wrapped gifts. Sarah's mood had brightened and, at her mother's invitation, she began to distribute parcels from under the Christmas tree.

'Children first,' said Rick, and his father cheerfully agreed. Despite the lingering scorched smell from the kitchen, Beth felt that the day was coming under control.

She noticed Mark smiling at her. 'Honey, why don't you go upstairs and change. We'll wait until you come back to open the presents.'

At first Beth thought that Mark was talking to his girlfriend. Although Beth agreed that Lena did indeed need to change, it soon became apparent that his remarks had been directed towards her. What a nerve. And Lena looked understandably put out about Mark calling Beth *honey*.

Beth was ready with a cynical retort, when Sarah – always the peacemaker – whispered, 'You do look a bit of a mess, Mum.' Beth bit her tongue. Thank goodness for Sarah. She couldn't afford to argue with Mark today. It wouldn't hurt to change her clothes if it would keep him happy.

'Don't be long,' said Rick, beside himself with anticipation.

Beth hurried upstairs and took a look in the mirror. It was all she could do to smother a laugh. Flushed face and tangled hair. Clothes dishevelled and soiled from crawling through the garden. Ruefully she thought of the good impression she'd hoped to make.

Looking in her wardrobe, she chose a simple yet elegant green silk blouse and teamed it with a pair of tailored cream pedal pushers. She evaluated herself in the mirror as she brushed her hair and decided she liked her choice. She looked coolly comfortable, with just the right hint of sophistication. A little foundation and lipstick completed the look.

Beth hurried downstairs, eager to get the day back on track.

'Mum's back!' shouted Rick, unnecessarily.

Mark eyed her approvingly as she entered the living room to take her place beside her children. The ritual of opening presents began. Beth had chosen her guests' gifts with great care. For Mark, she'd selected a small but expensive abstract painting by a fashionable artist whose work he loved. Lena received a bottle of French perfume. Both seemed pleased, particularly Lena, who visibly relaxed and proceeded to smother herself and Sarah in the costly fragrance.

At least it helped to hide the burnt smell, thought Beth, as she frowned at Rick for coughing in a pointed and exaggerated way. She distracted him by suggesting he pass out the last gift – a small, exquisitely wrapped parcel.

Rick read the card. 'It's for you, Mum – from Dad.'

'Are you sure?' Beth had already received an ugly crockpot with a card reading, *From Mark, Helena and Chance.* Lena's choice no doubt.

Rick plonked the mystery gift on his mother's lap and went back to hunting under the tree for presents he might have missed. Lena looked unhappy and sat forward in her chair.

'Open it,' urged Mark.

Inside was a velvet jewellery case. It contained a magnificent emerald necklace and matching earrings, all set in white gold. 'Are these real?' Beth asked, already knowing the answer to her question.

Mark laughed with pleasure. He crossed the room and placed the pendant around her neck, moving her hair aside to fasten it.

'They're gorgeous, Mum,' said Sarah. 'Can I try them on?'

For a moment Beth was too confused to respond, but one look at Lena's furious face spurred her into action. 'I can't possibly accept these,' she stammered.

Lena stood up. 'I'm going to check on Chance.' The baby was asleep in another room.

Beth groaned inwardly. Mark's foolish present threatened to

completely derail her plan. How could she promote her case with Lena now? She wanted to slap Mark, yet she needed him on-side too.

Excusing herself, Beth removed the necklace and chased after Lena. She found her in the spare bedroom, changing Chance's nappy and looking like she might cry.

Beth quickly explained that, of course, she would not accept the jewellery, and that she understood why Lena was upset. Mark was an overly generous person, that was all. He didn't understand how inappropriate his gift was. Lena seemed mollified. Beth insisted that she wanted them to be friends and even mocked Mark's poor judgement. 'Men,' she laughed. 'They have no idea, have they?'

Lena managed an uncertain smile.

'Here,' said Beth, reaching out her arms. 'Let me take Chance and give you a break.'

Lena hesitated, then passed the child over. Beth bounced him on her knee and was rewarded with peals of laughter. 'Oh my, he's so big. How much does he weigh now?'

'Eight kilos,' said Lena. 'He's growing out of his baby capsule. What sort of carrier should I buy next, do you think?'

Beth breathed a relieved sigh. They played with Chance and discussed car seats for a while. When they returned to the living room, Sarah was parading around in the emeralds, much to the delight of her father.

Beth escaped to the kitchen. The challenging task of rescuing Christmas lunch still lay ahead. Although the ham, pudding, and vegetables were history, she decided she could salvage the turkey. Under the blackened skin, much of the meat was edible, if a little dry. With the help of some canned ham, she managed to prepare an acceptable meal of cold meat, salad and cranberry sauce. Not such a bad outcome. It was too hot for a cooked dinner anyway. They finished lunch with tinned plum pudding and brandy custard, with the addition of a pavlova she'd prepared the night before, topped with cream and fresh strawberries from the garden.

The meal, together with generous amounts of wine, lifted everybody's spirits. Before long, Lena was happily prattling away to her hostess as if they were old friends.

Rick was playing air shots with his new cricket bat in the living room. Mark held up the matching ball. 'Backyard game?'

'Yay!' chorused the children.

'Any more takers?' Mark looked expectantly at the two women, who shook their heads. A shrug. 'Your loss.' He followed the kids outside, after first pouring himself a large glass of chardonnay to take with him.

Lena sipped her mineral water, looking cross. 'Mark is drinking such a lot these days. I barely drink at all.' She pointed to Beth's white wine. 'Do you know how many calories are in that?' Lena didn't wait for Beth to answer. 'Mark takes advantage of me being sober. He always has a designated driver and never has to be responsible about alcohol.'

Beth was a little sceptical about Lena's complaints. The Mark she used to know rarely overindulged, but she made comforting noises just the same. She sensed that the young woman was lonely, unhappy even, and her heart softened towards her. Beth was also increasingly hopeful of successfully broaching the subject of custody with Lena later that afternoon.

'Chance likes you,' said Lena, as he pulled at Beth's buttons. They talked about baby sleep routines, nappies and introducing solids. Lena was hungry to learn of Beth's experience as a mother. She was really quite sweet when you got to know her.

Mark came back in with the kids. Perspiration plastered strands of hair to his face. He plonked his empty wine glass on the table and wiped his brow. 'Phew, it's hot out there,' He looked at the empty bottle in the ice bucket. 'That's not a bad drop. Got any more?'

Lena glanced at Beth, frowning and shaking her head. Beth pretended not to notice. She cared nothing for Mark's state of sobriety or otherwise, and she certainly didn't want to upset him. 'There's more wine in the laundry fridge.'

Mark took the empty bottle and left the room. Too late, Beth remembered the snake. She handed Chance to his mother, leapt from her seat and rushed after Mark. As she reached the laundry, she heard a loud curse. Mark burst back through the open door, almost knocking her over. 'Are you mad?' He gestured angrily towards the offending duffel bag that lay fair and square in the middle of the laundry floor. As they watched, it quivered.

Lena followed hot on Beth's heels. She screamed when she spied the animated bag. Nothing Beth could say was able to calm either of her guests. She tried hard to keep her head, but when Mark threatened to drown her precious snake by throwing the bag in the dam, Beth finally lost her temper.

'Don't you dare touch that bag! I apologised for walking out on you at lunch, remember? Well, I take it back. You're such a cold bastard, I'd walk out on you now if I didn't live here.'

Despite her white-hot anger, Beth couldn't help noticing that Mark looked genuinely hurt by her outburst. Since when could words hurt Mark?

Lena's pain was more understandable. 'Lunch?' she asked. 'You two had lunch?'

Mark and Beth ceased personal hostilities and held their breath. Without another word, Lena returned to the living room and began to gather her things. Beth followed, attempting to explain, but Lena ignored her.

When Mark came in, he wasn't so lucky. His infuriated girlfriend turned on him in a rage. 'Expensive jewellery, secret lunches – what else don't I know about?'

Mark said nothing. He couldn't win this one.

Lena strapped Chance into his capsule, picked up her perfume and grabbed the car keys. Sarah crept forward. She put Chance's gift, a soft toy elephant, in the capsule beside him and gave him a swift kiss.

Mark began to collect his things. 'It looks like we're going,' he said lamely.

'Correction. *I'm* going,' shrilled Lena. 'You can stay and finish your lover's spat with snake woman here.' She turned to leave, paused for a moment, returned for the emeralds, and then swept self-righteously out the door.

Beth looked on aghast, expecting Mark to remonstrate with his girlfriend, but he seemed resigned, even indifferent to her departure. 'Go after Lena,' she ordered. 'Now!'

Mark sighed and did as he was told.

Beth heard some shouting, then the sound of the Mustang speeding away. A quick look out the window revealed Mark still standing in the driveway. Sarah and Rick exchanged smiles. They couldn't help feeling happy that their dad had stayed.

Beth sank down on the couch and started to sob. Her clever plan had come to nothing. It was easily the worst day of her life. The children rushed to comfort her, and as she looked into their earnest faces, her tears dried. Beth began to see the funny side of things.

'Why did Lena leave?' asked Rick.

'Mum put the snake in the laundry,' whispered Sarah.

'Oh.' Rick nodded as if this explained everything.

Beth couldn't resist a smile, pleased that the kids seemed okay and that she hadn't completely ruined their Christmas.

She went to find Mark, who was drinking again out on the verandah. As he met her gaze, she was taken aback by the vulnerability in his eyes. She had not seen it there before.

'Listen Mark, I've rung a local wildlife park. They can take the snake. I won't be gone more than an hour. Come inside and watch the kids until I get back please.'

He nodded agreement and followed her inside. Beth took his half full wineglass. 'I think you've had enough.'

'Let's play Uno,' said Sarah, producing the deck she'd got for Christmas.

Beth left Mark and the children playing cards. She fetched the snake from the laundry and stowed it in the back of her station wagon. Then she set off, confident at least that nothing more could go wrong on this sweltering Christmas Day.

CHAPTER EIGHTEEN

Mark listened to Beth's car leave and examined his feelings. Lena's accusations echoed in his head, yet he felt nothing. He remembered the hurt in her eyes as she took their child and left, yet he couldn't dredge up any emotions regarding her sudden departure: not disappointment, not anger, not surprise. Nothing.

Mark poured more wine, aware he was getting drunk and not caring. Although he wasn't sure why he bothered. Drinking no longer dulled the pain. There was no pain to dull. He felt strangely numb, sealed within a protective cocoon of his own indifference.

His thoughts turned to Beth. Hang on a minute, there was pain after all. He pictured her sitting forlornly on the porch with that snake-filled duffel bag beside her. Cool and elegant, always the gracious hostess, presiding over the make-do Christmas dinner. Reaching out to Lena and helping her with baby Chance. How many ex-partners would do that? She really was adorable.

His father, Robert, had warned him against leaving Beth. 'That girl's perfect for you,' he'd said. 'She grounds you. Without her, you'll lose your way.' How right Dad was, thought Mark. Why hadn't he listened?

Mark valued his father's opinion highly, as did everyone. Robert

York possessed the rare ability to succeed in the business world without compromising his integrity. As CEO of a large financial institution, he was renowned for his balanced, consultative management style combined with a certain fearlessness. He loved to take a measured risk and then defy the odds and the pessimistic predictions of the pundits. But he never played dirty. Robert was respected by all and admired for his courage and vision. Unfortunately, that courage didn't extend to his dealings with his wife, Mark's mother, Vanessa.

As Mark's frozen emotions thawed he began to feel better. Sarah came in. 'Dad, can we go down to the stable?'

'Sure. You can show me how you ride that pony again. Cheer us both up, eh?'

Before long, the delighted girl was trotting a reluctant Skittles in circles before her admiring father. The blazing sun beat down on Mark's hatless head, forcing him to seek the shade offered by the stable eaves.

Although he kept one eye on his daughter, his thoughts remained with her mother. How could he convince Beth that he still cared? She wanted everyone to think that she was so capable, so independent, yet today's events had demonstrated otherwise. She needed protection. Beth was too soft for her own good and always had been. By contrast, Lena seemed grasping and selfish. Beauty wasn't enough to compensate for such flaws. He wondered what he'd ever seen in her.

A paper wasp buzzed harmlessly past him on her way home. Mark ducked in fear and watched her fly off behind the stable. Cautiously he followed and discovered her nest. The innocent insect bore scant resemblance to a European wasp, but Mark was no naturalist. For him, all wasps automatically deserved to die.

An idea was forming. This was one practical problem he could solve for Beth. She'd been searching for the wasp nest, and now he'd found it for her. He could destroy it before she arrived home. How grateful she'd be for his help. Being on the receiving end of Beth's gratitude was a tantalising prospect.

Mark hailed his daughter, telling her that he needed to go back up to the house to get something.

'I'll come with you,' called Sarah. 'It's too hot out here anyway.' She rode Skittles up the path alongside her father, chatting away happily, never asking him what it was that he required from the house.

Sarah led Skittles behind the garage to hose him down, while her father went to the shed and selected a sturdy shovel and two cans of insect spray. Armed with these tools he returned to the stable to destroy the nest. For the native wasps, it would prove to be a fatal case of mistaken identity.

In an effort to be thorough, Mark decided to inspect all four stable walls. Peering cautiously up into the darkness under the eaves, he could at first see nothing. Gradually his eyes adjusted to the contrast between bright sun and deep shade. Now he could make out the array of little pots and spouts belonging to the potter wasps. He disturbed a large tiger-striped wasp that was just commencing to build in a corner. This single sighting confirmed his suspicions and thus sealed the fate of all.

Such was his fear of insects, especially biting and stinging ones, that his courage almost failed him. However alcohol-fuelled bravado, combined with an overwhelming desire to impress Beth, spurred him on.

Not for a moment did he pause to consider the miraculous ingenuity and parental devotion of the nest builders. He didn't stop to marvel at the staggering investment of time and energy represented by the building and provisioning of the sturdy mud nurseries. He harboured no sympathy for the innocent, developing wasplings whose lives he was poised to take so needlessly.

With forceful strokes of the shovel, he pounded the little nests, fearful all the while of encountering an angry wasp. Being ignorant of the potter wasps' biology, he didn't realise there were no adults to protect the helpless brood. He pulverised each ruined nest beneath his boot, killing or mortally wounding the babies within. He then sprayed them with insecticide, just to be on the safe side.

One potter wasp flew towards the carnage, complete with a mud pellet held in her mandibles. She had just begun to build, but now her embryonic nest was laid to waste. The commotion combined with the vile smell of the insect spray warned her to give the site a wide berth. In confusion, she flew away. She would begin her work anew tomorrow, unaware that Mark had smothered the eaves in a residual surface spray. This toxic legacy would doom to sickness and death any future wasps who tried to nest there.

Well satisfied by his work and emboldened by the lack of defence, Mark moved on to the paper wasp colony. Despite the obvious differences in form between the mud and paper nests, he failed to appreciate that there could also be a difference in the behaviour of the residents. He raised the sharp shovel and gave the delicate, umbrella-like shape a savage jab.

The force of the blow broke the narrow stem securing the nest to the roof. It hit the ground at his feet, retaining its shape thanks to the durable wasp-made paper of which it was woven.

Wasps on guard in and near the nest sprang into instant action. Mark found himself buzzed by a dozen or more, all aggressively pressing their attack. One landed on his hand. He shook it off in alarm and sprayed insect killer profusely into the air. But it was too thinly diffused to disable the angry wasps. One alighted on his ear and delivered a sharp sting. He yelled out as three more stung his forearm. Another stung the nape of his neck.

Fear increased his pain as a powerful panic gripped him. The natural world had always been alien to him, and ignorance added to his alarm. He'd read about attacks involving hundreds of wasps. He didn't know that the twenty or so native wasps defending the wrecked nest comprised almost the full complement of its adult workers.

Mark abandoned his tools of destruction and ran.

An icepack or two later, Mark was in better spirits and feeling pretty proud of himself. He had risked his own well-being to rescue his family from a serious threat to their health and safety. As his fear subsided, his self-satisfaction grew. Between the wasps and the snake incident, it was clearer than ever that Beth needed him. She just couldn't see it yet.

Sarah came in, having finished hosing down her pony and turning him out. Mark was sitting in the lounge room, drinking a cup of coffee and balancing a pack of frozen berries on his neck.

'What happened to you, Dad?'

'I had to do an important job for your mum,' he said rather grandly. 'Finally solved her wasp problem. I got a few stings, but that didn't stop me.'

'Where was the nest?'

'Down at the stable. There were a few of them actually. The place was infested with them.'

Sarah's face fell at her father's words. 'You didn't do anything to the nests at the stable, did you? Mum loves those nests.'

'Don't be silly, Sarah. I happen to know that your mother has been looking for those wasps for ages.'

'But Dad, those weren't European wasp nests. They were natives. Mum loves those nests and spends hours watching them. She's going to go ballistic.'

'Nonsense. A wasp is a wasp,' said Mark, dismissing his daughter's warning. He waited for Beth, confident that she'd thank him on her return.

Sarah went to warn Rick what their father had done, confident that they had both better make themselves scarce.

CHAPTER NINETEEN

When Lena reached Melbourne, she turned off the freeway at Toorak Road as usual, but she wasn't going home. The long and harrowing drive had given her time for some much-needed soul-searching. A subtle paradigm shift had occurred in her brain when she observed Mark's crestfallen face after Beth's furious outburst. There was no doubt about it – he was in love with his wife again.

Inconceivable as this was, it explained a lot: Mark's loss of libido, his neglect of her needs, his impatience with her spending and his indifference to their son. It all fitted together in Lena's mind like a completed jigsaw.

Distasteful as this realisation was, it didn't come as a complete surprise. Intuition told her that Mark no longer loved her – not the way he used to. She'd been pressing him to get a divorce from Beth so that they could marry. His reluctance should have sounded alarm bells, yet complacency had clouded her perception. Now her vision was crystal clear.

Lena required both to be loved and to be in love at all times. She did not respond well to a vacuum in that area of her life. A shrink once told her that this was because she lacked a sense of her own identity. Well, whatever the reason, she found her current situation intolerable.

Lena didn't blame Beth. As far as Lena was concerned, all was indeed fair in love and war, and she wouldn't waste time being bitter about her rival. Beth had somehow outwitted her and emerged as the unlikely victor. Good luck to her.

Mark, on the other hand? His cold betrayal of her and their son was unforgivable; a wound so deep it cut straight to her heart. Grimly, she vowed to make him pay.

Her immediate need, however, was to relieve her current overwhelming state of misery. Lena didn't intend to go home and wait there alone for her faithless partner. She already knew the self-help she required. All that remained was for her to solve a few practical problems.

Twenty minutes later Lena arrived at an elegant two-storey home in the leafy bayside suburb of Brighton. She grabbed her baby bag from the back seat. Chance had woken up crying. Lena tried unsuccessfully to quieten her son, then gave up and hauled his capsule from the car.

Carting her baby in one hand and the bag in the other, Lena struggled up the white granite steps. She hoped that Mark's father would open the door. Robert was a sweet man, a true gentleman who'd always been kind to her. Mark's mother on the other hand? Snooty Vanessa had taken an inexplicable dislike to Lena right from the start.

Vanessa opened the door and found herself confronted by a tearful Helena and her screaming baby. Despite the pair's obvious distress, her first instinct was to not ask them in. She distinctly remembered telling Mark to come for drinks at five o'clock and it was barely three. Such rudeness should not be excused, lest it be encouraged.

Lena marched in anyway, dumping the baby's bag on the tiled floor. Vanessa peered hopefully out of the doorway looking for Mark.

When it became clear that he wasn't there, the reluctant hostess closed the door and frowned at her unwelcome guests.

'You're too early, my dear. Where is Mark?'

Even in the middle of her own wretchedness, Lena had enough presence of mind not to criticise Mark in front of his mother.

'We've had a fight,' she said.

'Is he alright?' asked Vanessa.

Is *he* alright? Typical, thought Lena. What about me? I'm the one who's crying here. A shaft of anger pierced her despair and helped her to collect her thoughts. 'I just needed to get away for a bit.' Lena pasted on a smile. 'You understand, don't you?'

Vanessa clearly did not. 'My dear, you can't stay. I have a house full of people. Robert is entertaining some important colleagues this afternoon and we are simply not prepared for extra guests.'

Lena wasn't listening. 'Here, take bub for a minute. I need to freshen up.' She placed Chance in the arms of his astonished grandmother and escaped to the guest bathroom to fix her hair and make-up, and to put on Beth's emeralds. She admired herself in the magnificent mahogany-framed mirror. The jewels flashed and sparkled against her golden skin, lifting her spirits.

In contrast, the only thing rising in Vanessa was her displeasure. It didn't take long for her to realise that her grizzling grandson was hungry, wet and soiled after his car trip. Vanessa looked up hopefully as Lena hurried back from the bathroom. Lena gave her an encouraging smile and bestowed a lingering kiss on Chance's cheek.

'You don't mind, do you? I really must sort things out with Mark. Give Chance a bottle if he's hungry. There's powdered baby formula in the bag.'

'But my dear ...' Before Vanessa could object, Lena was out the front door.

. . .

Shortly afterwards, she pulled into the carpark of the Belmont Hotel and made good her escape from painful reality. An enormous wave of relief crashed in, sweeping away Lena's black mood. It was replaced by a familiar tingle of anticipation.

As she entered the venue, a keen pair of eyes followed her. Jason Black worked at the hotel as a security guard. He was a well-built young man with regular features, short dark hair and an engaging, boyish smile.

Jason had observed Lena many times before. She always followed the same pattern of behaviour. After making a brief visit to the ladies room, she played the poker machines for hours at a time, pausing occasionally to approach the bar and refresh a glass of chilled mineral water, with a twist of lime.

When she first arrived, she'd roam from machine to machine in a restless, distracted fashion. Within half an hour she settled on a particular machine and was thereafter loyal to it.

Such an attractive woman, flying solo, could not fail to attract attention. She drew many admiring glances, with none more admiring than Jason's. He'd made a habit of keeping an eye on her, half convincing himself that it was his professional responsibility to look out for such a vulnerable young patron. Yet deep down he knew his interest was intensely personal.

Jason was, purely and simply, besotted. She intrigued him in a way unmatched by any of the other pretty girls he saw there. For a start, single and presumably available young women usually arrived in pairs or small groups, mingling in the bars as well as the gaming rooms. Lena always came alone. She often arrived early in the morning, breezing in moments after opening time. Only committed gamblers arrived so promptly. It was odd though, thought Jason. She didn't fit the profile of a problem gambler. Lena wore no wedding ring, and bore scant resemblance to the general run of dour, daytime house-wives who played the machines with vacant eyes.

Once Lena bestowed her favours on her chosen machine, the

envious Jason couldn't help feeling that she treated it rather like a lover. Her slim, sensuous fingers played with the buttons, flicking over their metallic surface in a flirtatious fashion. With an intensity reserved for Jason only in his dreams, her big blue eyes opened even wider as she watched the reels dance and spin. When she won, she laughed out loud and tossed her head. Soft, blonde curls caressed her face and bare shoulders in a way that aroused Jason's desire, often in an embarrassingly physical way.

When she lost, her lips took on a petulant pout, making them look larger and more luscious. Yet her sparkling eyes retained their twinkle, and it was clear that her losses did not detract from her enjoyment. She seemed utterly unconcerned about the speed and amounts of her credit card withdrawals. This was not a woman on a budget. Only when she went for a meal was her vivacious expression replaced by one of boredom. Hurrying to the bistro, she picked disinterestedly at a seafood salad or fruit platter, then returned to her machine with shining eyes and a spring in her step.

However, even Jason was surprised to see the object of his infatuation arrive late in the afternoon on Christmas Day. Apart from some groups of young people avoiding tiresome family get-togethers, only a few lonely elderly folk were trying their luck today. She looked particularly dazzling, and there was a single-minded determination about her that Jason hadn't seen before. He wandered after her, trying to look casual, determined to stick close.

Scouting the gaming room, Lena assessed her options. Anxiety ebbed away as if she were meeting old friends. Her gaze wandered from one machine to the next. There was *Follow the Stars* with its astrological symbols, and *Cleopatra* with exotic depictions of scarabs, snakes and mummies. *Adonis* caught her eye with its paintings of muscular male bodies, as did *Panther Magic*, covered with sensual big cats. The mythological creatures of *Unicorn Dreaming* beckoned, beside jaunty scenes of lizards in top hats and suits on the machine named *Cash Chameleon.*

So many machines to choose from. *Orchid Mist*, romantically festooned with flowers. *Enchantress*, boasting magical images of witches and wizards, wands and broomsticks. *Koala Mist* was adorned with cute furry animals, while *Rocking and a'Reeling* carried pictures of Elvis-like figures with guitars and sideburns.

For some reason, Lena felt herself drawn to a machine she hadn't played before. It had always frightened her a little, with its brooding African jungle scenes. On this day, however, it perfectly suited her dark mood. Lena settled at the machine named *Black Rhino* and began to play.

Jason wasn't the only one to notice her. Seated next to Lena at a gold-embossed machine entitled *Winning Touch*, was a short, elderly, rather overweight man, with receding grey hair and huge, round horn-rimmed glasses. They made him look like a wise old owl. He stole the occasional sideways glance at her as she sank deeper and deeper into the comfort of her gambling.

Today, Lena wasn't driven by the excitement of a potential win. She was in it to lose, to punish Mark. With few emotional weapons left in her arsenal, deliberate financial sabotage was an obvious tool of reprisal. Inserting a hundred dollar note into *Black Rhino's* throat, she wagered ten dollars with every spin. Thirty seconds later, she'd lost the lot. Perfect. Her elation grew as she proceeded at this staggering rate of loss.

The greater the toll, the more Lena revenged herself. Periodically she received payouts, and familiar feelings of happiness and warmth claimed her. She quickly gambled away these windfalls. For Lena it was a win–win situation. She could vent anger and savour success all at once – the perfect foil for her misery.

Every aspect of the experience served to soothe her. The rattle of the coins. The flashing lights and colourful symbols that were, for Lena, imbued with mysterious hidden meanings. The catchy up-tempo music and rock anthems that played when she won a jackpot. She even loved the smooth sensation of sliding banknotes into the slot. Her hands craved to push those buttons, to make the reels spin with wild abandon. It gave her a powerful sense of control.

Sometimes her fingers coaxed win after win from the machine, and adrenaline surged through her body. At other times, the whirling images and flashing lights lulled her into a type of trance. Occasionally, she stroked the machine or slipped the silk scarf from around her neck, covering the screen for fun and luck. When the reels stopped spinning, Lena slowly removed the scarf, the action accompanied by surprised little *oohs* and *aahs*. It made her feel sexy and desirable, like she was dancing some sort of poker machine striptease and the *Black Rhino* was her lover.

A voice penetrated Lena's hypnotic daze. It took her a little while to comprehend that the gentleman from the neighbouring machine was speaking. This startled her, as she'd found that gambling was one of the few times that she didn't attract much attention.

'Allow me to introduce myself. My name is Konrad Smith. Come, my dear. Come with me and take a break. I wish to share coffee with you.'

Lena's initial resentment at the intrusion gave way to relief as she met the man's gaze. It had been a long time since she'd seen such open friendliness in another's eyes.

She rose unsteadily to her feet. Her back ached. Her legs were stiff and stinging with pins and needles. Her eyes were sore and dry from unbroken hours staring at the screen. She squeezed them shut in an attempt to lubricate them. Bright symbols still floated and twirled on the inside of her eyelids. A wave of dizziness came over her, and she felt her heart race.

Lena staggered slightly and a nearby security guard moved forward and offered a supportive arm. She took the old man's arm instead.

'Thank you, Konrad. I'm Helena, Lena for short, and I do need to stretch my legs. Coffee would be lovely.'

Soon the pair were seated before steaming cups of cappuccino. Konrad took off his glasses and cleaned them with a paper napkin. 'To have a fifty percent chance of winning on the *Black Rhino* you would have to press the button 6.7 million times.' Lena sipped her coffee. 'To do so would take 391 days of continuous twenty-four-hours-a-day play.'

'That could be arranged,' she said, coolly.

He tilted his head. 'It would cost nearly $630,000.'

'Good,' said Lena.

Konrad sighed and put his glasses back on. 'Have you no family? I myself have not. So I come to this place where the food is cheap and plentiful and, occasionally, I make a connection.' He took her hands in his and patted them.

Lena felt a catch in her throat. The old man's kindness melted her defences and she began to unburden herself. With some encouragement, she confided to Konrad all that had happened that day and more. She told him of her loneliness, her feelings of betrayal, her fears for the future; in a great stream of consciousness, she poured out her grief and anxiety. When she'd finished, an immense sense of relief engulfed her, threatening to unleash a torrent of tears. Konrad squeezed her hands fondly, then indicated their fellow gamblers.

'We are, all of us, here for the same reason. We fear an empty place in our souls. This game permits us to trust in fate. Fate is neither scientific nor logical. When we gamble, we defy rationality, and thus we defy the limits of our human condition. We become transcendent.'

Lena listened, fascinated. Konrad's words seemed filled with meaning and wisdom.

'Are you a religious woman, my dear?'

Lena shook her head.

'I myself have lost my faith,' he whispered.

'I never had one to begin with.'

'Aah, then we are both bereft,' said Konrad. 'We have no God. We live and die for nothing. We have only this material world that reduces everything to science. Take the moon, for example, which is now the focus of geological analysis rather than the subject of poetry.'

'What has this got to do with poker machines?' asked Lena, her eyes growing large.

Konrad warmed to his topic. 'Fate replaces religion. Old truths wane, and our new faith is located in the notion of chance. The magic of luck will transform our lives and thereby logic and mystery can once more coexist.'

Lena was transfixed. Her thoughts turned to the various attempts she'd made to add purpose to her increasingly empty life. Crystals, Tarot cards, astrology – she'd flirted with them all, much to Mark's disgust. Yet the vacuum at her centre remained. Mark's increasing emotional distance made her even more acutely aware of the aimlessness of her existence. She tried to make sense of Konrad's words.

'So you think there's a spiritual basis for gambling?'

'Of course, my dear. Our faith in chance gives us back our hope, does it not? In a godless world, all of us here seek salvation through gambling.'

Jason stood nearby, trying to eavesdrop on the gorgeous young woman and her unlikely escort. Today was the first time he'd heard her voice properly – musical but with a husky depth to it. He thought she sounded just like Marilyn Monroe. And he'd learned her name – Helena, like the beautiful Helen of Troy.

Many had tried to chat her up and many had failed. Her expertise at rejecting unwelcome attention had more than once dissuaded Jason from making his own advances. Until now, she'd avoided contact with all but the waitstaff. So it puzzled him why Helena had suddenly taken up with a pensioner.

Jason wasn't close enough to follow their conversation, but to judge by the intense expression on her face, she was hanging on the old man's every word.

Before long, the pair headed back to the gaming room. On the way, Helena made another of her frequent stops at the automatic teller machine. She withdrew a large sum of money and divided it, giving a sizeable chunk of cash to her elderly companion. They both resumed their gambling at adjacent machines. Smiling sideways glances and the occasional arm touch indicated that they'd achieved some degree of intimacy. Jason felt a dryness in his throat. He had a very uneasy feeling about this.

CHAPTER TWENTY

Beth sat on the dusty ground of the stable, head in hands, beside the crushed remains of the paper wasp nest. Anger and sorrow gripped her so tightly she found it hard to draw breath. Mark's ignorant act of destruction was a vile finale to a day she'd begun with such high hopes.

She struggled to find a way to deal with what he'd done. The power of her grief over the massacre of the harmless little insects surprised even her. Their death, so unjustified and unfair. Their queen's extraordinary industry and devotion, all gone to waste, while the true culprits still flourished in the fallen tree, their illegitimate claim to dominance only strengthened by Mark's misguided violence. The irony overwhelmed her and she began to cry, softly at first. Soon she wailed like a child, tears streaming down her face and clogging her nose. Tiny flies, attracted to the salty liquid, alighted on her cheeks.

In a while she rose from her seat amidst the carnage, her wailing replaced by shuddering sobs. Several European wasps arrived to investigate the remains of their hapless competitors. Beth swiped at the little vultures, but the smell of insecticide drove them off. They were too wise to scavenge these contaminated corpses.

Pity for the paper wasps was all tangled up with her own fears. She faced the same enemy. She must not lose her family as the unfortunate wasps had lost theirs. Mark did not understand what he would destroy with his hasty, ill-considered custody grab. The deeply satisfying, loving relationship shared by Beth and her children was invisible to him. She had no doubt that he would ruin her life as carelessly as he'd wiped out the wasps.

Seeking some comfort, Beth inspected the eaves, hoping to find a nest that had escaped Mark's ruinous rampage. Not one. She felt the tears welling again but choked them back. Taking some deep breaths, she tried to compose herself. Each time her thoughts wandered to the plight of the helpless wasplings, she curbed them. Each time her eyes wandered towards the now empty stable eaves, she averted them. She tried not to wonder about whether the insects died quickly or endured slow suffering deaths. Such thoughts would hamper her ability to deal with Mark – and deal with him she must. He was still at the house.

Beth washed her face under the tap, dusted off her clothes and combed her fingers through her snarled hair. If she took too long going back inside, Mark would come looking for her. She couldn't bear that. She wanted to encounter him on her own terms. At last she felt calm enough to make her way slowly up the path.

Her heart broke at the sight of a foraging paper wasp, buzzing jauntily towards the stable with a fat blowfly gripped in her jaws. Beth tried not to imagine the wasp's confusion upon arrival at the nest site, only to find all sign of her home and family obliterated. Without the security and motivation of her mother and sisters, she too would soon die of despair.

Beth shook her head as if to ward off such thoughts. As she reached the top of the path, she knew the worst thing about confronting Mark was that he would be unaware that there was even a problem. She marvelled at the depth of the chasm between them, one that Mark couldn't see, despite its magnitude. Perhaps she might be able to use this to her advantage.

On entering the house her face was a mask of control. She burned with words that she dare not say. Her self-discipline must be complete if she was to avoid a lapse into anger. Mark appeared at the kitchen doorway, an expectant look on his sun-flushed face. Beth did not trust herself to speak. Silently she condemned him. Reaching for the kettle, she made them both a strong coffee and checked to see if the children were about. No sign. They were probably holed up in their rooms, waiting for the fireworks to begin. As minutes ticked by, Mark became visibly puzzled by Beth's silence.

'Aren't you going to thank me?' he said at last.

'Why would I do that?'

'Because I got rid of those bloody wasps, of course. You and the kids could have been seriously hurt. Look how badly I was stung.'

Mark proffered his forearm on which could be seen several painful-looking red welts. Beth was thrilled. Her wasp friends had not died without a fight. Mark turned down his collar to reveal another angry-looking swelling on his neck. Beth knew she was expected to respond sympathetically, but couldn't bring herself to do so.

'You killed the wrong wasps.'

'Killed the wrong wasps? What do you mean? A wasp is a wasp.'

Provoked by Mark's foolish words, Beth's mask momentarily fell away, and a look of loathing passed across her features. She turned aside to drink her coffee, hide her feelings, and plan her words.

Mark laid his hand on her shoulder and spun her round with force, showering them both with spilt coffee. Beth's composure did not falter. She had herself on a very tight rein.

'I'm sorry you were stung,' she lied. 'But you did kill the wrong wasps. The European wasp nest is in the fallen tree. I might need a professional pest controller to get rid of it.'

Mark's anger abated. 'You should have told me. Then I could have killed all the little blighters at once. Well, at least I've saved you the cost of having the exterminator treat the stable.' He drained his cup and gave her his most dazzling smile. 'So no harm done, eh? Oh, except to me of course.'

He was still fishing for sympathy. Beth met his gaze coolly, her bitterness still well concealed. But she couldn't keep up appearances for ever. Beth's steely self-control was slipping and her anger was growing.

'Actually, I really liked those native wasps,' she said, struggling to say no more.

Mark was charmed. Why, this woman couldn't harbour an unkind thought, not even for wasps and snakes. As he gazed at Beth he felt a surge of love and a fierce desire to protect her.

'It's not such a good idea that the kids go back with you this afternoon,' she said. 'You and Lena have some things to sort out first. Why don't you get going and give me a ring later this week? You can take the old jeep to get home if you like.'

Beth's mention of Lena shifted Mark's focus in a most disagreeable way. Oh, yes – Lena. He supposed he had better go talk to her, yet he was loath to leave Beth. Rick and Sarah emerged from the bedroom, amazed to find their parents being civil to each other.

Reluctantly Mark kissed his children goodbye, apologising for changing their holiday plans. Beth took his cue and offered her own gracious apologies for the lunch fiasco. The children watched, incredulous. Beth noted, in a detached kind of way, that despite the coffee, Mark was still a bit drunk. Under normal circumstances she would have discouraged him from getting behind the wheel. As it was, she endured his clumsy kiss and watched him drive away.

CHAPTER TWENTY-ONE

❧

As Mark was leaving, Aureole, a tiny golden honeybee, was going about her daily business in Beth's garden. She buzzed away from the daisy bushes that bordered the driveway in a mass of brilliant yellow.

Her route took her into the path of the oncoming jeep as Mark drove from the house. Tired from the day's foraging, and heavily laden with pollen and nectar, her flight was laboured and slow. Too late, she became aware of the moving vehicle. In a clumsy attempt to avoid it, she changed direction, but her brain did not accurately judge the speed of the approaching danger. Only the rush of displaced air preceding the old jeep saved her. Caught up in the mini maelstrom, she was hurtled aside in the nick of time.

As the turbulent air settled, the frightened bee alighted on a nearby fence rail to steady her nerves. Her racing heartbeat slowed and she rested her aching wing muscles. For a while she considered returning to the hive. After all, she already carried two large baskets of pollen on her hind legs. But enthusiasm got the better of her and, shrugging off her weariness, she buzzed away to find fresh flowers.

. . .

Aureole was a bee in the prime of life. At one month old, she'd only recently graduated to foraging and she loved her new job. Until two weeks ago she'd been a house bee, feeding on honey stored in the hive and tending to the queen, larvae and drones. As she grew stronger and more capable, she began to produce wax and graduated to comb building.

However, her favourite task was to greet the older bees when they returned to the nest weighed down with scrumptious nectar and pollen. She helped to collect and store this bounty, snacking as she went, freeing the foragers to return to the field. Aureole loved doing this so much that she often shirked construction duty, and hung around near the hive entrance waiting for their arrival.

As each bee landed in the doorway, a guard examined the newcomer with her antennae. If the bee passed inspection, she was allowed to enter the hive. Members of the colony had a special odour that identified them as bees of good standing. Occasionally, bees lacking the correct odour passport attempted to enter. They were quickly identified as intruders by the guard bees, who grabbed them, mauled them, and dragged them from the hive. Only occasionally, if the foreigner was laden with food and acted in a confident manner, she would be allowed to pass unharmed.

No such allowances were made when the interloper was a robber bee or wasp. When one of these was discovered, the defending bees made a joint effort to sting it to death.

From inside the hive entrance, Aureole detected the exhilarating fragrances of the vast world beyond. Her sense of smell was a hundred times more acute than that of humans and her noses, located in her antennae, constantly searched the air. A returning worker carried with her the tempting aroma of honeysuckle and a crisp, clean hint of eucalyptus. The young bee buzzed with excitement, impatient for the opportunity to explore.

However duty called and Aureole retreated into the hive's dim interior. After a good feed of honey she began to secrete beeswax. It hardened on her abdomen and flaked off in clear flat sheets. She chewed and softened the wax flakes and added them to the comb, instinctively forming hexagonal shapes.

Aureole paused in her work to watch the breathtakingly beautiful dances of her older sisters. On the surface of one of the combs, the returned foragers performed intricate pirouettes, full of meaning for their hive-mates. Aureole gazed at one particular bee as she commenced to dance.

The bee turned rhythmically in graceful circles, alternately clockwise and counterclockwise, forming a precise figure eight. Soon her loops overlapped in a complicated pattern that entranced her audience. As she performed amidst the mass of admiring bees, their excitement became palpable. They began mimicking her actions to learn her dance, all the while touching her with their feelers. Sometimes she paused and regurgitated some of the nectar she'd collected to a lucky member of the crowd.

Her movements became more elaborate. She ran in a straight line before executing a 360-degree turn to the left. Another straight line ended in a 360-degree turn to the right. As she swirled and twirled, she waggled her abdomen in a precise form of body language.

That day she'd discovered a fresh patch of flowering Christmas bush. Her mesmerising performance provided vital information about the location of the nectar-laden bell-shaped flowers. In this way, she accurately communicated their distance and direction from the hive. The length and vigour of her display showed the assembly that her find was of great value.

After the dance was over, many of the bees left the hive, keen to search for the new nectar source. Aureole wistfully watched them go. She followed the foragers to the entrance and longingly buzzed her wings. To her delight, this action caused her to rise several centimetres into the air. She experimented with her new ability, practising changes of elevation and direction, at first tentative and clumsy.

After a few minutes she grew bolder, flying outside the hive entrance, thrilled with this newfound freedom. Her senses were bombarded with colours, sounds and smells. For the very first time,

Aureole went exploring. Like the young wasps, she was not born knowing the area surrounding her home. She needed to learn about it, using distinctive landmarks observed on these early orientation flights.

In order to interpret the dance of her sisters and to navigate effectively, Aureole also needed to memorise the sun's path across the sky. It would take almost five hundred foraging trips before she was sure of the ecliptic.

Just as with humans, the bee world had its slow and fast learners, its average, dependable workers and its explorers. Aureole was proud to be an explorer, or scout bee. She often left the hive simply to search for new flowers, returning if successful to advertise her find. There were few such bees in the colony. Like humans, most were followers, who worked steadily under direction, but never took the initiative themselves.

The honeybee hive was in a gum tree hollow, five metres above the ground. The bee tree grew in a gully bordering Beth's stable paddock. Earlier that season, a pair of black cockatoos had chosen the hollow to raise their family, hatching a pair of healthy chicks.

When the chicks were two days old, honeybees had invaded their nest. The swarm had escaped from the neglected hives of a neighbour. The damage wrought on the environment by these introduced European honeybees was on a par with that caused by the European wasps. Australian fauna had evolved alongside harmless stingless native bees and their modest hives. By contrast, the invasive honeybees poured into the nest en masse, attacking the helpless chicks.

The parent birds desperately tried to defend their offspring but were driven back by the insects' vicious stings. One of the tiny chicks managed to escape the hollow, only to fall injured to the ground. Within hours, the unfortunate baby bird died from dehydration and shock. The remaining chick was ruthlessly slain within its nest. Heartbroken, the parent birds flew off nursing painful stings, their chances of successfully breeding shattered for another year.

Although the bees had escaped from a domestic hive, they were in no real sense domesticated in the way that a dog or a horse was. *Apis mellifera*, western honeybees, could only be persuaded, not forced, to nest in a convenient artificial hive so that humans could more easily rob them of their honey.

Bees had been prized since the stone age, when honey was first collected from hives deep in the wild forests of ancient Europe. White colonists had introduced the western honeybee to Australia and they quickly went feral. Highly adaptable like the European wasps, these bees had no trouble finding nesting sites in their new habitat.

Native Australian hollow-dwellers could not compete when faced with this aggressive newcomer. Encounters with gentle native bees were no preparation for dealing with the honeybees' agonising stings.

Each time a honeybee stung a larger animal it caused the bee a fatal injury, her abdomen torn, and entrails cruelly ripped from her body along with the venomous barb. The disembodied sting, embedded in the flesh of the victim, continued to pump poison through attached muscles. The brave bee soon died; like a fanatical suicide-bomber, no sacrifice was too great for the protection of queen and colony.

Once a hollow was colonised by honeybees, it remained unoccupied by native fauna well after the insects vacated the hive. The honeybees also threatened the survival of native bees by competing for available flowers with maximum efficiency.

Aureole, of course, neither knew nor cared that the legitimate tenants of her nest hollow had been displaced by robbery and murder. She only knew that the welfare of the colony was paramount. She gradually extended her orientation flights to include Beth's dusty, dry paddocks and verdant gardens. She learned to slake her thirst at the birdbath that miraculously remained brimming with cool, fresh water even after days of relentless heat. She learned to recognise the blooms that yielded the most prized pollen and most copious nectar.

Now she could not only interpret her sisters' dances, but she could perform ones of her own. Swelling with pride, she twirled about the golden honeycomb, passing on the mysterious secrets of ancient bee lore to a new generation. Within a few weeks of her maiden flight, Aureole had become a skilful explorer, revelling in the freedom and satisfaction of her new life.

After her near miss with the jeep, Aureole continued foraging. She wanted to impress her younger sisters with how much pollen she could collect, and this desire helped overcome her weariness and fright. Faltering in flight at first, she buzzed off to the canopy of a scarlet-flowering gum tree that stood at Beth's front gate. She'd almost used up the supply of honey in her stomach and was looking forward to replenishing herself from the hive's stores. But nothing could divert her from her duty while she still had the energy to fly.

She moved about the vivid blossoms, scraping off pollen with her mouthparts and legs. Even her plump body was covered with hairs that trapped the loose pollen grains. She looked like she'd been sprinkled with gold dust. When Aureole could carry no more pollen, she used her long proboscis to suck nectar from the flowers until her crop was full to bursting. Satisfied at last, she flew home as the late afternoon sun beat down upon the thirsty garden.

CHAPTER TWENTY-TWO

Mark left the quiet country road and turned onto the highway leading into town. He was more tired than he'd thought. Perhaps he should have pushed for an invitation to stay at Beth's for the night. Now that was a delicious idea.

It was a long drive home and he missed having cruise control. The old jeep's crackling radio droned away, lulling his drink-blurred mind into a dangerously sleepy state. The wheels began a slow drift across the highway.

An ear-shattering blast from the horn of an approaching semi-trailer startled Mark into alertness. With a mighty effort, he wrenched the steering wheel sideways, narrowly missing the oncoming vehicle.

The near miss left him shocked and shaken, but it also left him thanking his lucky stars for the gift of life – a life that no longer lacked purpose. A few short weeks ago he would have felt differently about a brush with death. He might even have welcomed it, such was his despair. Yet now he had everything to live for. He was going to win Beth back.

Mark gave up trying to coax more speed from the ancient jeep and settled into the slow lane, pondering his mortality. What if he had died? What effect would that have had on the various people in his life?

His partners at work would waste little time replacing him. He might have been taken on as the golden boy: talented, even brilliant at times – but nobody was indispensable. The relationship he shared with his colleagues was one of cutthroat rivalry. Every day he dealt with their jealousy. They'd probably be glad to be rid of him.

And his mother? Vanessa would no doubt say *I told you so.* She'd predicted nothing but disaster ever since he'd hooked up with Lena. The funeral would give her a magnificent excuse for a party, where she could legitimately be the main object of attention and sympathy. How she would love that.

His father was a different matter. Dad loved him and had made genuine attempts over the years to get closer. Mark was grateful for that, even though neither of them quite knew how to achieve it. Still, Dad had tried, and that was what mattered. His father would miss him.

And Beth? Poor Beth. She'd be sorry then that she'd been so cold to him. He could picture her, dissolving into inconsolable sorrow at the terrible news. And his children, shattered and lost at the death of their father. He rather enjoyed the thought of Beth in mourning and filled with regret for rejecting him. Yes, she sure would be sorry then.

Beth and the kids relied on his child support. Her part-time job at the riding school had only ever meant pocket money, and according to Sarah she'd quit for some reason. How would she cope if he died? Then it occurred to him that she remained the sole beneficiary of his will and multimillion dollar life insurance policy. Mark had promised Lena to update his affairs when they moved in together, but he'd never got around to it. A happy oversight. It was a source of pride, knowing that he'd be there to support his family, even after death.

What about Lena? His knuckles showed white on the wheel. She'd also be devastated by his death. Her ride on the gravy train would well and truly be over.

The sun was sinking low in the sky when Mark pulled into his driveway. Rosy rays glinted off vast windows set in the ultra-modern concrete facade of the architect-designed townhouse. The style was apparently the height of fashion, yet despite its grand design, the place had never felt like home. He parked behind Lena's Audi, feeling lighter and more centred than he had for months. His annoying neighbour was staring at the beat-up jeep with a wrinkled nose as if he didn't believe such a thing could exist in Brighton.

'She's a beauty, isn't she?' Mark gave the jeep an affectionate slap, raising a cloud of dust. The man opened his mouth to speak, but Mark interrupted him. 'Sorry mate, she's not for sale.'

Mark grinned at his neighbour's horrified expression. He and Beth had bought the jeep ten years earlier while looking to buy a horse float. Not being made of money back then, they'd gone to a farm to look at a second-hand one. Beth had loved the float, but even at a bargain basement price, it was still at the top of their budget.

'Tell you what,' the farmer had said. 'I'll throw in that old jeep over there as a sweetener. That way you can tow the float home today.'

Mark had inspected the jeep with doubtful eyes. 'Does it even work?'

'Built to last and runs like a dream,' said the farmer. 'Don't make them like that anymore, they don't.'

They'd done the deal and Mark had been proved wrong. The black jeep might look like it was on its last legs, but it had never given them a moment's trouble. He'd grown to love it.

Mark stood leaning on the jeep for the longest time, watching the sky and wearing his rose-coloured glasses. More happy memories crowded in. The birth of his first child. Buying his first home. Falling in love for the first time.

He'd met Beth on a holiday in southern France. She'd been visiting her parents there, after her maths professor father landed a job at the University of Lyon.

He recalled his first sight of her – twenty-one years old and sitting at a Chambery bar. Copper-coloured hair fell in a bronze mane down her shapely back. Her sparkling emerald eyes flashed with fun as she regaled her friends with some silly story. He couldn't help staring. Then she'd noticed him too. As their eyes met, he'd felt a deep sense of connection, as though he'd known her forever.

It hit him now that all the significant moments of his life were linked inextricably to Beth. Mark craved to recapture that bond. He didn't doubt that he could win his wife back, for that's what she still was – his wife. It was simply a matter of time. He'd never failed at anything except for his marriage, and it was time to put that right. Certain obstacles lay in his path – Lena, for one thing. Yet buoyed by his new optimism, Mark was confident he could find a way.

He locked up the jeep, took a deep breath and headed for the front door, not looking forward to dealing with his angry girlfriend. Wait, where was his Mustang? Not in the driveway. Mark checked the garage. Not there either. He went inside. The lights were off and all was quiet. Lena and the baby weren't home.

The shrill ring of the landline interrupted the silence. It was his mother. 'Did you know that your mobile is turned off?'

'Yes, Mum. Sorry.' He'd done that on purpose so Lena couldn't bother him.

'Wherever have you been? I've left five messages.'

Of course. He and Lena had promised to pop around to his parents' place. Hurriedly he made his excuses. The last thing he needed right now was his mother on his back.

'I don't think we can make it, Mum. Chance has a bit of a fever.'

'Does he? And just exactly how would you know that?' asked his mother in a voice dripping with sarcasm.

Mark knew he was caught out in his lie, but wasn't sure how.

'You don't know, do you?'

What was she talking about?

'Chance is here, with us. You and Lena must come to collect him immediately. He simply ruined my Christmas afternoon tea.'

Mark could hear a baby crying in the background. His confusion grew. If Chance was at Mum's place, why wasn't Lena there too? His silence only served to further infuriate his mother.

'Mark, are you still there? Put Lena on. You've no idea how much trouble she's caused. Your father is off chasing around to buy baby formula, of all things. Lord knows, she only left enough for two feeds and that has long gone.'

There was another uncomfortable pause before Mark finally spoke. 'Lena isn't here.' It was Vanessa's turn to be speechless. 'Mum, tell me exactly what happened.' His calm front belied Mark's growing anger.

'Lena left the baby with us this afternoon. She said you two had argued and needed time to sort things out. You mean she didn't go home?'

'No.'

'Then you had better come to collect him yourself. Chance simply won't settle, and I am at my wit's end. You know I've never been good with babies.'

This was true. Mark wondered briefly how he'd ever survived infancy. 'Of course, Mum. I'm on my way.'

Mark took time out to brew himself a coffee and think things through. He didn't have a clue where his wayward girlfriend might be. He had no idea what Lena did during the day, or who her friends were. All he thought she did was sleep and shop.

He tried ringing her again, but her phone was turned off. Perhaps she'd left a message on the landline? The first five were all from his mother, each a little more frantic than the previous one.

It was the final message that interested him. Someone from the Belmont Hotel had found Lena's mobile phone. Curiosity, anger and suspicion all competed for top spot in Mark's mind. But before he could solve the mystery of his missing girlfriend, he needed to collect his son.

Mark wasn't exactly a hands-on dad when it came to babies. He never had been. He believed they were pretty much the sole responsibility of their mothers or nannies, at least until they could walk. Consequently, his parenting skills in that regard weren't great. In fact, he'd never actually been alone with his youngest son. But what choice did he have? Leave Chance with Mum? He could just imagine how she'd take that.

The shock of Lena's disappearance had totally destroyed Mark's positive frame of mind. He felt cheated out of his happiness and laid the blame fairly and squarely on his girlfriend.

Mark left the house in a foul mood. He took Lena's Audi and drove the short trip to his parents' house. When he arrived, he was greeted by the screams of his baby. Chance was being rocked, gingerly and not very effectively, in the arms of his grandfather. Vanessa was entertaining a small group of guests separately in the living room. She gave Mark a curt wave and returned to her hostess duties.

Robert's relief to see him was almost palpable. Mark exchanged Christmas greetings with his father, apologised for the inconvenience caused, took the crying child and turned to leave. Robert put his hand on his son's shoulder and handed him Chance's baby bag, replete with disposable nappies, formula, several new rattles and some beautifully wrapped Christmas gifts.

'I forgot to bring your presents,' said Mark, feeling at a loss.

'You have a lot on your plate, son. Everything else can wait until you sort things out with Helena.'

Mark gave him a grateful smile, wishing that he could stop and talk to his dad – share his troubles with someone who cared. He was about to do just that when Vanessa called her husband. Robert excused himself and hurried off.

Mark felt like he'd been slapped. Typical. Neither one of his parents had asked him what was wrong. They hadn't even asked him how he was. Perhaps it was just as well. He would have been unable to come up with a satisfactory answer to either question. Mark took his son and left.

/ CHAPTER TWENTY-THREE

Within minutes of their leaving, Chance fell asleep in his baby carrier. Mark glanced at his sleeping son in the rear-view mirror and saw him as if for the first time. His cherubic face was still damp with tears and pale hair fell in one wispy, golden lock across his forehead. His miniature fist grasped the new blue teething ring given to him by his grandfather. He looked like the child of a stranger.

It occurred to Mark that he really had no relationship with his infant son. He'd behaved in an appropriately excited way when Chance was born, but had felt burdened by a heavy secret. He'd only been going through the motions. The child was little more than an afterthought linked to his primary relationship with Lena. As Mark's relationship with Lena deteriorated, his interest in his little son also diminished.

By contrast, Mark's experience with the birth of his first two children was one of great joy. He'd felt a deep sense of pride as he'd held his newborn babies. He remembered the look of wonder on Beth's face as she inspected her perfect little bundles, the profound gratitude he'd felt towards his wife – the sense of anticipation about their shared future with these children. How had they lost their way?

Chance stirred in his seat. Please don't let him wake up. Mark swore softly. Why should he be forced to take responsibility for a baby that he felt no connection with? Mark drove on through the night, his mind consumed by a cold resentment towards Lena.

At a little after nine o'clock Mark pulled into the Belmont Hotel carpark. There weren't many cars about. Most people had better things to do on Christmas night. But look, there was his red Ford Mustang parked at the back. He parked beside it.

As Mark got out of the car, he remembered Chance. The baby still lay fast asleep. With barely a backward glance he locked up and strode into the hotel. It took him only a few minutes to check the bistro and bar areas. No Lena.

Mark found her in the gaming room. He walked over and stood behind her chair, calling her name. She did not respond. She didn't even notice when he tapped her shoulder, so deeply absorbed was she at playing the stupid machine. Mark swung her chair around to face him.

For Lena, being ripped away mid-gamble was like being shaken from a trance. It took a few moments for her befuddled mind to even recognise Mark. No, it couldn't be. How had he found her? This was her safe place and he didn't belong.

Confusion turned to fear as she took in the look of fury on his face. She turned to her new friend Konrad who'd been playing the adjoining machine, but he'd moved away. She could see him watching from a distance.

Jason had noticed Mark on his arrival. The security staff were trained to head off trouble before it began, and Mark definitely looked like trouble. Jason could barely believe his eyes when the angry-looking man marched straight up to the beautiful young woman of whom he was so enamoured.

The pair's raised voices gave Jason an excuse to intervene.

'Excuse me, sir. I must ask you to leave the young lady alone.'

'Piss off,' said Mark, without turning around.

The girl looked directly at Jason for the first time, beseeching him for help. Her beautiful blue eyes were wide with worry and alarm. Jason was almost grateful to this oaf of a man for giving him the opportunity to finally meet her.

'Right, mate,' said Jason. 'I'm afraid you're going to have to come with me.'

'Didn't I tell you to piss off?' said Mark. 'I'm not going anywhere without my girlfriend.'

This statement struck Jason with a physical jolt of disbelief. Surely this gorgeous creature was not with this jerk? His eyes searched her face for any sign of denial, but he saw none.

'Listen, Lena,' the man said, his voice tight. 'We're leaving, right now. You have a lot of explaining to do.'

Lena took stock of her options. Once the initial shock of seeing Mark had worn off, she reminded herself that she was the aggrieved party. She should be angry with him, not the other way around, and she sensed an ally in the guard.

'I'm not going anywhere with you,' she said. 'Go back to your crazy wife – and you can take these with you!'

With an angry yank, Lena tore off the exquisite emerald necklace and threw it to the ground. The delicate gold chain snapped, spilling the brilliant jewels to the floor like a river of sparkling raindrops. The earrings soon followed. These, however, she hurled straight at Mark. They missed their target, twinkling in the air for a moment before hitting a screen and sliding into the gap behind a poker machine.

Mark watched, grim-faced, as Lena destroyed the expensive gift he'd so lovingly chosen for Beth. It didn't matter. He'd replace it with something even more special. Right now he needed to get Lena home with Chance where she belonged.

'I said, you're coming with me!' Mark roughly grabbed her arm and pulled her from her chair.

By now the guard had called for backup, and another burly security officer arrived. Lena squirmed from Mark's grasp, rubbing her upper arm where he'd manhandled her.

'I'll wait for you outside,' said Mark in a menacing voice. 'You'd better come.'

The two guards moved in, escorting him from the room.

The broken emerald necklace lay discarded on the floor, forgotten by all except Konrad. He hesitated a little before putting on his spectacles. Then he shuffled over, laboriously lowered himself onto his hands and knees, and began combing the carpet for lost gems.

Mark stood in the foyer, half expecting Lena not to show. Ah, there she was, exiting the gaming room with that stubborn look on her face. Mark didn't want any more trouble. All he wanted to do was take her and leave.

He'd already apologised to the hotel staff who hovered nearby, monitoring the situation. Smiling, he gave them a wave to show that all was well. Once again he took Lena by the arm, gently this time, and guided her out through the double glass doors.

Lena propped out the front of the hotel, refusing to go any further. 'I'll talk to you, Mark,' she said, 'but I'm not going *anywhere*.'

A pulse started in his throat.

Jason stood nearby, watching. He could catch snippets of their conversation, and it was clear that they were getting back into an argument. He moved closer.

The girl, Lena, seemed reluctant to leave with the man who was her boyfriend, yet also apparently had a *crazy wife*. Jason couldn't make sense of it.

'Mark, I don't understand why you want me to come home with you.' Lena sounded genuinely puzzled. 'Why not ask Beth instead?'

'If you think I'm going to leave you here to gamble away all my money, you're insane.'

Lena recoiled. 'You're the one that's insane if you think I'm going with you.'

Jason silently cheered as Lena swivelled on her heel. When she turned to face him, he noticed something odd about the red top she was wearing. The bright silk pulled tight over her generous breasts was growing steadily darker.

'What sort of a mother are you?' the man said, his voice full of scorn. 'Look, you're leaking milk. How long has it been since you fed our baby?'

Lena spun back around. 'I'm a better mother than you are a father. When do you ever give our baby a second thought? If you must know, Chance is with your mother. It won't hurt her to give him a few top-up bottles for once.'

'No, Chance is not with my mother. He's all alone in the carpark while his mother is out gambling.'

Jason was now close enough to hear each word. Lena was a mother? The surprises just kept on coming. The man took her by the arm again, and this time he successfully managed to guide her to the carpark. Jason followed, unnoticed by either of them.

Lena could hear a baby's frightened cries coming from a silver Audi in the carpark – her silver Audi. She ran to the vehicle, banging on the window and shouting for Mark to hurry. Then she gave herself a mental kick. This was her car. She had a key right there in her bag. Lena wrenched open the door and grabbed Chance from his carrier.

Mark arrived, followed by Jason, who waited in the shadows.

'Strap him back in,' ordered Mark. 'We're going home.'

Lena ignored him as she attempted to comfort the wailing baby. Mark tried to take the child from her arms. Lena screamed and pulled away.

Jason stepped into the light, alarming them both. 'Do you want to leave with this gentleman?' he asked Lena.

'No.' She gave Mark a defiant stare. 'No, I don't.'

Mark turned on Jason. 'Look, mate. This is my girlfriend and my child and my car. If I say we're going home, then we're going home.'

'I'm afraid not, sir. The young lady doesn't want to go with you.'

At this, Mark swore loudly, opened the back door and attempted to physically bundle both mother and child inside. Lena screamed and pulled away, causing Chance to be shoved against the car door.

In one swift movement, Jason swung the surprised Mark around by his right shoulder and dealt him a powerful punch to his stomach. The blow left Mark doubled over, winded and gasping for breath. Lena looked from her groaning boyfriend to her handsome saviour.

Jason nervously met her eyes, a half-smile on his face. 'I probably shouldn't have done that.'

It was Lena's turn to smile. Before Mark had time to compose himself, she grabbed the baby bag from the back seat, complete with the Christmas gifts from Mark's parents. Jason took it from her, leaving Lena free to soothe her screaming child.

'We'd better get you two back inside,' said Jason, urging her away.

Escorted by her newfound champion and with Chance safely cradled in her arms, Lena returned to the hotel.

Mark leaned against the car, eyes squinted shut in shock and disbelief, surprised by just how much his stomach hurt. A rush of nausea made him vomit. Miserably, he wondered if his spleen might be ruptured.

As minutes ticked by and the pain eased, Mark's anger also waned, replaced by an overwhelming weariness. He should go back inside to report the assault and make that bastard pay. He should reason once more with Lena. He should retrieve his son. But he was physically and emotionally spent. Christmas morning seemed light years away.

Mark stumbled over to his own car, pleased to at least have that back. With shaking hands he locked up the Audi, found the spare Mustang key in his wallet and eased himself into the sports car. He drove home in a daze and fell into bed, too tired to think.

CHAPTER TWENTY-FOUR

Jason waited for Lena outside the Belmont Hotel parents room. He shifted his weight restlessly from foot to foot, craving a cigarette although he'd given up a year ago. Competing emotions made his stomach churn. First, the good news. He'd finally met the girl that he'd had a crush on for months. He'd even rescued her from a bad situation and so earned some degree of trust and gratitude.

The bad news was that she came complete with a boyfriend and baby. Not to mention the fact that he'd probably wind up on an assault charge. Would her jerk of a boyfriend come back in to file a complaint? As the minutes ticked by with no sign of him, Jason started to relax. Perhaps, against the odds, his luck would hold. There weren't any witnesses, and no security cameras covered that end of the carpark. He was confident that Lena wouldn't implicate him, so the charge would be hard to prove.

In a short while Lena emerged with her baby, who looked sleepy and satisfied. She gave Jason a warm smile and he thought he would burst with happiness.

'How's the little fella doing? He looks a lot happier now.'

'Doesn't he? I think he was as much frightened as hurt. Imagine Mark leaving him alone in the car like that. I can't believe it.'

An awkward silence ensued. There was the small matter of what would happen next. As if reading Jason's thoughts, Lena said, 'I can't go home, not tonight.'

Jason nodded agreement. A plan was forming. He had nothing to lose. 'You and the baby could come home with me. I'm off shift in ten minutes.'

Lena studied Jason. His expression was hungry and intense. She'd ached for months to see that look in Mark's eyes. 'Okay,' she said, easily. 'I'll go home with you.' Jason gave her a nervous grin, looking like he couldn't believe his luck. 'Let me just go say goodbye to my friend,' said Lena, remembering Konrad.

She found the old man sitting once more at his machine. He raised his gaze as she approached, his eyes filled with concern. 'Are you all right, my dear?'

'I think so,' she said. 'I thought you might like to meet Chance.'

Konrad regarded the sleepy child with a smile of pure delight. 'He is too beautiful for words. My life is empty of children. It stirs many wonderful memories for me to see this child.'

She felt an unfamiliar sense of pride upon hearing his words. Few people in her life had responded to Lena and her baby with the sort of sympathy and affection displayed by Jason and Konrad tonight. Lena craved the acceptance and praise that was missing in her relationship with Mark. She would take it wherever she could get it.

The old man followed her out to the cafe. He cooed over Chance until Jason emerged in his street clothes a few minutes later. Konrad looked back and forth from Jason to Lena. 'So, you and your son do not go home tonight?'

'No,' admitted Lena, suddenly embarrassed. Would he judge her?

'Then take care, my dear,' was all Konrad said.

Jason helped Lena to gather her things. 'We can take my car,' she said. 'It has a baby carrier.'

If he was surprised by the Audi's soft leather seats, decorative oaken inlays and multimedia display screens, he didn't show it.

Half an hour later they arrived at Jason's small ground-floor flat. He opened the front door, wondering what the evening might hold.

Helena extracted her sleepy child from the car and carried him inside. Pushing two lounge chairs together, she fashioned a makeshift cot where Chance fell straight asleep. Now she turned to Jason, who was bringing in the baby's bag. She walked towards him boldly, put her arms around his neck and whispered, 'Thank you.'

'Helena—'

She nibbled his ear. 'Call me Lena.'

Having this gorgeous girl standing so close was too much for Jason. He could feel her warmth, smell her perfume, see the smooth sheen of her polished skin. He swore he could even hear the beating of her heart.

Jason dropped the bag, bent his head and let his mouth find hers. Lena parted her lips and stood on tiptoe to meet his tentative kiss. Was he coming on too strong? With an effort, Jason backed off. Holding Lena's head gently in his large hands, he checked her expression for any sign of doubt, realising with a jolt how disappointed he would be if she stopped him. But it seemed that Lena was not in a shy mood. She smiled and pulled him close. When he hesitated, she closed her eyes and pressed her open lips to his.

It was all the encouragement Jason needed. He took her hand and led her to his bedroom, acutely aware of the unmade bed and discarded clothes on the floor. He hoped that she wouldn't notice in the dark.

Playfully, Lena pulled at his belt and unbuttoned his shirt. With extravagant care, he undressed her. He thought her astonishingly beautiful. Her breasts, now no longer engorged with milk, were large, soft and shapely. Her flawless skin glowed golden brown. Her body was slim yet sensuously curved, well-proportioned with generous hips and a soft, yielding waist. Jason caressed her all over, kissing her tenderly, hoping against hope that this was no dream. Praying that she would not change her mind or regret her decision.

Lena revelled in Jason's ardour. Since Chance's birth, she'd almost forgotten how it felt to be the object of a man's lust. Lena wanted so very much to be wanted. In some ways, she defined her self-worth by the extent to which men hungered for her. Jason's powerful desire reminded her that she was, after all, a seductive and successful woman.

But her infidelity was also motivated by revenge. If Mark didn't appreciate her, she would find someone who did. And Jason proved to be an excellent lover, considerate yet assertive enough to take charge. This suited Lena very well. While not an imaginative partner, she certainly was an obliging one when aroused. The frustration of the last few months added to her passion.

Jason was in heaven. Weeks of fantasy had become reality. They made love over and over again, Lena responding willingly to his every move. Hours later, tired and satisfied, they slept in each other's arms until daylight crept in the window.

Jason woke as the room brightened. He reached for Lena but found himself alone. Had she stolen away during the night? A gut-wrenching wave of disappointment threatened to overwhelm him.

But the sounds of someone moving about in the kitchen calmed his fears. Jason lay, head pillowed in his hands, and relived the events of the previous evening. He was in love. No, love was too small a word for it. Jason was gripped so mightily by emotion that he found it hard to breathe. He ached for Lena, even though she was just in the next room. His body would burn until he could see her. The world had changed, all certainties vanished. This was uncharted territory. Of one thing he was certain – he needed her in his life.

Jason sat up and tried to gather his thoughts. A sudden terror that she was about to leave rocketed him out of bed and into the kitchen. Lena was sitting at the table breastfeeding Chance, wearing nothing but Jason's old towelling robe.

He was ridiculously pleased to see her. A broad grin spread over his face and he felt himself getting hard again. 'Good morning, gorgeous.'

'Good morning.' She flashed him a brief, distracted smile. 'Would you be a darling and get me a cup of tea? Strong with a dash of milk. I always get thirsty after feeding bub.'

Jason pulled on some shorts and busied himself in the kitchen. Lena laid Chance on the lounge chairs and went to shower and dress. When she emerged from the bathroom, Jason was waiting with tea and toast.

Lena sat down and silently sipped her tea, staring out the window. A new awkwardness was rising between them. The easiness and intimacy of the night before seemed to have vanished. Jason sensed his happiness slipping away.

'You don't need to go back,' he urged. 'Stay here, at least for a day or two.'

'That's very kind,' she said. 'But I really do need to get home. Mark – that's my boyfriend – Mark and I have a lot to sort out.'

Her use of the word *boyfriend* and the mention of his rival's name filled Jason with jealous misery. He despised the man who could legitimately claim Lena as his own. Yet he couldn't think of any way to keep her without sounding desperate, and nobody liked desperate.

So many questions he was dying to ask. Why was Lena with a dropkick like Mark? What was she doing out gambling on Christmas Day? Why did Mark have a wife if he was with Lena? But she was busy with Chance, and it wasn't the time.

Barely believing his own folly, Jason helped Lena gather her things and put them into the Audi. Before long they were driving back to the hotel so that he could collect his car. Jason took a rather convoluted route in order to cadge a few extra minutes with Lena. Perhaps he could change her mind about going home? But when Jason tried to persuade her, she dismissed his arguments.

'Leave it, babe. I have to get back and talk to Mark.' She looked out the window. 'Why is it taking so long? Didn't we already pass that church?'

Jason sighed. He could put it off no longer.

They turned into the hotel carpark and pulled up beside his old Holden. He searched in vain for something more to say, but drew a blank. In the end all he could manage was, 'Make sure to put my number in your phone.'

'I can't,' she said. 'I must have left it in the gaming room.'

'We'd better go inside and fetch it then.'

She shook her head. 'Not now. Can you find it and keep it safe for me?'

That was something, at least. It meant that Jason would see her again. He found a pen and notepad in the glove box, scribbled down his phone number and pressed it into Lena's hand. 'Call me if you need me.'

She offered him a dazzling smile, causing his heart to jump with hope.

'What the heck, call me even if you don't need me,' he said, feeling bolder. He drew her to him and kissed her goodbye. Reluctant as he was to let her leave, he knew it was time when she leant over to open his door.

'I really must go,' she said, with a hint of irritation in her voice.

Jason tickled Chance under the chin. 'See you, kid. Look after your mum for me.'

He got out and Lena quickly moved into the driver's seat. With a brief nod, she pulled away, leaving Jason standing in the carpark, wishing like crazy that he'd done something differently. The anti-climax was almost unbearable.

Lena drove home slowly, taking stock. Jason's apparent infatuation with her was flattering. She would miss him. With Jason she felt important, powerful, and irresistibly beautiful. One night with him and her self-esteem had soared. Yet as sweet as her night of passion had been, Lena did not intend to leave her treacherous partner just yet. She had unfinished business.

The mere thought of Mark made her blood boil. How dare he treat her so shabbily. Well, she would show him. Like Jason, she was consumed by a new passion. However, unlike Jason, it was not for a new lover. It was for revenge – although she regarded it more as justice. As the spurned party, she held a legitimate right to even the score.

What was important to Mark? Status? Money? Beth? He valued all of the above in roughly that order. It was only fair that he should lose those things. With a little planning, Lena felt confident that she could accomplish it. However, right now she was exhausted and needed to sleep. Maybe later on, at the hotel, she would discuss her plans with Konrad. His advice might be useful.

CHAPTER TWENTY-FIVE

It hadn't rained at Benbullen for more than a month. Each morning dawned clear and bright, like the one before it and the one to follow. The prolonged dry caused food shortages for many of the inhabitants of Beth's garden, though this was not true for Zenandra and her children. They positively thrived on the sort of hardship that defeated others.

Beth relied entirely on rainwater and the house tanks were almost empty. She could no longer afford to water her plants. Colourful nectar-filled blooms withered and died on desiccated stems. Honeyeaters and butterflies foraged in vain throughout the dying garden. Until now, the European wasps had also relied heavily on those succulent flowers for food. Undismayed, they demonstrated their resilience by quickly identifying an alternative source of sweet sustenance.

Dotted about the expansive lawns were more than a dozen conifers of various sizes and shapes. Their stately upright growth habit added a formal charm to the grassy slopes bordering the parched garden beds. Scale insects infested the trunks and branches of these trees. The tiny insects derived their name from the presence of an armoured scale that entirely covered their bodies.

Newly hatched female scale nymphs were only active for a week or two before settling down to feed. That brief period of freedom was the last they would ever know. While the males remained free, riding the winds in search of sex and food, the females were condemned to a life of confinement. Securely attaching herself to a stem by her beak, each little scale nymph became deeply and permanently embedded in the host plant. A waxy scale gradually formed over her. Beneath this protective covering, the legless female insect remained imprisoned for the rest of her life.

These tiny insects provided an unlikely food source for the nectar feeders in Beth's garden. While feeding on plant sap, the scale insects excreted the residue through a waxy anal tube. Droplets of sugary honeydew accumulated on the ends of these tubes and became more concentrated over time. A variety of birds, insects and reptiles included honeydew in their diet. During dry summers and cold winters it provided an abundant, high-energy food source when few such foods were available.

That year however, the European wasps had entirely monopolised this vital resource. They swarmed over the trees in huge numbers. Some hovered with expert precision, plucking the sweet droplets in mid-flight. Others crawled about the foliage, lapping as they went. Sometimes they fell from the trees, feebly beating their wings, temporarily intoxicated by fermented honeydew.

Intruders were not only fiercely repelled by the wasps – they were often eaten. Honeydew was also a main energy source for bees, but now any bee risked her life if she ventured too close to the honeydew trees.

Zenandra's daughters were developing a taste for honeybees. As prey became scarcer, the wasps became bolder and more determined. It had only taken one attack on one unfortunate bee to bring this abundant new protein source to the attention of the entire colony. Now any bee was fair game.

Not only was bee meat perfect fare for wasplings, but the adult wasps prized the nectar and pollen that spilled from the dying bees' butchered bodies. Soon the wasps not only targeted bees near the honeydew trees, but began to actively seek them out in other parts of the garden. The wasps required every ounce of energy they could muster for, deep within their underground home, a renovation project had commenced.

Like houseproud humans, worker wasps frequently rearranged the nest furniture. Nest envelopes were modified to provide more space for brood cells. Old cells were torn down and building materials recycled. Sometimes whole sections of the nest were walled off when they became inconveniently distant from the centre of colony activity. But this new renovation was by no means routine. A fresh urgency motivated the workers. The nest was abuzz with the news that construction of the royal brood chambers was underway.

Only the most experienced architects laboured on the brood cells that would contain the future drones (males) and queens. All previous offspring, although female, were sexually incomplete. This was partly due to malnutrition. When Zenandra founded her colony, she alone constructed the nest, laid the eggs, hunted and fed her young. It was therefore no surprise that the first generation was a little undernourished. Subsequent generations, however, had droves of capable older sisters to keep house and hunt for them.

It was a distasteful truth that these common babies were deliberately underfed by their nursemaids. They were also deprived of nutrition in another way. The larvae produced a drop of sweet saliva whenever they were fed. This liquid was eagerly sought after by the adult wasps. Unscrupulous workers often moved over the brood combs, giving the feeding signal and accepting the larval offerings, but providing no food in return. If trickery didn't work, greedy adults sometimes abused the wasplings in an effort to extract the prized fluid. Recalcitrant babies were seized roughly by their heads, dragged part way out of their beds, and then jammed back down hard until they produced a sweet droplet. Malnourished wasplings could not achieve sexual maturity after metamorphosis. Zenandra would brook no rival for her sovereignty among the labour force.

The queen also loved these sugary larval secretions, and when a worker offered her a droplet, Zenandra drank it with relish. She took time out from her furious egg-laying duties and rested awhile on an area of comb filled with pupating young. Nearby, her devoted daughters laboured on the construction of the new brood cells – cradles fit for queens. They were almost twice as large as ordinary worker cells, with thicker, more durable walls, and roomy enough to comfortably accommodate their royal occupants.

The queen observed the scene with satisfaction. Her life was about to turn full circle.

Twelve months ago, Zenandra had herself been a young royal, born in her mother's nest. When she emerged from her cocoon, the entire colony had gathered to admire her special size and beauty. She'd preened herself, buzzed her wings and imperiously demanded food. Her deferential sisters had scurried to oblige.

Zenandra was raised with the best of everything. Future queens enjoyed an abundance of the finest fare the colony could provide. For several weeks, she and the other princesses had idled around the nest, putting on weight and strengthening their wing muscles. Drones were also emerging. The males, although slightly smaller than the queens, were far more aggressive. They were forever scrapping with each other and harassing their nest-mates.

These adolescent royals were lazy liabilities to their sisters. They never hunted. Instead they demanded food from returning workers, substantially increasing the colony's workload.

As late summer had turned to autumn, Zenandra's mother had ceased her egg-laying. The colony was nearing the end of its growing season, and social life became increasingly disrupted. The old queen was dying, worn out by the effort of nest building and endless egg production. She huddled in a corner of the comb, too cold and weak to even ask her daughters for food. Her wings hung in tatters, and her once-glorious colours were fading fast.

Without their queen's wisdom and direction, a kind of madness had overtaken the wasps in Zenandra's birth nest. Some workers clumsily commenced to lay eggs themselves in a vain attempt to revive the colony. Inexperience sometimes led them to lay more than one egg in a cell or to feed each other's eggs to existing larvae. Occasionally these worker-laid eggs were successfully raised to maturity. But the offspring produced by these virgin mothers were inevitably useless males.

Upon the death of their old queen, true anarchy had reigned. The wasps failed to care even for the healthy larvae that remained. Some wasplings simply starved. Some were ripped from their cells and cannibalised, their meat fed to other larvae or shared amongst the adults. Zenandra herself partook of this gruesome fare. Some were roughly ripped from their cradles and discarded at a distance from the nest, quickly falling prey to ants. Soon the brood consisted of nothing but a few shrivelled larvae and persistent pupae, whose metamorphosis was retarded by the cooler temperatures of autumn. Eventually the adults, including Zenandra and the other young royals, abandoned the nest altogether.

It was with a sense of single-minded purpose that Zenandra had departed her birth nest for the last time. With the confidence of youth, she decided to see how high she could fly. Up and up she spiralled, losing all bearings, aware only of the vast, formless landscape beneath and the shining, blinding clarity of the sky above. Immense joy overtook her as she dipped and swerved, testing her flight skills to the limit. Passing birds showed some interest in the swooping insect but made no attempt to attack. Her brilliant colouring alerted all to the danger of her sting.

Tired at last, Zenandra dropped from the sky, eager for rest and something to eat. She searched the uniformly grey-green bushland for a promising place to land. A flash of scarlet attracted her attention and she flew in its direction.

Within a few minutes she arrived at a bank of red-flowering bottlebrush. Hungrily she crawled over the flowers, sharing the sweet nectar with a host of other insects. She was not in predator mode, and the native bees and brightly painted butterflies had nothing to fear from her – not yet.

After eating her fill, Zenandra had explored beyond the bottle-brush. Ahead of her lay a green oasis within the dry bushland – Beth's garden. Surrounding the house lay extensive beds of exotic blooms, interspersed with drought-resistant clumps of Australian native plants. Dotted over the green lawn were a multitude of tiny yellow and white daisies. Several stone birdbaths, brimming with water, stood about the gardens. A large variety of insects already lived here, and she noted the abundance of potential prey .

Zenandra alighted on the roof of Beth's tool-shed to rest. She was not the only wasp attracted to this welcoming place. Half a dozen drones of her own species had come here too. Their primary raison d'etre was sex. They could not expect to survive the coming winter, as could a large and healthy queen such as Zenandra. A drone's biological clock ticked fast. Their need to pass on their genes required them to mate quickly before the cooler weather killed them, and thus their libidos were overwhelming.

It had not taken long for the drones to become aware of the young virgin queen. Her body emitted a chemical attractant, a pheromone, irresistible to males. One by one, the drones detected this chemical signal and began their search. An eager male discovered Zenandra hovering uncertainly above a birdbath, contemplating how to safely slake her thirst. Vividly coloured bands on her body showed that she was fertile and ready to mate. The scent and sight of her spurred the young drone into a sexual frenzy.

Dispensing with pleasantries, he dived down and grasped her in mid-flight. Straddling her body, he gripped her tightly beneath him with his legs and mandibles. Caught by surprise, Zenandra at first perceived the drone's actions as an assault. Aggressively, she extended her sting. This gave the enthusiastic drone a clear pathway to her genital opening, known as a gonopore. With a sharp downward twist, he drove the tip of his abdomen deep inside her. With a shock of plea-sure, she relaxed and drew her sting partly back into her body. The drone, while still astride his queen, stroked her softly to keep her calm. It would be fatal for him if she mistook his purpose.

The pair had come to rest on a yellow daisy flower striped with shadows. They remained there, camouflaged, until mating was over. The extraordinary gentleness of the drone was partly self-serving. Startling his lover could result in an attack. Yet there was no doubting the shared sensuousness of the encounter. He vibrated his antennae against hers all the while – an action that seemed to mesmerise the young queen. When mating was complete, he spent a long time caressing her feelers with the curved tips of his own. He was more fortunate than a honeybee drone, whose violent act of procreation resulted in catastrophic injuries to his abdomen and certain death.

As the wasps' sexual excitement waned, the male slowly withdrew from Zenandra and dismounted from her body. They rested for a few moments, side by side, grooming themselves and regaining their strength.

Within a few minutes the male wasp returned to a state of high alertness. He tilted his head from side to side, sensing the presence of another receptive queen nearby. Soon he buzzed away, consumed all over again with the urgency of his sexual needs. The sheer physical effort of the drone's mating behaviour would soon kill him, but not before he succeeded in his mission to transfer his genes to the new generation.

Zenandra took a while longer to recover from the encounter. Unlike her doomed mate, she had the luxury of a generous life span by insect standards. She could expect to live for fifteen months or more. However she repeated this courtship ritual with different suitors on different occasions over the coming days. Multiple matings increased her chances of collecting a sufficient supply of healthy sperm, which she stored deep inside her.

At last her womb was replete with the seed of the next generation and her sexual energy was spent. The sperm collected over this one wild week would remain viable over her entire lifetime, available whenever she needed to fertilise her eggs. Zenandra would never mate again.

Her body ceased to produce the volatile odour which so aroused the drones. Her vivid colours faded a little. She signalled her unwillingness to mate in other ways too, by adopting a slower, less showy flight pattern and fleeing from any interested drone. When a persistent young male failed to take the hint, she used her sting to physically block the opening to her gonopore – a kind of waspine chastity belt. Eventually the amorous drone abandoned his attempt. After all, there were other young queens in the garden available for nuptial flights.

For the remainder of that autumn Zenandra had enjoyed all Beth's garden could offer. She fed on windfall apples and peaches, growing fat and sleek. She explored the surrounding bushland by day, suiting herself as to where she went and where she slept. On warm nights, when the full moon illuminated the garden, she defied the diurnal customs of her kind and soared up into the darkness towards the dazzling, silver orb. Spiralling higher and higher, among the moths and other nocturnal insects, she experienced great joy and a feeling of being in unison with creation.

As the days lengthened and grew colder, Zenandra fed furiously, building up her body reserves for the ordeal of hibernation. One cold day she disappeared into Beth's garden shed, finding a snug bed in the fingertip of an old leather gardening glove. Cooling temperatures induced in her body a deep torpor – a state very much like death. She became unresponsive to touch, light and sound. A minute quantity of glycerine in her blood functioned as a natural anti-freeze, and in this condition she could endure temperatures well below freezing. Her metabolism slowed to the point where it could not be measured.

Zenandra had entered a state of suspended animation that even halted ageing. She remained corpse-like until the following spring, when rising temperatures and longer days triggered a physiological resurrection. The queen rose from the dead to establish the flourishing colony beneath Beth's fallen tree.

She'd had an extraordinarily successful life, but Zenandra was not done yet. Her destiny remained incomplete without the survival of this new crop of royals. Nothing must interfere with that grand purpose.

The wasps were now forced to increase their ruthless hunting efficiency. Royal larvae required abundant, high quality protein. Although the local native wasp population had, over time, been destroyed, the European wasps still faced competition for food from other wasps of their own species. An uneasy truce existed between these tribes. The pressure was on, and life was about to become even harder for the little creatures who made their home in Beth's garden.

CHAPTER TWENTY-SIX

Beth trotted Shannon down the drive on a loose rein. The mare's fine black coat was lathered with sweat, and veins stood out as shiny sinews beneath her satin skin. With nostrils flared wide, the mare gulped down lungfuls of fresh air, her heart beating fast. It had been a hard morning's ride. Galloping at punishing speeds through the bush was Beth's latest way of releasing tension. Shannon thoroughly enjoyed these wild rides, though she was a little puzzled by the change in tempo. Riding with her mistress had previously been a much more sedate affair.

Horse and rider headed down the hill to the stable yard, both looking forward to a refreshing drink. Beth dismounted and swore under her breath when she saw the empty trough. The dry summer had left water reserves low in the stable tank. Bits and pieces of rotting leaves, usually safely at rest on the bottom, now found their way into pipes and mechanisms, obstructing the flow. Such blockages had plagued the stock tank system for weeks. Beth was left with no alternative but to use the dwindling house supply to fill the troughs until her handyman found time to fix it. That could be a while. Ted seemed reluctant to visit since the wasp attack. How would he feel, she wondered, if he knew that she hadn't destroyed the nest?

Beth unsaddled her tired mare. A slight movement in the empty trough caught her eye. A little money spider was trapped by the steep, slippery sides. These particular spiders were favourites of hers. Showing them kindness was meant to bring good fortune. Beth looked about for a stick with which to rescue it. As she leant over the trough with a leafy twig, a European wasp buzzed in. It seized the unfortunate spider and deftly amputated all eight of its legs. Seconds later it was gone, carrying its disabled, but still living victim, back to the nest to suffer a terrifying death.

Beth was frozen with sadness and guilt. If only she'd acted more quickly. Split seconds sometimes stood between life and death, and death now stalked the insects of Beth's garden. Despite her empathy with the European wasp queen, she conceded it was time to exterminate the nest.

Disturbing tales about the wasps were starting to circulate. A neighbour told of finding a dead cow one evening in his paddock. He returned early the next morning on his tractor to remove it. The entire carcass was covered by thousands of European wasps. He was unable to get anywhere near it, such was the aggression of the swarm. Other scavengers, like kites and foxes, were savagely attacked and driven off. Even flies attempting to blow the bloated body were seized. So the cow remained rotting where it lay, disappearing beneath a seething mass of black and gold wasps.

Many similar stories were doing the rounds. The one that provoked the most disquiet was that of a stockman whose horse stumbled onto a nest up in the high country. The outraged wasps attacked in their thousands, making his mare bolt over the rough, timber-strewn ground. The wasps gave chase. A hidden wombat hole caused the horse to fall heavily, throwing her rider. The stockman made a dash on foot to the safety of a farm dam. When he finally went in search of his mare, he found the unfortunate animal quite dead and covered in feeding wasps.

When he returned days later to recover his bridle and saddle, a gruesome scene confronted him. Gaping sockets indicated where the wasps had eaten away the animal's eyes, possibly before death. The shape of the horse's body was grossly distorted by masses of stings, causing ugly swellings and lesions all over its hide.

Beth had heard these rumours, but regarded them with scepticism. Now she wasn't so sure. Her late summer garden, which should have been abuzz with a wide variety of insects, seemed barren of life. Even the frogs in the dam had fallen silent. Beth loved to hear the evening symphony of frog calls. This summer, not even the croak of eastern banjo frogs, quaintly known as *pobblebonks,* broke the stillness at dusk.

Beth had assumed that the absence of frogs was due to the dry. But yesterday, having ventured down to the dam to investigate, she was surprised to discover that the water level, although low, was perfectly adequate to sustain the frog population.

Again Beth stood at the water's edge, sensing that the dam had changed in some undefined way. Then it struck her. The rippled surface, usually swarming with water boatmen, dragonflies, midges, and a host of other aquatic insects, was calm and empty. Peering into the murky shallows, she saw no sign of the water beetles, nymphs, and tadpoles that usually flourished there. A patch of blue-green algae spread a toxic bloom across one corner of the dam. Without the usual aquatic inhabitants feeding on it, the algae was thriving unchecked.

Were the wasps somehow responsible? Perhaps the frogs couldn't compete with them for food. But as Beth turned to go, she saw something that indicated the wasps were playing a more direct role in the disappearance of the amphibians. Two partly decomposed frog corpses sprawled from under a log, little arms outstretched. Tiny hands with open fingers seemed to beseech Beth for help. Six European wasps were busy slicing frog flesh. Whether the insects were predators or scavengers seemed immaterial. The dam's once vibrant ecosystem was destroyed and, once again, the wasps were the likely culprits.

Beth could not disregard the mounting evidence, and the attack that morning on the spider confirmed her decision. The European wasp nest must go. So many people had told her that: Ted, Mark, Karen – Noah. What had he said? *Destroy that nest before you have a truckload of trouble on your hands.* Why had she ignored him?

Beth watered her mare from a bucket, then turned her out and returned to the house. Exploring extermination options on her laptop was a grim task. None of them were pretty. Killing was an ugly game no matter how it was done. For the umpteenth time she missed Noah. Noah would understand how she felt. He was perhaps the only person in the world who would.

The ringing phone came as a welcome distraction. To her astonishment it was Lena. Beth hadn't spoken to Lena since the disastrous Christmas lunch more than six weeks ago. She'd spoken to Mark though. Not that she'd forgiven him for destroying the nests, but she'd put aside her anger because of his change of heart regarding the children. He was paying them attention again – calling them, messaging them, keeping his temper. He'd even come up midweek a few times outside agreed access times to surprise them. Lord knows what Lena thought about that. Of course Rick and Sarah had loved these unexpected visits, and because Mark had been on his best behaviour – no physical advances – Beth hadn't objected. Letting him see the kids as much as he wanted might persuade him to drop his custody bid.

'I'd forgotten what a great mother you are,' he'd said a few days ago, after turning up out of the blue for dinner. Afterwards, he'd helped clear the table and pack the dishwasher. 'I'd also forgotten what a great butter chicken you make. Maybe the children *are* better off with you. They'll certainly eat better. Lena can't boil an egg.'

Beth had dropped a plate as her heart leaped with hope. 'Of course they're better off with me,' she'd whispered, after checking Rick and Sarah weren't in earshot. 'We both know that.'

To Beth's amazement, a large tear welled in Mark's eyes and tracked down his cheek. He took a deep breath and knuckled it away. 'Can I talk to you? I don't have anybody else.'

He told her about his unhappiness at work and his problems with Lena. 'I sometimes wish I'd never met the woman.'

'Don't talk like that,' said Beth, troubled by the coldness in his tone. 'What about Chance?'

A flash of resentment showed on his face, one so brief that she might have imagined it. 'Yes, of course,' he said. 'I didn't mean it. It's just one of those things you say …' His voice trailed off.

Beth smiled as if she understood.

Mark had reached for her hand. 'We could give our marriage one more try. That way we'd both get what we want – the children, I mean.'

It had taken Beth a moment to recover from the surprise. She'd withdrawn her hand and brushed the suggestion aside, making light of it. 'You and Lena are going through a rough patch, that's all. You'll be singing her praises in a week or two.'

Beth hadn't believed her cheery prediction any more than Mark had. It was clear his relationship with Lena was seriously on the rocks. How would the jealous young woman react if she knew that Mark had suggested a reconciliation with his wife, even in jest? Was that what Lena's phone call was about?

'Beth?' said Lena. 'Are you still there? We need to talk. Please, it's important.'

First Mark and now Lena. Beth scrubbed a hand over her face. What was she – their relationship counsellor? 'Well, we're talking now, aren't we?' she said.

'No, I mean in person. Can I come to see you? Would this afternoon suit?'

Beth was thinking on her feet. Perhaps this could work to her advantage – an opportunity to tell Lena about the extent of her partner's betrayal. The girl deserved to know the truth about Mark. And as a bonus, the truth would further subvert their shaky relationship and damage Mark's chance of victory in the family court. Beth had spoken to a lawyer, who'd confirmed that Mark would never get the children without Lena's support.

'Okay. The kids get home on the bus at 4:30 though. You'll need to be gone by then.'

Beth put down the phone, feeling more than a little confused. This meeting could suit her own agenda. What she didn't understand was how it would suit Lena's. Did Lena intend to warn her off Mark? A needless exercise. He made Beth's skin crawl. But she would not confide this to Lena. Let the girl believe what she wanted. Let her jealousy grow. Beth owed Lena no favours.

CHAPTER TWENTY-SEVEN

Two hours later Lena arrived on Beth's doorstep. She spent a while tapping the brass knocker, while Beth observed her from an upstairs window. The young woman held Chance in one arm and used the other to knock at the door. She then peered in the window, waving and calling to catch someone's attention.

Lena was dressed in her trademark halter-necked top and cut-off jeans, her slim brown legs teetering on top of shiny, stiletto-heeled sandals. After what must have seemed to Lena an inordinately long time, Beth descended the spiral staircase to receive her visitor – pleased that this little encounter would be very much on her terms.

Beth opened the door. 'Come in, you two.'

'Thanks, my shoulder's aching,' Lena hitched Chance a little higher in the crook of her arm.

The baby must have been be nine months old by now – engagingly alert with a melting smile. Beth suddenly saw Rick in Chance's sweet face. The resemblance unnerved her. Lena put the baby on the lounge room floor with a toy or two and refused Beth's half-hearted offers of hospitality. Her eyes were red and puffy.

'No coffee, thanks.'

Beth indicated a chair and they both sat down. There was a

prolonged silence, with neither party eager to launch into a conversation that promised to be tricky at best. Finally, Beth's curiosity got the better of her.

'Is this visit about Mark?'

'My whole life is about Mark.' Lena wrung her hands together and blinked a lot, the very picture of despair. 'I suppose you know that he thinks he's in love with you again.'

Beth sighed. Her plan to fan Lena's insecurities now seemed foolish and cruel. She searched for something kind to say that might still serve her own purpose. She failed.

Lena rubbed her eyes. 'Can I ask you a question?'

Beth wanted to say no. She wanted to say that she should never have agreed to this meeting and that Lena should leave. The brittle silence stretched between them.

Lena's foot began a rhythmic tapping. She stared at Beth, looking like she might cry. 'I need to know if you want Mark or not.' Still Beth didn't speak. 'I came all this way to ask the question. You could at least answer me.' Still nothing. 'I'm actually trying to do you a favour.'

This foolish remark finally provoked a response. 'Doing me a favour?' Beth looked askance. 'What exactly do you want from me?'

'I told you. I need to know if you still want Mark. If the answer is no, then I'll go and leave you alone. If the answer is yes, then I should warn you about something.'

Beth shifted in her seat. There it was. Did the girl think that she could came and bully her in her own home? 'Look, Lena, if your relationship is in trouble, that's your problem. Coming here and making threats won't help. If you want to keep Mark, go talk to him.'

'But I don't want to keep him,' said Lena, with such wide-eyed sincerity that Beth didn't doubt her for a second.

'Didn't you come here to warn me off? You're not making any sense.'

'I asked if *you* wanted Mark. I never said that I did.'

Confusion swept over Beth. She had mistaken Lena's purpose and was now firmly on the back foot. If Lena was telling the truth, then all Beth's fears for her children were unfounded. It meant that Mark had no stable de facto relationship, and the courts would not prefer him as a custodial parent. This was truly wonderful news. Still, the question remained. What exactly did Lena want? Why her sudden interest in Beth's relationship with Mark?

'You don't get it, do you?' said Lena, regarding Beth's astonished expression. Beth shook her head.

'Mark doesn't love me anymore.' Lena's voice was filled with resignation and pain. 'He doesn't even seem to love Chance. He's made me so miserable these last few months. He's made me feel completely alone, like I don't have a friend in the world and that this beautiful baby I gave him is worthless. His family treats me like dirt. He barely even talks to me. Oh, unless he's yelling about me spending too much of *his* money. There isn't even any action in the bedroom.'

Lena gulped back a breath and continued. 'Well, I can tell you one thing. Mark's going to pay for what he's done to me. Why should he just get you back and live happily ever after, like me and Chance never existed? I don't want him to get away with it. So, I need to know if you want him back. I hope you don't. That would be perfect. But if you do, I have something to tell you that might change your mind.'

Beth had heard enough. She was uncomfortable with both the intimacy and intensity of Lena's outburst. The girl was clearly unhinged. Anyway, Beth knew all that she needed to know. Mark would not gain custody, so there was no need to deal with Lena dishonestly. Beth actually felt a great deal of sympathy for the young woman. It seemed Mark had treated her with callous indifference. Yet it was still time for her to leave.

'It sounds like you've had a truly terrible time, Lena, but this really is between you and Mark. I'm not prepared to continue this discussion. Sorry, but you need to go.'

As far as Beth was concerned, the visit was over. To emphasise her decision, Beth stood up and walked to the door.

Lena followed her, stopping only to scoop up Chance, who had happily wiggled his way halfway under the couch. 'You stuck-up bitch! If you think that you and Mark can just take up where you left off and play happy families, then think again. Mark won't have his fancy job or his money by the time I'm finished with him!'

Beth went outside and walked past Lena's car in an effort to avoid her. Lena followed, shouting. 'Wait. Do you want Mark or not? I won't leave until you tell me.'

Beth increased her walking pace and headed through a gate that led to the stables. Dell, the collie, bounced eagerly along the path ahead. Behind her, Beth could still hear Lena calling out for her to stop.

A flurry of excited barking distracted Beth. In the paddock past the fallen tree, Dell had ambushed an echidna that was going quietly about his business of eating ants. He'd discovered a large mound of meat ants and was excavating it with strong front digging claws, harvesting the agitated insects with his long, sticky tongue as they crowded around. The furious ants were unable to penetrate his spiny hide with their stings or serrated jaws.

Momentarily Beth forgot about Lena and climbed through the fence to fetch Dell who, unlike the echidna, was in danger of being bitten. By now the echidna had half-buried himself into the ground, his vulnerable face and underbelly tucked safely away. Only his formidable spines, swarming with ants, were exposed.

Beth called to Dell, urging her away from the danger. A sudden bloodcurdling scream startled them both, and they swung around in the direction of the noise. A sickening sight greeted them. Lena, down on her hands and knees, was scrabbling around, reaching for something on the ground by the fallen tree. To Beth's horror, she realised that Lena was reaching for Chance.

The young woman had followed Beth, climbing through the fence while carrying the baby. As she hurried over the uneven ground in her strappy high-heeled sandals, she must have tripped – falling heavily near the log and triggering a defence attack from the wasps within.

Lena's screams were joined by those of her child, as the helpless infant, lying almost directly on top of the hive, bore the full brunt of the attack. Defying the angry insects and enduring scores of painful stings, Lena rescued her baby and lurched off in pain and panic, followed for several metres by the angry swarm.

Beth sprinted to the injured pair. Lena was standing by the fence, frozen to the spot, staring at her child who lay screaming and rigid in her arms. A tiger-striped wasp emerged from behind Chance's ear and crawled over his face. For a moment the two women stood speechless, too horrified to move. Then Beth sprang into action, flicking the wasp away and easing the baby from his mother's grasp. 'Get through the fence – quickly. Chance needs a doctor.'

The terrified young woman met Beth's gaze, then obeyed. At a stumbling run they made their way back up the path to where the cars were parked. Beth opened the passenger door of Lena's car.

'Put him in his car seat and get your keys. I'll drive you to the hospital. Now!' She paused to look at Chance. So far, his breathing didn't seem to be affected, if the volume of his cries was anything to go by. But his exposed limbs and face were covered in dozens of white weals with central red spots. Every inch of his skin was inflamed and swollen. Even the top of his head showed ugly welts through his fine blond hair.

Beth was well aware of the danger the child was in. Even without specific allergies, victims of a mass envenomation could suffer systemic reactions. Their entire circulatory and respiratory systems could fail. When Beth factored in Chance's tender age, the possibilities were truly terrifying.

With a massive effort she composed herself and turned her attention to Lena. The girl was sobbing with pain and fear, her own body and face covered in stings. Her skimpy outfit had provided almost no protection from the attack. With eyes red from crying and her hair damp with sweat and tears, Lena looked about fifteen years old.

Beth repeated her instructions as calmly as she could. 'Lena. Put Chance in the car. Are your keys in your bag? Where is it? We need to hurry.'

'In the house,' said Lena in a faltering voice. She placed the screaming child in his car seat, while Beth ran to fetch Lena's tote bag and packs of frozen peas from the freezer. Grabbing some tea towels to wrap them in, Beth ran back to the car, urging Lena to apply the cold compresses to the baby's inflamed skin.

With a grim face, Beth began the thirty-minute drive to the local hospital emergency room. During the interminable trip she failed to fight back tears. If only she'd exterminated the nest. Guilt welled up and settled like a terrible weight on her chest. But deep down, so deep that she barely knew it herself, she grieved for the wasp queen and the fate that inevitably awaited her.

Beth and Lena sat in triage at the hospital emergency room, taking turns to nurse the inconsolable child. Chance had been briefly assessed on their arrival and they'd been told to wait. This in itself was reassuring. To Beth's untrained eye, the baby seemed to be suffering no more than pain and swelling. His constant crying, although gut-wrenching, was probably a good sign.

Beth put a consoling hand on Lena's shoulder, regarding her with a new compassion. The young mother's deep distress for her child was etched all over her swollen features.

Lena looked up at Beth, eyes filled with a desperation that was instantly recognisable to any mother – the expression of someone who finds themselves powerless to comfort their child.

Chance's red, bloated face was distorted into a mask of agony. His howls were quieter now, coming in long, tired wails which for some reason were more disturbing than his earlier full-throated screaming. Lena must have also been suffering, yet the girl seemed oblivious to her own pain, fixing all her attention on comforting Chance.

Beth's thoughts turned to Lena's surprising revelation. So Mark had denied his partner affection and intimacy, isolating her and her baby at a time when a woman needed an excess of love and support. What was it that Lena had said? 'He's made me feel completely alone.' Beth's heart went out to the young woman. Then she remembered Lena's wild threats to ruin Mark and a small chill ran through her.

'Where the hell is the doctor?' cried Lena, just as a young intern and a nurse approached. The nurse took a short history as the stern-faced doctor examined the baby.

'We're going to admit him,' he said after a moment or two. In a quiet, reassuring tone he tried to calm Lena, explaining that the admission was precautionary but advisable considering the number of stings. Still crying, Chance was placed in a cot and wheeled away from his protesting mother by the nurse.

Another nurse arrived with some hospital forms. 'We need you to fill these out for us, and then we'll show you straight up to the ward. Don't worry, your baby is in the best of hands.'

Beth began to feel that it wasn't her place to stay. She turned to Lena. 'Let me ring Mark for you. He really should be here.'

'No.' Lena shook her head, looking flustered.

'But you shouldn't be alone, and I really have to go. My kids, you know? They'll be coming home from school.'

For the first time that day, Beth saw Lena smile.

'Yeah, actually I do know your kids. They're terrific.' It was now Beth's turn to smile. 'Don't worry about me,' said Lena. 'I've rung somebody. They won't be long.'

Beth relaxed, presuming that Lena had called her mother or maybe a friend.

The nurse came back and urged Lena to hurry up with the forms. 'You're needed in the ward,' she said. 'And yes, your baby is stable.'

As Lena turned to go, she gave Beth a heartfelt hug.

Beth suddenly remembered the original purpose of Lena's ill-fated visit that day. 'The answer is no,' she said.

Lena looked puzzled.

'That question you asked me earlier, about Mark? No, I don't want him back.'

Lena hugged Beth again, tighter this time. Tears trickled down her cheeks, moistening Beth's collar, before she disappeared into the lift after the nurse.

Beth sat awhile, processing the awful events of the afternoon. She glanced at her phone and got a shock when she realised how late it was. Rick and Sarah would be home soon. She texted them to say that she was running late. It was only when Beth reached the carpark that she remembered she didn't have her car. She called Karen who agreed to pick her up within the hour.

There was nothing to do but return to the emergency room, sit by the door and await her lift home. Now that the immediate crisis had passed Beth actually felt worse. If only she'd destroyed the nest. The image of Chance's tiny, swollen face and frightened eyes constantly hijacked her mind's eye. She dissolved into soft sobbing. When she rose to find a less conspicuous seat, her legs almost buckled beneath her. It was all she could do to keep from falling.

Beth found a seat in the far corner of the waiting room. As she quietly struggled with her feelings, she noticed a young man come in and approach the counter. Something about him held her attention.

He turned from the counter and she got to see him properly – exceptionally attractive, with something of a young Mark about him. His confident walk and boyish good looks reminded Beth of what had drawn her to her husband fifteen years earlier.

Lena appeared from the lift, eyes swollen from crying. She looked about as if searching for someone. Beth wondered if Lena looking for her. She rose unsteadily to her feet. But to her surprise, the handsome young man bounded to Lena's side and extended a muscular, well-tanned arm around her shoulder.

A brother, perhaps? The two seemed to be around the same age. Then the young man took Lena in his arms and tenderly kissed away the tears from her eyes. So, Lena had a lover. Beth edged her way to the door, reluctant to be noticed, although there seemed to be no fear of that. Lena was entirely focused on her male companion, allowing Beth to slip away unseen.

She spotted Karen's battered Land Rover arriving and waved her down. They drove off in silence. Karen glanced occasionally at her friend, but didn't press for an explanation. Once they'd cleared the town limits and turned up the road leading to the mountains, Beth related the extraordinary events of the day.

Karen was horrified to hear about the wasp attack, but for some reason she took the news about Lena's mystery boyfriend in her stride.

'You're not surprised?' asked Beth.

Karen gave her an odd sideways glance. 'I should have told you. Paul heard some rumours at the cricket club.'

'But Mark doesn't play cricket there anymore.'

'I know, but plenty of people still know him. The gossip mill grinds on'

'What sort of gossip?'

The silence yawned between them. Chatterbox Karen was being unusually reticent. 'Well?'

'Okay … there's talk of Lena running around right under Mark's nose. Either he doesn't know or doesn't care. Seems he's having problems at work too, mucking up some important deals. He's aggro when anyone tries to talk to him and won't listen. If he keeps it up, his job could even be on the line.'

Beth was more than a little annoyed at her friend for keeping this information to herself. 'It's nice to be the last to find out.'

'It's only hearsay and I know how much you hate people spreading rumours. None of it might be true. I didn't want to worry you.'

Beth considered Karen's words, conceding that she'd often expressed a dislike for gossip. Yet this was different. This could impact her children. 'You should have told me so that I could make up my own mind,' Beth said, sharply. 'Have you left anything out?'

Karen shook her head and they drove on in silence. After a few minutes, Beth relented and began a conversation to change the subject and ease the tension. But in the back of her mind she was going over all her friend had told her. It seemed that Mark might be in serious trouble.

CHAPTER TWENTY-EIGHT

~

From Zenandra's point of view, the attack on Lena and the baby had been a terrific success. The nest always buzzed with pride when they repelled intruders, though in truth the colony rarely felt threatened. Few dared to challenge them, and those like Lena who unwittingly ventured too close would never repeat their folly. Zenandra and her kin reigned over the garden as apex predators. Even snakes and dingoes acknowledged the wasps' supremacy, affording them a wide berth and meekly relinquishing their prey to the hungry hordes if required to do so.

The pair of wedge-tailed eagles that nested annually in the valley beyond Beth's garden feared the wasps from bitter personal experience. Earlier that season they'd watched helplessly as a swarm of wasps descended on their fledglings and devoured the eyes of the living chicks until only gaping hollows remained. The eaglets did not die immediately but lingered on for an agonising few days. The heartbroken parent birds abandoned them, realising that there was no point trying to raise their blind babies. After the chicks died, the insects returned to strip their tiny frames bare of flesh. The skeletons remained in the nest as testimony to the wasps' invincibility.

Within the colony, the royal brood chambers swelled with the precious kings and queens who would form the next generation. Some advanced larvae already lay pupating, their molecules magically reassembling themselves into an adult form. The colony now contained thousands of individual insects, each going about their own business in an apparently random way. But this was well-organised chaos. Mysterious communications between hive-mates allowed the nest to function as a single living organism.

The honeybee population was also on the rise. Aureole and her sisters had to provide more and more food for the hive. Foraging for nectar among the withering blooms in Beth's wasp-infested garden was now too dangerous. The bees were forced to search further afield. It was flowering season for the towering eucalypt forests surrounding Benbullen. Now honeybees joined the throng of nectar-feeding insects and birds attracted to the lofty blossom-covered treetops.

Aureole was now middle-aged for a honeybee. During the busy summer season, bees often worked themselves to an early death. She could probably only survive for another few weeks before her wings became too tattered to fly. A wing-damaged worker, unable to return to the hive after a day's foraging, soon fell victim to predators, cold or hunger. Yet for now Aureole remained productive and healthy, enjoying her soaring flights into the canopy of the giant mountain ash and messmate forest.

To start with, the canopy had been a safe place, shared with harmless creatures like stingless native bees, pollen wasps, butterflies and honeyeaters.

But the European wasps soon discovered this rich resource high in the treetops. They were present in ever-increasing numbers, dining on nectar and preying on the other insects.

Aureole dodged another wasp. It was a close call. She checked her pollen baskets, decided that they were full, and set off home. Momentous developments were afoot in the hive, and she was determined not to miss any of the excitement.

Two weeks ago, a critical turning point was marked in the history of the honeybee colony – swarming day. Up to half of all the workers in the hive, having gorged themselves on honey for days, had left the hive. Of the thousands departing, none would ever return.

The adventurers had been joined by their queen. Over the past few weeks she had almost ceased egg production. Her once bloated body was now trim and ready for travel. Some mysterious motivating force propelled the old queen to abandon her nest and join her restless daughters on their flight into the unknown.

They flew for an hour or more before the bees leading the swarm settled on the branch of a tall wattle tree growing on the edge of a forest clearing. Soon the rest of the adventurers joined them, including the queen. They formed a large, seething ball of bees and remained like this for more than a day. During this time, scout bees flew off in various directions, searching for suitable new homes for the swarm.

When they discovered a possible nest site, the scouts returned and danced to advertise their find. Other bees followed these directions and flew to investigate the new accommodation. If impressed, they returned and voted in favour with their own dance of approval. It was all extraordinarily democratic, and the decision was not made hastily. Several sites were explored, with some bees dancing for one location and then changing their minds upon viewing another. The combined consciousness of the swarm helped to decide, with each individual bee having her say. Once the choice was more or less unanimous, the swarm moved off to take possession of their new home.

The swarm chose a nearby tree hollow. A pair of late-nesting kookaburras inhabited the space with an almost fully-fledged nestling. Fortunately for them, the chick was mature enough to escape the tree cavity upon the arrival of the honeybee vanguard. The kookaburras would need to find a new nursery next year, never an easy task in the rapidly shrinking forest.

Back in the original hive, all might have seemed lost with the departure of the queen. Yet an attempt was underway to provide a line of succession. The abandoned workers planned to transform six perfectly normal larvae into infant queens.

Each baby bee lay horizontally within its own little waxen cradle. Worker cells were the smallest. Drone cells were slightly larger. Queen cells were not only the largest, but were also of unique construction. Echoes of waspine evolution could be found in the six inverted thimble-shaped chambers that hung vertically from the edges of the honeycomb.

Before leaving, the old queen had performed one last vital service to give the deserted hive a chance of survival. She deposited a single egg into each of the empty royal brood chambers. Although these eggs were identical to the thousands of others that she'd laid, they were destined to become new queens. The future of the colony depended entirely upon the successful rearing of these bees.

Four days after being laid, the eggs hatched. These special grubs received the food given to all honeybee babies during their first few days of life – royal jelly, produced in the glands of young worker bees. After the third day of life, larvae designated to become drones or workers had this special brood food diluted with a mixture of honey and pollen. By contrast, the future queens continued to be fed exclusively on royal jelly. As the precious larvae grew, their cells were enlarged and finally sealed. The six new queens lay quietly transmuting, suspended in their peanut-shaped cradles, unaware that they faced a race against time for survival.

Aureole arrived home just in time to witness the emergence of the first young queen. A crowd of admiring onlookers gathered. The queen was larger and more vivid than her worker sisters. Her long abdomen extended beyond her closed wings, which took several minutes to unfurl. It took some time for her soft body to harden and gain strength. Workers jostled each other, competing for the privilege of feeding the new monarch.

The young queen, however, seemed restless and much too distracted to eat. She began to search the honeycomb for the cells of her royal sisters who had not yet emerged. The crowd of worker bees understood what was to follow, and a kind of bloodlust overtook them. The virgin queen was to perform her first duty – the murder of the other queens.

With the active assistance of her subjects, she discovered a second queen cell. She clambered onto it, stabbed her formidable sting through the wax seal, and stung the unfortunate occupant to death in her bed. She slaughtered the other queens in the same manner, while her worker sisters encouraged the vicious rampage. In fact, when the new queen was a little slow to find the final cell, the workers themselves ripped open the cap and stung the last queen to death as she attempted to emerge.

Exhausted by her crimes, the queen rested. Meanwhile, her subjects unceremoniously disposed of the bodies of her victims, unfazed by the fact that they had been their devoted nursemaids only hours earlier. The hive only required one queen.

Pleased as Aureole was with the successful arrival of her new sovereign, she wondered if she might have been wiser to throw her fortunes in with the old queen. Though the intrepid swarm faced the challenge of establishing a new home, they did have the advantage of an experienced monarch with proven fertility. And they had escaped the growing threat of the wasps. Aureole fell asleep that night regretting her decision to stay.

Next morning, she woke to a commotion. All around her, bees were making a mad scramble for the entrance of the hive. The air was thick with the odour of alarm. Through her legs and antennae, Aureole could feel the vibration of thousands of agitated bees.

She joined the throng heading for the entrance. It was just past dawn, but the day was already oppressively hot. As she neared the hive opening, daylight penetrated the gloom, but her vision remained blocked by the crush of bees. All she could do was wait impatiently while the crowd moved slowly and inexorably towards the light. It was half an hour before she could see the danger for herself.

A vast gathering of airborne shadows swooped outside the entrance. As Aureole worked her way forward, she saw that the shadows belonged to European wasps, attacking in their thousands. As the defending bees spilled through the hive entrance, they were set upon by the wasps. The larger and heavier attackers forced the stricken bees down to a broad branch below the hive. Here they butchered their living victims, carrying away the juicy abdomens and leaving the bees to die.

The honeybees possessed few defences against a coordinated mass attack of this kind. Their stings were unable to effectively strike the wasps, who grasped them headfirst and swiftly decapitated them. By the time Aureole reached the entrance, the scene of carnage was truly appalling. Nearby branches and the forest floor were littered with corpses. Everywhere there were wasps, dissecting the dead and dying bees and flying away with body parts.

Aureole, filled with fury, launched herself bravely at the nearest wasp. Taken by surprise, it grasped her awkwardly, allowing her lethal sting to penetrate its soft underbelly. Once she had the tip embedded in her adversary, the sting automatically worked its way in deeper and deeper, all the while pumping venom.

There are barbs present in the extremity of a bee's sting that prevent its withdrawal from the skin of a human. It is ripped from the bee's body as she attempts to fly away, and she soon dies from the injury.

However, Aureole could remove her sting without damage when using it on the wasps, whose chitinous covering did not hold onto the barb as would the elastic skin of a mammal. Thus, she was able to safely extract herself from the dying body of her enemy. Savouring the sweetness of victory, she paused for a moment and then valiantly went on to use her sting with deadly force on several more wasps.

Eventually her luck ran out. The invading force noticed the damage being caused by this determined little bee. Three wasps combined to attack her. Overwhelmed, she died, despairing for her young queen.

The battle raged for hours. Terrified birds and insects steered clear of the fury. The sheer number of buzzing combatants caused the baking air to throb with sound. Inevitably, the larger and heavier wasps prevailed. At the height of the struggle, honeybees died at the rate of one per second. This frenzied pace continued until most of the defenders were dead. The wasps began to fly directly into the hive, jubilant at the prospect of robbing the bees' rich store of honey.

In the royal brood chamber, news of the rout reached the new queen. With no escape tunnel, she could do nothing but wait in the dark for the final attack to commence. A large contingent of the royal guard remained to protect her.

A wasp appeared at the chamber entrance. It was quickly despatched by the queen herself. More arrived, singly at first, and then in twos and threes. For a time, the bees mounted a fierce resistance and many wasps died. But they couldn't hold out forever. Eventually, a steady stream of wasps overpowered the exhausted guards and moved in for the kill. In total darkness, having never seen sunshine, the murderous young queen met her own violent end.

With the honeybees defeated, the victorious wasps rested before seeking out the hive's rich honey stores. They gorged themselves, oblivious to the increasing distress of the neglected and hungry bee larvae. These helpless babies would soon be slaughtered themselves and fed to the growing wasp hordes. Zenandra could indeed be proud of her children. The capture of such rich spoils virtually guaranteed the future of their colony.

CHAPTER TWENTY-NINE

Mark threw back the sheet as early light framed the window blind. He checked his phone – eight o'clock. Might as well get up; he couldn't sleep anyway. Mark swore and rubbed his back. Bloody mattress. He'd paid a fortune for the designer sofa bed in the spare room. Nobody had used it until now and just as well. Some sort of metal bar dug into your spine in the middle of the night like a medieval torture device.

Chance's cries sounded from down the hall. It had been three weeks since the wasp attack. The baby had spent twenty-four hours in hospital before Mark even found out about the incident, and then it was the doctor, not Lena, who'd informed him. Chance came home with his skin covered in bruises and blotches. He wouldn't settle and grizzled constantly. Mark wondered if his son's misery had as much to do with the tension in the house as with his injuries. He and Lena were living their lives at a kind of impasse. They barely talked to each other, allowing individual resentments to fester and grow.

Chance's cries grew louder. Mark hurried in the opposite direction. He did a quick check of the kitchen to be sure Lena wasn't already up. Empty. He should have known. The lazy bitch never emerged from her room before ten o'clock. Mark made a coffee and, although it was Sunday, decided to go to the office. Better than hanging around home, and he had some loose ends to tie up with an important account. The last thing he needed was a second client complaining about him.

Mark called Beth before leaving, but she didn't pick up. It had happened a lot lately. He blamed bad reception in the hills. She wasn't avoiding him, he was sure of that. Their relationship was better than it had been for years.

Beth had told him the circumstances of the wasp attack when she'd rung to ask about the baby's welfare. His throat had cramped in anger. How dare Lena visit his wife! She could have spoiled everything. Mark could not, would not, lose his growing emotional connection with Beth. Without it, he feared plunging back into emptiness and despair.

Mark's fury with Lena was deeply rooted in this fear. It overcame his natural compassion for his child. It clouded his perception, leaving him coldly indifferent to the suffering of his partner and blind to the danger she posed.

Mark left the townhouse, closing the door softly behind him. The air was hot and oppressive, the sky sulky and grey. He set off for the office, lost in a delicious daydream about reuniting his original family.

Jason rubbed his eyes, unsure of the time or what had woken him. The bedroom was stiflingly hot. He fumbled for his phone and swore. Great, he'd only had two hours sleep. Last night's eight-hour shift had turned into an eleven-hour shift when he'd been put on the door of the hotel nightclub. He'd only finished at seven o'clock that morning.

Jason checked his phone again. No texts or missed calls from Lena. Disappointment swept in. He pushed the heels of his hands into his eyes and squeezed his lids shut. He should go back to sleep. Lena's lovely profile swam into view and she turned to him with that teasing smile. Jason snatched at the half-remembered dream, despairing as it slipped away. He couldn't bear it. Someway, somehow, he must convince Lena to leave her boyfriend. Jason turned over in bed, restless, mind too busy to settle. He missed that girl like a limb.

According to Lena, Mark remained unaware of her affair. Jason found it hard to believe that any man could be such a fool. She'd concealed her infidelity by confining their encounters to a series of daytime trysts that left Jason hungry for more and frustrated by the subterfuge. He loved her, and was unhappy with the role of cuckold in which he'd been cast.

The three of them – Jason, Lena and little Chance – often spent the day together. They went for trips to the beach and picnics in the park.

Lena took Chance to see Jason play cricket. As he opened the batting for the local side, the beautiful young woman stood on the sidelines, cheering his every run and trying to explain the rules to the baby. His surprised teammates mistook them for Jason's family and were openly admiring of his gorgeous wife. If only it were true.

In the evenings, when Jason was unable to steal time with his lover, he retreated to his flat, no longer interested in any kind of a social life that didn't involve Lena. Night after night he sat alone at his computer, escaping into a cyberworld of games and fantasies. With an avatar that looked a lot like Lena, and a few clicks of the mouse, he could make all his dreams come true.

Jason longed for an honest, legitimate relationship with the woman he wished to marry as soon as she left Mark. Lena had promised to say yes, but first she intended to inflict some serious financial damage upon her wealthy boyfriend.

Jason got up for a glass of water and a leak, deciding it was too early to call Lena on a Sunday. He opened the bedroom window and frowned at his phone, willing it to ring.

Her preoccupation with revenge worried him a lot. He wished that she would focus a little more on her future with him, instead of on her past with Mark. Yet if Lena needed to punish the bastard to find closure, Jason would go along with it. He hated the man who felt he had a rightful claim to her.

The ping of a text came from his phone. Lena – she was coming over later. Jason felt the tension in his body slip away and he climbed back into bed. He could sleep now.

The front door closed – the softest sound – but Lena heard it. She exhaled. What a relief. She always held herself in so tight when Mark was home. His presence in the house made it hard to breathe.

Although ignorant of the affair, Mark was now aware of Lena's gambling habit. He'd promptly cancelled her credit cards and imposed a strict limit on her daily withdrawals. This had failed to curtail her regular visits to the hotel.

Lena didn't go there just to play the pokies. Her handsome lover worked there and she enjoyed his attention, of course. But she also looked forward to the companionship of her elderly friend, Konrad. Lena's own father had abandoned her and her mother when Lena was ten years old. With Konrad, she experienced the sort of unconditional approval and acceptance that she imagined a loving father might offer.

It was unusual for her to have a relationship with a man that was not based on sex, or convenience, or social climbing. Konrad seemed to appreciate her for who she was – no more, no less. He was generous with his wisdom and advice. Lena felt valued and needed by the lonely old man, who could nearly always be found at the venue enjoying the free coffee and snacks, or playing the machines, carefully and sporadically, to conserve the modest cup of coins he allowed himself.

Thanks to Jason, Lena was not too inconvenienced by Mark's attempts to curb her spending. He kept her supplied with as much cash as he could afford on a security guard's wage. Although she could no longer squander thousands in an afternoon, she had enough to enjoy a few games at the side of her mentor.

Lena frequently give any cash she had to Konrad, preferring

merely to chat and watch him play. They made for an odd couple – the lovely girl and portly old man.

Jason didn't trust Konrad. 'The old guy is taking advantage,' he'd warned her more than once. Lena didn't pay any attention, believing he was merely jealous of the position Konrad held as her most trusted confidant.

Lena confessed to Konrad her bitterness over her sham of a relationship with Mark and her vengeful plans for the future. Unlike Jason, Konrad seemed to understand that she couldn't move forward until she somehow made Mark atone for his betrayal. He convinced her, if she'd ever doubted it, that justice required that she settle the score. In Konrad, Lena found all her ideas and opinions reflected and affirmed. In his own way, the old man was as seductive as her young lover.

Lena had never been interested in her personal finances. With Konrad's advice and encouragement, she set about to remedy this. A search of Mark's home office and an investigative trip to the bank revealed some fascinating information.

Their luxury home was in joint names, an accounting ruse apparently, according to a tax agent's letter. A line of credit existed for half of the property's multimillion dollar value. That wasn't all. Mark was using accounts held in Lena's name to income split for taxation purposes. She cursed herself for not paying more attention. How many times had she signed bank documents and provided sample signatures without ever questioning what they were for? It soon became clear she could legitimately access these funds. However, she had ambitions to put a much larger hole than that in Mark's pockets.

Lena's previous laissez-faire attitude now worked to her advantage. Her naivete had caused Mark to lower his guard. He'd dismissed his partner as being incapable of involving herself in their financial affairs. But it is never wise to underestimate the enemy, and things were about to change.

Lena fed Chance a jar of baby food for breakfast and put him in his bouncer in front of the television. Then she went into Mark's home office and sat down at his desktop computer. Fingers crossed. Yes, it turned on without requiring a username. Now she tried to access their bank accounts. Okay, passwords and pin numbers were required, and she couldn't access his password manager.

Undeterred, she systematically emptied the contents of the desk draws. Mark always said to keep hard copies. An exhaustive search revealed nothing. Lena replaced the items as neatly as possible, hoping it would not be too apparent that things had been disturbed. She needed to think this through. Mark was a careful person who wouldn't leave important information lying around.

Lena had an idea. In their bedroom, a small safe sat on the floor of the biggest wardrobe. It contained her more valuable jewellery, but it also contained a small document file. She hurried upstairs, entered a number into the safe's keypad and opened it.

She soon found what she wanted in a manila folder. Two little cards with passwords and account details for their bank. She found other information too – lists of numbers relating to Mark's accounting practice. Lena didn't know what they were for, but she took photos of them with her phone, just as Konrad had suggested.

After replacing the contents of the safe, she returned to the office. The codes gave access to various accounts in her name. How foolish she felt, looking at her own fiscal information for the very first time. One gave access to the line of credit, and yet another was for Mark's personal accounts and investments conducted through the bank.

Sifting through the files, Lena found that they weren't quite as well-off as she'd imagined. Mark had been constantly complaining that her gambling had drained his funds. Maybe that was true. She'd lost a heck of a lot. Or maybe Mark's preoccupation with winning Beth back had made him neglect their affairs. It didn't matter. He'd have even less money by the time she'd finished with him.

The morning wore on. In between attending to Chance, deciphering the computer records and making copies, her investigation was taking longer than Lena had expected. She was fairly sure that Mark wouldn't come home. He'd taken to spending weekends at the office. Still, she couldn't be certain, and her nerves were a jangled mess.

It was almost lunchtime before she was satisfied with her work. Lena logged off, hoping that Mark would be too complacent to notice the time of the last login. She tidied up and was taking a final look round when her phone rang.

'What's happening, baby?' said Jason. 'I thought you were coming over.'

'On my way. Actually, I can't wait to see you. There's a favour I need to ask.'

'Ask away. Just hurry up will you, babe? I miss you.'

Lena dressed Chance quickly. She left with sweaty palms and a racing heart, thinking about her upcoming conversation with Jason. Today she would discover how far he was prepared to go to prove that he loved her.

On Monday morning, Mark couldn't find his laptop anywhere.

'Did you leave it at work?' asked Lena, sweetly.

'If I'd left it at work, I wouldn't be looking all over the damned house.' Mark swore beneath his breath and left without it.

As Mark drove away, Jason slipped from his car. He was parked opposite the townhouse, in a spot that offered a clear view of the driveway. Lena opened the front door for him as he approached, ushering him inside and through to an office.

'There.' She pointed to where Mark's laptop lay on the desk, along with a sheaf of pages filled with cryptic numbers. 'But won't Mark get a text if you mess with his bank accounts?'

'Two factor authentication makes an account harder to hack, but not impossible.' Jason took a phone from his pocket. 'Try texting Mark.'

'Why, what should I say?' Lena looked confused.

'Say *I love you.*'

'You're joking.'

'Go on,' said Jason. 'Humour me.'

Lena sighed and tapped something into her phone. A text sound chimed from Jason's mobile. He flashed her a playful smile. 'I love you too, baby.'

'Let me see that,' said Lena, laughing. Jason passed over the phone, where her message to Mark showed on the screen. Her eyes grew large. 'This isn't your normal phone.'

'No, it's a burner that I'll chuck when we're done. I used the bastard's personal details to temporarily port his mobile number.'

'You're a genius.' Lena sounded amazed. 'How?'

'Don't ask. Just know that I'll receive any security codes sent via SMS for the next few hours.'

Jason slipped on a pair of thin cotton gloves and set to work, matching up passwords and codes with Mark's client and trust account numbers. It didn't take too long. After less than an hour Jason pushed his chair back from the desk and looked at Lena, examining her face for any sign of hesitation or doubt. He found none.

'Well?' she asked, with a faint smile.

'Do you really want me to go through with this?'

Lena's smile broadened. She gave him an encouraging kiss.

Jason swallowed hard and began to transfer large sums from client trust funds into Mark's personal and investment accounts.

Ten minutes later Jason stood up. 'There,' he said, astonished by what he'd just done.

Lena, who'd been watching entranced as bank balances magically tumbled and climbed, gave a cry of delight.

A jolt of pure fear hit Jason, and he toyed with the idea of undoing his crime while there was still time. But one look at Lena's face was enough to quell his regret. She was not about to change her mind, and he was not about to disappoint her. The die was cast.

'Don't fiddle with anything else,' he warned. 'We don't want money turning up in your accounts. You'll be under enough scrutiny as it is.'

Lena nodded, eyes shining. She's not the only one who'll be under scrutiny, he thought to himself, staggered by the extent of his folly.

Jason's anxiety was tempered by his excitement over Lena and Chance moving in with him. His flat was modest but comfortable, and he owned it outright. He could use it as collateral for a loan on a larger place, somewhere with a backyard for Chance. Jason would happily work day and night to make Lena happy.

They'd booked a removal truck to arrive at lunchtime to collect Lena's things and a few sticks of furniture. Tonight, and every other night from now on, Lena would belong to him. His longing for this to happen outweighed his fear. He was in so far over his head now that the only path lay forward.

'Jason honey, you'd better leave,' said Lena. 'We don't want anyone to see you. I'll follow the truck over to your place this afternoon.'

Jason couldn't wait to escape. It was the first time he'd been impatient to leave Lena's side. He took off down the street at speed. Maybe once he was home, the pit of dread in his stomach would disappear.

As soon as Jason was gone Lena returned to the office. She had one more task to complete. Logging back onto the internet banking site, she opened the line of credit account linked to the house. It was in her name. She had every right. Taking a piece of paper from the pocket of her jeans, she carefully typed the account number it contained into the *transfer to* box. She then selected the maximum amount of credit available and typed this figure into the *amount of transfer* box. After confirming the transaction, she sat back for a moment, satisfied that now Mark could not afford to keep the house after she left. Then she rang Konrad to tell him it was done.

CHAPTER THIRTY

~

The ant grasped a fluffy bee head in her giant jaws. The ground beneath the honeybee tree, strewn with the remains of the bloody battle, provided easy pickings for the bull ants that lived on the edge of Beth's garden. They possessed a keen sense of smell located in their antennae, and the aroma of death attracted them in great numbers.

As they entered the vacated battlefield, their large compound eyes took in the thousands of velvety golden orbs, sticky on one side with smeared bee blood. The bull ants, like the wasps, had plenty of their own young to feed, and this windfall was most welcome.

As the worker ant returned to her nest, she repositioned her load a little to maintain her balance. Not that the bee head was much of a burden. She was huge by ant standards: forty millimetres long, armed with toothed mandibles for biting and a potent venom-laden sting. Her tough, chitinous body was glossy black and boasted, in certain lights, an iridescent green sheen. She was from an ancient lineage, unchanged in form and feature from her ancestors trapped in resin over fifty million years earlier. In size and shape she resembled a wingless wasp, but compared to that distant relative, the social structure of her nest was much more primitive.

Her colony consisted of several hundred individuals and their mound measured more than a metre wide – its surface decorated with pebbles and pine needles, leaves and twigs. Beneath the ground lay dozens of rough chambers, connected by passages and extending deep below the earth. Multiple ant holes allowed for flexible escape plans and rapid defence of any part of the nest. The proud insects wouldn't suffer the same fate as the imprisoned honeybee queen, trapped behind the single hive entrance, waiting in the dark to die.

The worker ant entered her nest mound and greeted her queen, who was herself venturing out on a trip to the forest to collect bee heads. In contrast to the bee and wasp queens, it was hard to distinguish the bull ant queen from her offspring, as she was approximately the same size. This was no pampered housebound princess, but instead a long-lived warrior queen, who ranged side by side with her daughters, defending and hunting with them. More than ten summers ago she bore wings, participated in her single nuptial flight, and then established her colony. Most of the sperm she received a decade ago remained alive inside her, available whenever she needed to fertilise her eggs. With luck, she could expect to lead the colony for many years to come.

The bull ant queen had few maternal instincts. She believed in tough love. Her eggs were not tenderly placed in intricately designed cells like those of the wasps and bees. By contrast, she dropped her eggs randomly around her untidy underground chambers.

Neither the queen nor her workers gave the young much attention. Feeding was a rough and ready affair. The adults dropped unchewed lumps of dead insect near the larvae, and then left them to fend for themselves. These babies needed to learn to eat raw meat right from the start. This caused them to be so aggressive that they cannibalised their weaker siblings if given half a chance.

The grubs were covered with rough, spiky hairs to protect them from their fierce sisters. They pupated in cocoons as tough as leather and emerged without assistance as fully functional and highly independent adults. In one respect, however, they did display a fierce allegiance to each other – nest protection. In defence, these insects were courageous, defiant, and supremely confident. They possessed a painful sting and were well known by animals and humans alike for their ability to use it. Thus, they were treated with respect by all and had few natural enemies. Even the ant-eating echidna viewed them as a meal of last resort.

Unlike the introduced European wasps and honeybees, this formidable native ant was a valuable member of her bushland community. Oddly enough, the bull ants performed a similar function to harmless earthworms, by excavating nests and thus aerating and improving the soil. They also kept the forest floor clean by scavenging dead or unhealthy animals. Bull ant adults were not vegetarians like adult wasps and bees. They might occasionally lap up sweet plant juices for variety, but otherwise they were dedicated carnivores.

After greeting her queen, the bull ant entered the nest and dropped the severed bee's head near several larvae. The hairy, eyeless, legless grubs sensed the presence of food and attempted to wriggle towards it. Indifferent to their struggles, the ant returned to the surface and headed back into the forest to collect more meat. She followed no scent trail, as other ants commonly did. Having lived in the garden for three years, she knew her way around perfectly well by sight.

As she approached the bee tree, she noticed the human child. Resenting this intrusion, she decided to repel him. The boy crouched to examine the golden fluff that covered the ground and floated in little eddies in the light breeze. He reached down his hand to touch it.

The bull ant seized her opportunity. Using her powerful hind legs almost like a grasshopper, she propelled herself with surprising speed in leaps and bounds towards the child. It was a bold attack by such a tiny creature. She was an ant with attitude. Unseen, she landed on the back of the boy's hand.

'Ow!' Rick felt her bite. The ant pinched his skin so viciously with her serrated mandibles that she drew blood. He shook his hand wildly, trying to dislodge his attacker. But the bull ant's reputation for ferocity and determination was well deserved. She held on doggedly to her victim with jagged jaws and curled her abdomen underneath and upwards, thrusting her long, barbless sting into the soft skin of Rick's hand. Then she injected her poison, a combination of formic acid and a venom similar to that of wasps and bees.

It was like he'd been stabbed. With a scream, Rick ran off, dislodging the ant with a final flick of his arm. She landed safely on the ground, only a little worse for wear. The noise and pheromones produced by the initial attack motivated dozens more foraging ants to mount an assault. They took the offensive, jaws raised, pursuing Rick some ten metres along the path – a savage sisterhood programmed to attack.

Rick sprinted for the house, yelling for his mother. Beth, collecting salad greens for lunch in the vegie garden, heard his cries and came running down the path to see what was wrong.

For a horrifying moment Beth thought that her son had suffered a wasp attack. The recent incident with Chance still haunted her. What a relief to discover that Rick had merely suffered a bull ant bite. Excruciating yes, but not life-threatening.

Comforting her hurt child, she guided him up the path to the house and applied an ice pack to the swelling.

'Where were you when you were stung?'

'Along the forest path a bit,' Rick managed, his sobs abating. 'I saw this fluffy yellow stuff on the ground and I bent down to touch it. Then the ant bit my hand.'

'What sort of stuff?'

'At first, I thought it was wattle flowers, but it's the wrong time of year for wattle, isn't it, Mum?'

Beth gave Rick an analgesic to ease the pain and sent him to lie down in the family room with the icepack.

'Can I watch more *How to Train Your Dragon* episodes?'

Beth nodded and swept a lock of hair back from her son's face. Once the burning sensation in his hand eased and he was on the improve, she took her own walk along the bush path.

Several metres into the forest shade stood an old gum tree. A fuzzy, golden carpet circled the base of its trunk. How curious. As Rick said, it was the wrong time of year for wattle flowers.

She bent down for a closer inspection, wary of lurking bull ants. Several of them were carrying away the fluff in their jaws. Definitely not any type of blossom. Bull ants were meat eaters.

Beth studied the odd substance a while longer, scooping some up with a curled gum leaf for a closer inspection. With a jolt she recognised the tiny, severed head capsules of dozens of honeybees.

Beth gazed around in horror as the sheer scale of the massacre hit home. She stood up and spotted a tree hollow high above her with a steady stream of European wasps coming and going. Beth dropped the leaf and knelt down to examine the carnage on the ground. A few dead wasps lay among the thousands of bee heads. The invaders had suffered their own casualties.

Beth despaired for the creatures of her garden. This was not competition. This was annihilation. She'd put the task off for too long. The wasp nest must be destroyed and she would do it tonight.

Her sympathy and admiration for Zenandra remained undiminished. How could one not admire the sheer magnitude of the queen's achievements? In the space of a few short months, from a meagre and solitary beginning, one little insect had conquered Beth's garden and extended her dominion into the surrounding bush. No predators existed in this new homeland to challenge her imperial design. But fear tempered Beth's admiration. If a new generation of queens colonised the local bushland, the wasp scourge would become unstoppable.

Beth took a deep, shuddering breath. She'd already decided against a professional pest exterminator. This was personal. If she was to kill the queen, she needed the courage to do it herself.

Beth retraced her steps, slipping through the fence and making the familiar detour to the woodpile. There, beneath the dry grass and piles of old logs, lay the nest. To a knowledgeable observer, the constant to-ing and fro-ing of the worker wasps betrayed the location of the concealed entrance. She felt a mounting pity for the insects, going about their lives with no inkling of looming disaster. Yet Beth was as helpless and impotent as the wasps were to change what was coming.

She returned to the house in the scorching midafternoon heat to organise her chemical weapons. Everything was planned and ready to go. It had been for weeks, ever since the attack on Chance. Beth's regard for Zenandra had prevented her, time and time again, from following through on the task. There would be no reprieve tonight. The safety of her children and the ecology of her garden depended on it. She must not let mawkish emotions distort her judgement. The wasp queen would suffer no such sentimental scruples should their situations be reversed.

Rick's hand was still painfully swollen, but he was otherwise in good spirits, bingeing episodes of *The Dragon Prince* on Netflix. Beth didn't tell him that the fuzz in the forest consisted of severed bee heads. It seemed too gruesome. She made him a snack before going to the garden shed to check on her preparations. From a cardboard box she took a beekeeper's hat and veil, a pair of double-lined gauntlet gloves, a long-sleeved denim shirt, a face mask and some overalls. At the bottom of the box lay two tins of Carbaryl insecticidal dust, two cans of fast knockdown insect spray and some sheets of red cellophane. The only other thing she needed was a torch.

Beth carried the box and its contents to the verandah. What a blessing that Sarah was spending the night with Bec. She wouldn't have been so easily distracted as her brother.

Beth went inside to see Rick. 'Can I borrow that headlamp your dad gave you for Christmas?'

'It's at the top of my wardrobe,' he said, mouth full of toasted cheese. 'But it's got a loose connection or something. It keeps flicking on and off.'

Beth went to her son's room and searched through the jumble of clothes, tennis racquets, and computer games. There it was. She could strap it to her head like a miner's torch, leaving her hands free to fumigate the nest. But when she tested it, she found that Rick was right. The lamp only worked intermittently.

Beth settled for a large handheld torch. Using sticky tape, she covered the lens with cellophane. This created a red filter, a colour far less aggravating for wasps. White light could provoke an attack.

Beth piled her tools of destruction into a bucket and headed out the door to the woodpile. Leaving the bucket in the corner of the paddock, she ventured as close as she dared towards the nest and tried to imagine the scene underground.

~

There was Zenandra, now frail and aged, still laying eggs and fussing about the royal brood cells as the last hatchling queen escaped the prison of her pupal case. As she emerged, her delighted sisters thronged around, eager for the opportunity to tend her. Unsteady on her new legs, she clambered clumsily about the comb. Zenandra herself nudged her daughter towards a group of her recently emerged royal sisters.

The new queens occupied an area to themselves. A cordon of worker wasps protected them from the attention of the young drones, whose tendency to mount any other wasp drove every member of the hive to distraction. Their rowdy behaviour was heightened by the collective expectation that many royals were due to embark upon their nuptial flight on the following day.

Each royal would fly a predetermined distance from the colony and then seek a mate. Incest was discouraged. Queens would actively avoid drones carrying their nest scent, but there were ample numbers of unrelated European wasps in the local vicinity. Zenandra's children enjoyed good prospects of finding eligible suitors.

The excited young royals caused mayhem by practising their flying within the overcrowded nest. The boldest ventured beyond the entrance, taking short flights into the baking air of the late summer afternoon. Their devoted worker sisters were on hand to feed and water them upon their return. The nest took on a celebratory air, each wasp personally priding herself on the successful production of the next generation. After all, even the lowliest worker shared a genetic make-up with these young queens. Through them, all hoped for immortality.

Beth turned away from the nest. Stop it. How could she destroy the colony if she kept empathising so heavily with the wasps? She hurried back to the house, making a conscious effort to clear these disturbing imaginings from her mind.

It was only one o'clock. Time dragged on. Beth tried hard to distract herself, but nothing worked. Not reading or listening to podcasts. Not cooking or cleaning her saddles. Certainly not gardening. She couldn't bear to see a foraging wasp fly past.

At three o'clock, Mark rang. 'I'll pass you to Rick,' said Beth.

'Why is Rick home on a Wednesday?'

'It's a teacher conference day at school – pupil free. I thought that was why you called; because you knew the children would be home,' said Beth. 'Although Sarah's not here. She's at Bec's.'

Mark didn't speak straight away. 'Yeah, of course. Put Rick on.'

Beth was happy to oblige. Mark was no longer a threat. Beth actually felt sorry for him, in light of his problems at work and Lena's secret affair.

Mark hadn't asked for a weekend with Rick and Sarah lately. He said that his unhappy home situation didn't allow it, but he still called or Zoomed them almost every day. Sometimes he talked to Beth as well.

Pity caused Beth to listen. He talked of his problems with Lena and his dissatisfaction with his career. Apparently he and Lena had grown apart and agreed upon an amicable separation. He wanted a sea change; to seek a new, more satisfying path for his life. He questioned the value of the extravagant materialism he'd been chasing for years.

Beth was impressed by this shift in her husband. He was closer to the Mark of long ago, before ambition blinded him to the important things in life. During one of their conversations, lulled by his new improved attitude, she almost unburdened herself of her guilty secret; almost blurted out about Lena and her lover. It was only fair that he should know. But something in Mark's manner had stopped her.

Although he always spoke well of Lena and Chance, at times he used a cold, resentful tone that belied his words. Was it really an *amicable* separation? Beth couldn't quite believe that the bitter, tearful young woman who'd confided her loneliness and pain the day of the wasp attack on Chance, could so easily accept the split. Beth remained unconvinced that Mark was being sincere. A niggling suspicion warned her that he might only be telling her what she wanted to hear.

Rick chatted happily away, regaling his father with an account of his bull ant bite. After a few minutes he said, 'Dad wants to talk to you.'

Beth took the phone.

'I was wondering …' He sounded uncertain, a first for Mark. 'I was wondering if I could come over and see the kids?'

'What, now?'

'If it's okay? I haven't seen them for ages.'

Whose fault is that? thought Beth, uncharitably.

'You know how things are between Lena and me. I was hoping to spend some time with them at your place.'

Beth thought of her planned mission that evening to destroy the wasps, and the importance of it. She could just imagine Mark's heavy-handed offers to help, his gloating over the exterminated nest. How ignorant he would be of her ambivalence. How painful it would be to witness his callous satisfaction with the completed task. No, if there was ever a time when Mark was not welcome, it was now.

Beth took the phone into the kitchen. Once Rick was out of earshot, she lied about having friends over for dinner.

'What friends?' said Mark. It was almost a demand, and Beth raised her guard.

'You don't know them. Look Mark, ringing up out of the blue like this? It's not your week for access and Sarah's not even home. She'd hate missing out on seeing you.'

'Please, Beth. It's been so long …'

Beth heard genuine disappointment in his voice, sadness too. 'Come up on Sunday,' she offered.

'Okay.' He sounded a little brighter. 'That's great, Beth, because I need to talk to you about something.'

'Go on.'

'Not over the phone.'

'On Sunday then. Look, I really must go.'

A long pause. 'I've never stopped loving you, Beth. You need to know that. Until Sunday.'

Mark hung up. Beth stood holding the phone to her ear, too amazed to move. He loved her? Oh no, what had she done? Mark had mistaken her offer of a sympathetic ear for something more. And by allowing Mark to visit on Sunday outside the regular access schedule, it seemed that she'd unwittingly agreed to some sort of absurd date.

The back of her neck began to crawl. Beth contemplated ringing Mark back to retract the offer, but couldn't bear to hear his voice again. It was only Wednesday. She'd call him in a day or two, when he wasn't so emotional, and set him straight.

The phone rang again. She panicked for a moment before seeing the caller ID. Not Mark – Noah. A rush of relief claimed her. His was a voice Beth longed to hear. She'd held herself so tight these past few months, consumed with keeping her children safe, distancing herself from work and friends – from Noah. It had been a desperately lonely time. Hadn't she sacrificed enough for Mark?

Beth stared at the ringing phone, thinking ahead to the grim task she'd set for herself that night. Noah was one of the few people who'd understand how torn she was. Beth answered his call.

CHAPTER THIRTY-ONE

Mark had just ended his call with Beth, when Ruth came into his office. She didn't knock, but for once he didn't mind. Although Ruth was one of the colleagues at Blue Sky who he particularly disliked.

She gave him a quizzical look. 'What's that grin for?' When she received no response, Ruth placed a manila folder on his desk. 'The Horizon account. Jack asked me to take a look. I found a few errors and fixed them. No need to thank me.'

Mark didn't rise to the bait. He just waited patiently for her to leave. Even Ruth couldn't spoil the pure, cathartic joy of having told Beth that he loved her. The gush of pent-up emotion left him dizzy. From now on there would be no more prevarication, no more hidden agendas. He was going back to his wife.

Such was Mark's overwhelming impatience to see Beth that he decided to go home early. He'd change out of his suit and tie, shake off the grey world of work and pay her a surprise visit. This was too important to wait until Sunday. It was time to get this romance on the road.

As he prepared to leave, his PA popped her head around the door. 'Mr Gray wants to see you. He says it's urgent.'

Mark cursed beneath his breath. As the firm's senior managing partner, Gray's word was law. Even so, Mark almost decided to ignore the summons. He was a partner too, after all – not an employee subject to anyone's beck and call. As Mark tossed up whether or not to respond, Steve Gray himself entered the office, closing the door behind him.

'I'll get straight to the point,' he said. 'There is a serious discrepancy involving one of your corporate client's investment accounts. I've taken a disturbing call from Christopher Tyler. He claims that a large proportion of his funds are, well … he claims they're missing.'

Mark's frustration rose another notch. First Ruth and now this. Didn't anybody know how to read a column of figures anymore? Did he have to waste his whole afternoon proving his professional competence to these morons?

'That's nonsense, Steve, and you know it. Here, I'll show you.'

Mark sat down at his desk and accessed the Tyler account.

Wait … what on earth? That couldn't be right. A massive unauthorised withdrawal had been made that very morning. Fighting a rising feeling of panic, Mark tracked the funds. No, not possible. The final destination of the missing money was his own personal bank account. Steve Gray, looking over his shoulder, seemed equally flabbergasted.

'I had nothing to do with this, Steve, you must believe me!' Nobody spoke. 'Someone's hacked into the system. See this logon at 8:05 this morning? I never accessed this file then. I was still driving to work.'

Before Mark had finished his sentence, an ashen-faced Steve was dialling the police. After a brief conversation, he turned his attention to the shell-shocked Mark.

'Of course we don't believe you're responsible. But the fact remains that the money from Tyler's account has somehow found its way into yours. If the system has been compromised, we need to find out how, why, and by whom. I'd like you to check on your other client files while we're here, just to be sure.'

Mark brought a trembling hand to his forehead. His stomach churned. It was the same story right across his portfolio. Substantial unauthorised withdrawals had been made from all the client accounts, with the funds transferred directly to Mark. The men looked at each other, thunderstruck. A prolonged silence reigned as the enormity of the scandal hit home.

Mark couldn't breathe. He stood up and paced the room, feeling trapped by the four walls and the tinted windows that couldn't be opened to let in fresh air. 'You must know it wasn't me,' he said at last. 'I wouldn't be so stupid. Why would I embezzle my clients' funds, all on the same day, in one hit, transfer them to my own account where they could be easily traced, and then come in to work as if nothing had happened? I couldn't hope to get away with it. I'd have to be an idiot!'

'You're right,' replied Steve, soothingly. 'You'd have to be an idiot – or perhaps unbalanced in some way. To be honest we've all noticed you acting a little oddly of late. Not that any of us think you had anything to do with this ...' Steve placed his hands in his trouser pockets. 'But it's only fair to inform you, Mark, that we'll have to tell the police about the apparent strain you've been under recently.'

Mark's legs went weak. His supposed friends and colleagues were about to throw him under the bus. He flinched as Steve laid a hand on his shoulder.

'Why not go and wait in the boardroom, Mark? Try to calm down. I expect the fraud squad will want to interview you when they arrive. And remember, we're behind you all the way.'

Like hell you are, thought Mark, picking up his briefcase.

Steve held up his hand. 'Best if you leave that here.'

Mark frowned and left the office. But instead of taking the lift up to the boardroom, he pushed the button for the underground carpark.

A growing fear gripped him. What if Beth believed these lies? He needed to discover the truth so that he could prove his innocence. If he could just have some time in the privacy of his home office before the police came for him.

Breaking every speed limit, he arrived home to find a removal van parked outside his house. The men were raising the tailgate and preparing to leave. An astonished Mark glimpsed several pieces of his own furniture inside the van before the doors slammed shut. 'Hey! What do you think you're doing?'

'This your place?' asked a short middle-aged man in overalls. Mark nodded. 'Well, you'd better ask your missus, then.' The removalist waved his hand towards the house. 'She told us to take this stuff to an address in Kingston. If you've got any problems, ring head office.'

The man handed him a business card and a copy of the job sheet. Bewildered, Mark watched the truck drive away. He stared at the piece of paper. The world had gone mad. After a few minutes, he walked up to the front door and turned the key.

Mark almost collided with Lena coming out. She was struggling with Chance under one arm and a suitcase under the other. When she saw Mark, she made a valiant attempt to push past. He blocked her exit, wedged himself between her and the door, and managed to slam it shut. Lena stood in the hall, defiant and uncertain.

'What's all this?' asked Mark, his tone measured and menacing. Lena backed away. Chance saw his father and smiled.

'I said, what's all this?' He spoke more fiercely this time. The baby's smile dissolved and he began to cry.

'Do I have to spell it out?' said Lena. 'I'm leaving you. Now, get out of my way.'

She tried to push past him again. Mark slapped her hard. Caught off guard, Lena lost her balance and fell, dropping Chance onto the hard parquet floor. The howling child crawled towards his mother. Mark picked him up and shut him in the dining room. His cries intensified, although the sound was muffled by the heavy timber door.

'Give him to me!' screamed Lena, scrambling to her feet and running for the dining room.

Mark followed and slapped her again. This time, she managed to stay on her feet.

'Where were you going?' yelled Mark. It surprised him to see a look of triumph on her face.

'To live with Jason, that's where. You remember, the guy who punched you in the carpark? I've been screwing him for months.'

Mark took in the information, trying to make sense of it all. So, she had a lover. Though his pride was wounded, Lena's infidelity didn't pain him too much. He was ditching her anyway. It would be convenient for him if she moved on quickly.

'I should have known you were nothing but a tramp. Go on then, get out.'

Mark had expected Lena to collect Chance and beat a hasty retreat. But something in her expression suggested she wasn't finished, and that his indifference had stung her more than his anger. He'd hurt her. Now she wanted to hurt him back.

'I suppose you think you'll just return to your darling Beth. But guess what?' Lena spat out the hateful words. 'Beth doesn't love you or want you. She told me. Once she finds out that you're a thief, she'll despise you.'

Mark's eyes narrowed. So Lena knew about the accusations of fraud levelled against him. The extraordinary surprises of the day were fitting together in an unlikely way, and the fog of confusion began to lift. Lena had set him up. But how? She was as good as computer illiterate. She'd need help. The pennies just kept dropping. Of course – the new boyfriend. Bewilderment turned to rage. She'd said that Beth didn't love him, didn't want him.

Lena finally got her wish. A mask of suffering distorted his features. Closing his eyes tight, Mark gulped to loosen the knot in his throat. When he opened his eyes, they shone with malice.

'That's a damn lie!' He crossed the room to where Lena stood and punched her in the face. She avoided the full force of his fist by turning and ducking, but it was still a terrible blow. Mark caught her by the shoulders as she fell, shaking her violently. 'It's a lie. Tell me it's a lie! Beth still loves me!'

'It's not a lie,' whispered Lena through split lips.

Tears welled in his eyes as he was forced to consider that Lena might be telling the truth. With one final backhander, he hurled her to the floor where she lay slumped in a heap. Behind the dining room door, Chance screamed louder.

Mark stared coldly at the battered woman. She only had herself to blame for goading him like that. And with such a wicked lie.

The prospect of a new life with Beth was all that stood between him and total despair. Mark tried to reassure himself that such a future was still possible. Not with those damned allegations hanging over his head, it wasn't. First, he'd need to expose the true identity of the embezzler. He looked in his pocket and found the job sheet given to him by the removalist. Bingo! There it was – an address in Kingston. Leaving his injured girlfriend and crying baby to fend for themselves, Mark leapt into his car and drove off on a mission to clear his name.

CHAPTER THIRTY-TWO

Jason wiped beads of sweat from his forehead as he helped move the final item from the van into the house. He paid the men and retreated inside, out of the glare of late afternoon sun. He peered through the curtained window back along the street. The van was driving away. Still no sign of Lena. Where was she?

Jason turned on the television to listen to the cricket, then went to the kitchen to pour himself another shot of scotch. Stress over the bank fraud had made him have a drink to calm his jangled nerves. One drink had turned into another and he was already a little buzzed.

He needed to call Lena and find out why she was so late. Where was his phone? Jason looked in all the usual places: in pockets, under couch cushions, beneath the bed. No luck. A nagging suspicion told him he'd left it at Lena's house that morning.

He was still searching for the phone when he heard someone knocking. Lena! She'd never need to knock again. He'd had a key cut and put on a heart-shaped opal key ring for her as a welcome home gift.

Full of booze-heightened anticipation, Jason ran down the hall. He flung open the door, ready to sweep her into his arms. What the hell? It wasn't Lena standing on his doorstep – it was Mark.

His unexpected visitor shoved the open door hard against Jason's face. Caught off guard, Jason let Mark push past him into the flat.

They stood in the hallway, sizing each other up. Jason knew he would live to regret all those scotches.

'Surprised to see me?' said Mark. 'You're the thug that assaulted me in the carpark, right? Turns out you're a swindler and a bit of a backdoor man as well. I don't really care about that last part. Lena? You're welcome to her.' Mark was breathing hard. 'All I care about is you confessing to the police that you hacked my accounts. How did you do it? From my laptop? Maybe you were in bed with my girlfriend at the time.'

Mark's voice was thick with fury.

'Anyhow, we can do this the easy way or the hard way. You come with me to the police, right now, and I'll try to make it as okay as I can for you. We'll untangle this stupid mess with as little harm done as possible. I'll say that Lena put you up to it. That she's got a screw loose. That you were being blackmailed or something. If you don't go to the police voluntarily, then pack your bags and prepare for some serious jail time. I'll make sure they throw away the key.'

Jason's mind was racing at a million miles a minute, but the alcohol stopped him from thinking clearly. Then he noticed something disturbing about Mark, or more specifically, about his white shirt. It had what looked like bloodstains down the front. Fear for Lena and loathing for Mark hit him in a single blind impulse.

'If you've hurt her, I'll kill you,' he said in a low voice.

Mark laughed. 'She's not worth it mate. Don't worry, Lena's okay, though she's not quite as pretty as she used to be. Will you still fancy a slut with a banged-up face?'

Jason snapped. He lunged and threw a punch.

Although not an experienced fighter, Mark had the advantage of a clear head. Stepping aside, he dodged the blow, leaving Jason unbalanced. The violent scene in the hotel carpark flashed into Mark's mind. Time to return the favour.

As Jason swung to face him, Mark landed his own punch straight to Jason's stomach. Jason doubled over in pain. Capitalising on his advantage, Mark delivered another punch, this time a telling head blow that sent his opponent reeling into the wall.

Jason's head smashed against a large framed print, shattering the glass. Sharp slivers rained down. A large shard stabbed him above the eye. It looked like it went deep. More lacerations to his scalp left his hair sticky with oozing blood. Jason slumped to a sitting position on the floor with his back against the wall, a red stream running from his forehead.

Mark came forward for a closer look. Jason's left eye, barely open, was filled with blood still pouring from his split temple. He looked in a very bad way.

For the first time Mark considered his own culpability in these events. Lena and her lover had got what they deserved, but he was rational enough to recognise that the police might not see it that way. Jason and Lena were both beaten and bloodied, yet he hadn't suffered so much as a scratch. Arguing self-defence might be a stretch. Mark crouched down in front of Jason. The bastard seemed to be unconscious. Perhaps he should try to stem the bleeding. Mark looked around for something to use as a pressure bandage. That T-shirt on the corner airer might do.

Mark never saw it coming. Jason had been playing dead, all the while feeling around behind him for a piece of glass to use as a weapon. He'd come across something better – his cricket bat. Jason grabbed the handle and used his good eye to line up his target. In one smooth motion, he aimed for Mark's head.

The bat collided with a sickening thud. Mark went out like the proverbial light, collapsing to the floor. It took all Jason's self-control to refrain from kicking the prone man. But it was more important to get to Lena, and in any case, he was getting the headache from hell. Curse his missing phone. Lena would have been trying to reach him, asking for help, wanting to warn him. While he'd been waiting uselessly at home like a sitting duck.

Jason swore, grabbed his keys and stumbled outside. Mark's car was parked directly behind his own, blocking his exit. He went back inside and searched Mark's pockets until he found his car keys. Better take his phone as well.

The hammering inside his head was growing worse as, still bleeding heavily, Jason roared out of the driveway. Mark's Mustang was fast and powerful. Under other circumstances Jason would have thought it a dream drive, but tonight it was more like a nightmare. He struggled to control the car, which seemed to reach tremendous speeds with the slightest touch of the throttle. Every now and then he had to wipe the blood from his eyes. So much blood. He wasn't feeling well. It wasn't just the headache – he was dizzy and cold and incredibly sleepy.

Jason barely noticed running the red light. The outside world was fading. The squeal of brakes came to him as if through a thick fog. Narrowly missing the entering traffic, he careened through the intersection, picking up speed. His thoughts were now nothing more than an incomprehensible collage of images: scenes from childhood, snapshots of his mother and his beautiful Lena. Seconds later, he lapsed into unconsciousness.

Still accelerating, the car ran off the road, flipping over as it sideswiped a metal safety railing. It landed on its roof, slid down a steep embankment and slammed into a massive electrical power pylon. The Mustang burst into flames. Jason and the car were incinerated in front of a small crowd of horrified passers-by.

CHAPTER THIRTY-THREE

It was almost time. From the sanctuary of her upstairs bedroom, Beth watched the sun sink in a blood-red sky behind the distant mountain. It lingered interminably, shooting rays of crimson far into the twilight as if struggling to remain aloft. Finally, abandoning the fight, it vanished, plunging all into darkness. In a few hours the full moon would rise to light the night. But until then, only the brilliance of the stars pierced the blackness.

Sunset provided scant relief from the sultry heat of the day. Beth stood at her open window, acutely aware of an absence. The familiar night chorus was gone. Something had silenced the noisy nocturnal throng of cicada and frog calls. No crickets chirped in the garden. Even the resident mopoke owl had fled. Except for the hum of mosquitos on the outside of the insect screen, the evening was eerily quiet.

Astonishing how the European wasps, in such a short space of time, had fundamentally altered the natural scheme of things. Mosquitos, operating under the cover of darkness, thrived as never before. The wasps had eliminated most of their natural predators from the garden. After her grim find by the dam, Beth was certain that even frogs had fallen victim to the wasps. Whatever the reason, the choristers were gone and Beth hated the silence.

Convinced that it was finally dark enough, she went downstairs. Rick was chatting on the phone. Who said only girls talk for hours? thought Beth, catching snippets of what sounded suspiciously like gossip. 'I'm going outside for a bit,' she told him. Rick took absolutely no notice.

That was a relief. Beth was reluctant to tell the children of her plans to fumigate the nest. It still felt like a shameful thing to do. She'd kept it a secret from everyone – everyone except for Noah.

Noah had listened to her pour out her story. Of how she'd found the European wasp colony and yet allowed it to live. Of the havoc the insects had wreaked on the ecosystem of her garden, and her strange affinity with their queen. Of her dreadful guilt after the attack on Chance and the inexplicable grief she felt at her decision to finally destroy the nest.

Noah had been one of those who warned her about the wasps. She'd half expected him to say, 'I told you so.' Yet he hadn't interrupted or judged. He hadn't tried to solve her problem by insisting on destroying the nest himself. He'd merely listened and promised to be there for her. Beth wondered again if she should have asked him to help. But no – this was something she had to do by herself.

Beth collected the torch, covered neatly in its red cellophane, from the verandah table. Then she headed to the woodpile, the way ahead lit by the strange rosy glow of the torchlight. There, in the corner of the paddock, was the bucket containing the Carbaryl and protective clothing.

Beth put the torch on the ground and stripped down to her bra and underpants. She stood for a while, allowing the faint hint of a breeze to cool her by evaporating the sweat from her skin. She was vulnerable like this. If Zenandra could read her mind, it would be an easy job for the wasps to kill her now, unprotected as she was. But Zenandra didn't know. Until recently Beth had almost been an ally, at least in spirit. At the thought of the coming attack she felt a chill, despite the sweltering night. Her skin raised goose bumps and she fought against a wave of fear.

With nervous haste, Beth donned the loose denim shirt and overalls, along with the beekeeper's hat and veil. She tightly buttoned her sleeves at the wrist and pulled on the double-lined gauntlet gloves. Instead of vulnerable, she now felt over-prepared. Nonetheless, she continued to follow the instructions given to her by the council.

Always make sure you have a fast and easy escape route from the nest you are treating.

Good advice. Pulling off her gloves, Beth went back to the fence and opened the gate. If she needed to flee the paddock in a hurry, she didn't fancy having to stop to unlatch it.

All was ready. Taking a deep breath, Beth pulled the gloves back on and fitted the mask. She picked up her bucket and advanced to the nest entrance. A desire to get the dirty deed over and done with as soon as possible overcame her. Grabbing a tin of Carbaryl insecticidal dust, Beth smothered the concealed nest entrance with the cloying powder.

Seconds later, wasps appeared at the surface. With a can of fast-knockdown insect spray, she squirted the unfortunate insects, causing them to fall to the ground, mortally stricken. They contracted into feebly struggling balls.

With the wasps immobilised, Beth grabbed the hatchet and chopped at the ground, trying to gain better access to the nest space. She alternated clouds of Carbaryl dust with floods of insect spray whenever she encountered defenders. A sort of zeal descended on her as she pressed her attack. Despite the mask, at times Beth herself was almost choked by the thick haze of powder. When she thought that she'd adequately completed the task, she would go another round, alternately chopping, dusting and spraying.

~

Inside the nest, the first indication of trouble was the vibration of footsteps overhead. Guard wasps, only lightly asleep even at night, swarmed from the entrance hole to repel the attacker. Although primarily diurnal, wasps could see passably well at night. They erupted from the nest, incensed that their young royals should be threatened on the eve of their nuptials. Superbly confident as always, they didn't know that their luck was about to run out.

In the first seconds of the attack, the red light from Beth's torch deceived their senses, giving them no indication of the direction in which the danger lay. Instantly, they faced an onslaught of toxic mist. The chemicals' effect on the wasps was akin to that of a nerve gas attack on humans. The guard wasps first experienced a deterioration of their vision; vision that was already compromised by darkness.

Violent tremors gripped their tiny bodies as their nervous systems lost control, preventing the insects from performing coordinated movements. The active ingredient in the pesticide poisoned the wasps' synapses, causing a tortured, continuous stimulation of their nerves. It was a slow death, taking some stronger individuals twenty minutes or more of desperate struggle before they lapsed into a paralytic coma.

As the poison penetrated further into the nest, the young queens and drones also met their fate. Too excited to sleep, many were still buzzing about in anticipation of their virgin flight the following morning. As the effect of the poison took hold, they hoped that Zenandra might protect them. Those that could fled towards their queen, convinced that there they would be safe. Dozens of young royals died in front of her, suffering from dreadful, fatal tremors.

Zenandra watched the carnage. Her powerful will to live saw her battle free of the doomed and damaged nest. She crawled towards the light of the stars. Though dying, Zenandra strove for one final experience of freedom. In her mind existed an image of the night sky, remembered from long ago, before duty saw her nestbound. With painstaking slowness, she clambered from the ruined nest and inched her way up a mound of dirt towards the starlight.

By this time Beth had halted her attack. There was no longer much resistance. Dying wasps lay everywhere. With one last hatchet chop, Beth broke through the surface above the buried tree hollow and saw the actual nest. It resembled a slightly squashed basketball. The stem had dislodged from the roof of the cavity, causing the whole thing to fall to the floor. Despite this, the extraordinary strength of the wasp-made paper gave the nest a good degree of resilience, and it had mostly held its form. The ground around it was littered with the vanquished wasps, not yet dead, but shrivelling and shuddering as their brilliant colours faded to grey.

Despite her precarious situation, curiosity overtook Beth, and she rashly removed the red cellophane from the lens of her torch. She could see clearly now. Leaning forward to examine the nest more closely, she lost her footing on the uneven ground and landed, torch still in hand, prone on the ground with her nose only inches from the destroyed nest. Fear gripped her but then let her go, as she realised the insects were all incapacitated.

A wasp, much larger than the others, managed to crawl from the carnage towards Beth's outstretched arm. With the last of her strength, Zenandra clambered onto the glove and curled up, trembling in the palm of Beth's hand. By her size, and the state of her battered wings, Beth knew it was the queen.

Using one arm, she pushed herself awkwardly to her feet, all the while cradling Zenandra tenderly in her glove. With her deadly fervour spent, Beth walked a little distance away from the nest, then sat down on the grass and wept.

Thus Zenandra was spirited away from the scene of death and destruction to the peace of the warm, starry night. Grateful for this final service, Zenandra died, releasing her tiny spark of energy back to the bush.

Slowly Beth's weeping reduced to sobs. In the torchlight, she examined Zenandra's wizened little body and marvelled that, over the course of the summer, this inconspicuous speck of life had wielded such an influence upon her own seemingly far more important life. Recognising that Zenandra was finally dead, Beth made a shallow furrow in the soil and reverently deposited the insect's body in the earth. With her finger, she covered it over. After a minute or two, she stood up, walked back, and shone her torch down into the collapsed pit. She kicked some dry, crumbly clay over the crumpled, brown balloon and the withered wasps. Gathering her tools, she marched back home.

Beth felt oddly desolate. Intellectually, though, she understood that she'd acted properly. She had to try to put the grisly task behind her. She wished that Noah was there. What a relief it would be to have someone to talk to; to debrief as it were. Beth felt deeply alone. She stopped to lock the poison away in the shed and change out of her overalls before going inside.

Rick met her at the door. 'Your phone was ringing in the kitchen. It's Grandma York.'

Beth took the phone from him, thinking wryly that perhaps the only thing worse than having nobody to talk to, was having Vanessa to talk to.

'I'll take the call upstairs.' Rick ran off.

Beth was frankly astonished to hear from Vanessa at all. Perhaps Rick was wrong? But no, she recognised the distinctive, plum-in-the-mouth voice of her mother-in-law.

'Elizabeth, my dear, you must sit down. I have some terrible news.' A long pause. 'There's no easy way to tell you, I'm afraid. So I'll just say it. Mark is dead. He died this afternoon in a car accident.' Beth took Vanessa's advice and sat down on the edge of the bed.

'How?'

'It was a single-vehicle accident. The police seem to think that he lost control of his car for some reason and hit a pole. I've been told that it burst into flames. Apparently, there was no hope of saving him …' Vanessa's usually controlled voice disintegrated into a sob.

'My God, Vanessa, I can't believe it. I'm so terribly sorry.'

'Of course you are, Elizabeth, as are we all. You were so good for Mark. It broke my heart when you two parted. Why on earth Mark hooked up with that little tramp is beyond me. And your poor dear children? Our family must gather the courage and faith to be strong for them.'

Beth found her mother-in-law's sympathy for Rick and Sarah a little false. As far as she knew, Vanessa had neither seen nor spoken to the kids for months, and had merely sent them an email and money for Christmas. During Beth's marriage to Mark, Vanessa had subtly undermined her. But it seemed that now, in comparison to Lena, Vanessa found Beth a highly desirable daughter-in-law.

'I'll let you know of the funeral arrangements as soon as I can confirm them. Such a heartbreaking time for us all. Robert is beside himself.' Vanessa's voice broke. 'Please give our love to our grandchildren. God bless you, Elizabeth.'

'Of course, Vanessa. Is there anything I can do?'

'You are too kind, Elizabeth. And with you and Mark just beginning to set things back on track. It really is too tragic for words. Robert is in no state to make the necessary arrangements. I suppose I will just have to fill the breach. Try to rest, dear, and I will call you tomorrow.'

Beth sat for the longest time. A million questions crowded her head. Mark was dead. How would she tell her kids? How would this change her life? Could she manage without his financial support? Would she miss him? And what on earth was that stuff about getting things back on track? So, Mark had been misleading his mother about the state of their relationship. Was he genuinely deluded or just mischief-making? She would never know.

Beth tried to get her head around the news. Dead. Mark was dead. Mark, who always seemed so in charge, so sure that he could make things turn out his way. Beth's thoughts turned once more to her children; his children too. They had just lost their father. She remembered what Vanessa had said about the car bursting into flames, and the full horror hit her.

For the second time that night, Beth wept.

CHAPTER THIRTY-FOUR

Mark woke as the first shafts of sunlight filtered through the dusty venetian blinds. It took a few minutes for him to emerge from the stupor of sleep. Why did he have such an aching head? Then the events of the previous night came back to him in a rush.

Mark opened his eyes, gasping as he tried to move cramped limbs. His body was sprawled over hard floorboards, and he had a painful crick in the neck where his head had been jammed up against a television cabinet. An early morning children's show blared loudly. Putting his hand to his head, he felt a large bump, like the lump a cartoon character might get after being struck by an anvil.

Mark staggered to his feet and looked around, fearing that Jason might be lurking somewhere nearby. But after a cursory search it became clear that he was alone in the flat.

He had to get out of there. Mark checked his pockets for his car keys. They were missing, along with his phone. Mark tried to stay calm – he kept a spare key hidden in a magnetic holder under the car. But when he went outside, he discovered that his Mustang was missing as well. Dammit, he couldn't even phone a taxi.

Jason's car was in the driveway though – a clapped-out old

Holden. Mark ran a hand over his aching head. Right. He'd find Jason's car keys in the flat and maybe some aspirin for his head. Mark returned inside and began a systematic search of the kitchen.

The television droned on in the other room. Irritated by the noise, Mark went in to switch it off, but he couldn't find the remote control. He was searching for it under cushions when the news headlines came on.

A man who died yesterday in a single-car collision has been identified as Mark York, son of Robert York, prominent CEO of the Transnational Banking Corporation. Mr York died yesterday afternoon when he lost control of his car and hit a pylon. The car was engulfed in flames. Police are investigating the circumstances of the accident. More news at nine o'clock.

Mark turned to look at the screen. He recognised the scene – a nearby intersection. Footage showed the burnt out shell of a still-smouldering Mustang wrapped around a steel tower. He sank down on the couch, shaking as the news sank in. Jason had stolen his car and crashed it. What's more, he'd been killed. Mark closed his eyes and rocked back and forth. How would he ever prove his innocence now? The true culprit was dead, and he could expect no cooperation from Lena.

Mark went into the kitchen, took some headache tablets, made a strong mug of coffee and sat back down in the lounge room. Finding the remote, he switched channels, surfing the morning news shows. In a few minutes, another report came on. But to his horror, this time there was more information: *The deceased driver has been identified as Mark York, currently facing fraud charges.*

Fraud? Mark reeled backwards. He hadn't even had a chance to tell his side of the story. He lay down, heart racing, trying to process the events of the past twenty-four hours.

Then it dawned on him. Since everybody believed that he'd died in the crash, no one would be looking for him. Mark began to calm down. Carefully, he thought through the bizarre situation he found himself in. The police investigation into the embezzlement would be called off following the death of the major suspect. The fraudulent transactions would swiftly be reversed, appeasing the victims and absolving Blue Sky of further liability. Public interest in the whole scandal would soon die down.

Beth would be devastated, of course. His first impulse was to call and reassure her that he was safe, but he didn't have a phone. Maybe it was just as well. Much better to think through all possible scenarios before revealing to anyone that he was alive.

Then there was Lena. Well, she'd be happy – until she discovered that her new boyfriend had gone and got himself killed. But then she wouldn't know, would she? It would seem as though Jason had dropped off the face of the earth.

Mark continued to play out the probable events in his mind. Next there'd be a funeral and they'd settle his estate. He hadn't changed his will, so Lena would receive nothing except the house, and without the means to keep up the mortgage payments she'd have to sell that. That luxury townhouse would fetch a good price and there'd be plenty left over to help her raise Chance. It was all he could do for the boy.

Now to Beth. Everything else would go to her and the kids, even his substantial life insurance. She would gain an enormous financial windfall if he died. Now it was obvious – he must remain dead. A small voice inside him tried to warn of the insanity of his plan, but Mark wasn't listening. His break with reality was complete.

He would hold off from telling Beth of his survival. Being so honest, she'd find it hard to act out the charade without support. Best to wait until the commotion died down and they could be together. It pained him to allow her and the children to suffer such grief, but it wouldn't be for long. In a few months they'd head overseas – with him on a false passport – and begin a new life. Mark imagined Beth's surprise and delight when he revealed to her that he was alive. It would be a magic moment. But for now, he needed to lie low.

Mark turned down the volume of the television and closed the curtains in every room. Finding house keys in the kitchen, he dead-locked the doors, set the burglar alarm and lowered the steel shutters over the windows. Jason had been very security conscious. The place was like a fortress.

The flat was also well provisioned with everything Mark might need for a few days. The perfect hideout. Mark opened the champagne and ate the chocolates in the fridge. He explored further, discovering candles in the bedroom, and a freshly painted spare room sporting nursery friezes and soft toys. It was deeply satisfying to know that Jason wouldn't be playing house there with Lena.

A third room was set up as a kind of office. Mark noted with a frown that items of his own furniture were stacked in the corner. Judging by the amount of state-of-the-art IT equipment, Jason was quite the computer nerd. This confirmed Mark's suspicions that the dead man was responsible for hacking into his accounts. He sat down at the desk and found no problems accessing Jason's computer. Living alone meant that Jason hadn't bothered to set up passwords.

Mark surprised himself by going first to the York family website, created by his mother as a blog and calendar of upcoming family events. Mark had never actually visited it before. Nothing like a death in the family to bring people together. Bizarrely, he found a moving personal tribute to himself, penned by his father. An uncomfortable knot formed in Mark's stomach as he read his father's words of pride and grief.

'I profoundly regret that over recent years I did not adequately express to Mark how much he meant to me. It was my intention to rectify this situation and to forge a closer bond in the near future. There will forever be a wretched vacancy in my heart, knowing that I left it too late.

To those of Mark's friends and family who are left behind, do not repeat my folly. Shower those dear to you with your love, today and always. I would trade all my worldly goods for the opportunity to tell my son that I love him, I value him, and I'm proud of him. God willing, I'll have that opportunity when I meet my maker. Till then, may the Lord bless him and keep him, and have mercy on his soul.'

Tears welled in Mark's eyes – such an unfamiliar feeling. He longed to talk to his Dad, to say that he wanted it too – that closer bond. He wanted to say that he'd always found it hard to express his feelings and that the pressure of getting ahead had left him time-poor and hollowed out. Like father, like son. If Mark had a phone he would have called his Dad, then and there, whatever the consequences.

The moment soon passed. The original plan was best. With a firm grip on his emotions, Mark returned to reading the details of his funeral arrangements. How peculiar to read them.

A knock on the door startled him. He held his breath, staying still as a statue, hoping the visitor would leave. The intermittent knocking carried on for a long time. Then Mark heard noises from the side of the house. He jumped at a sharp rap on the window nearest to him. Then he heard Lena's voice. Whatever would he do if she had a key?

'Jason, are you there? Please, Jason, answer the door!'

More frantic knocking.

'Babe, what's wrong? Answer the door.' A pause. 'Mark's dead. I need to talk to you. Answer the door. Please, I know you're in there.'

Half an hour passed without Mark seeming to move a muscle. Eventually the knocking and calling ceased. He sneaked down the hall to the front door and raised the shutters a fraction, just in time to see Lena's car drive off. A note was stuffed under the door.

Babe, Mark was killed in a car crash yesterday. They were going to charge him with fraud. The police think it was suicide, but they still seem suspicious. They took his computer away this morning. They don't know about you. We should stay away from each other until everything calms down. Hope you're okay. Love Lena xox

So, Lena had what she wanted and was giving poor Jason the flick. She probably imagined that she'd clean up on both the life insurance and the estate, and didn't feel much like sharing. Mark felt a moment of sympathy for the man who'd been so callously used, but it was fleeting. The pain of the false accusations was too raw, not to mention the little issue of the affair with his girlfriend. Oh, and the punch in the guts. No, the bastard deserved to suffer, maybe even die for what he'd done. It seemed to Mark as if some universal force was dishing out justice, and who was he to argue?

CHAPTER THIRTY-FIVE

Lena arrived back home, parked in the driveway and laid her head on the steering wheel. Chance was at day care, so she was alone. Her injured cheek throbbed with pain and she wondered if it was broken. As the morning grew hotter and more humid, the heavy make-up she'd applied to hide the bruising was coming off. Lena looked in the visor mirror: her bruised face was purple and swollen.

What to do now that Jason had mysteriously vanished? They needed to get their stories straight. She could email him. But when she got into the home office she remembered the computers had been taken away by the police. She couldn't phone or text him. When she'd tried to earlier, Jason's ring tone had sounded from behind the printer on Mark's desk. Thank goodness she'd found it before the police did.

She went inside and bathed her injured face, flinching at how ugly she looked. Where was Jason? Could he be ghosting her? It had happened to a couple of Lena's friends – men dropping out of their lives without warning, imposing sudden radio silence. But those had been casual hook-ups, not serious relationships. Those couples weren't in the middle of moving in together.

The doorbell rang. Please, let it be Jason. Lena rushed to open the door. Mark's boss was standing there. She'd met him a few times at work functions.

'Mr Gray.'

'Please, call me Steve.' He stared at her battered face. 'May I come in?'

Lena blushed, although it probably wasn't noticeable through the bruising. She invited him into the living room, wishing she was wearing something more appropriate than a skimpy sundress. 'Sit down, please.'

Steve settled himself on the couch and Lena sat opposite. His eyes wandered to her stiffly crossed legs. 'Firstly, Helena, may I extend my deepest condolences for your loss. Such a terrible tragedy. Mark was a greatly valued friend and colleague.'

Lena didn't speak. Steve's tone was less than sincere.

He opened his brief case and took out a document. 'If you'd sign this? It allows for a discreet reversal of the fraudulent transactions, thereby avoiding a scandal and allowing the firm to protect its reputation. Is there something more you can do to help perhaps—?'

Lena sighed and went upstairs to the safe. She fetched the security codes – the same ones she'd given to Jason twenty-four hours earlier.

Steve closed his brief case with a satisfied snap. 'On behalf of Blue Sky Financial Services I intend to deposit a generous sum of money into your account, Helena. In appreciation of your cooperation, and to help with funeral and other testamentary expenses.'

'Thanks,' she said. 'That's very kind.'

'And if there's any way I can help on a more … personal level, do let me know.' Steve handed her a card with a phone number. As he rose to leave, he hugged her. His arms lingered a little too long around her bare shoulders, and his hands brushed her breasts as he let her go. Creep! She pulled free and opened the front door to see him out.

Lena was disgusted – not so much with Steve Gray, but with herself. What sort of a person was she? With a flash of insight, she realised that she'd always depended on men to fulfil her needs: happiness, security, status, money – even revenge. Couldn't she do anything for herself?

Her dependent plans always backfired anyway. Where were the men in her life now? Where was her father? Where were Mark and Jason and Konrad?

Konrad. Lena had heard nothing from her elderly friend since yesterday, when she'd transferred funds from the townhouse's line of credit into his account. He'd said it would protect the money from Mark's lawyers. Lena tried to phone him again but her call went straight to voicemail. She didn't bother leaving a message.

Instead, she jumped in her car and drove to his address. It turned out to be an old housing commission apartment block. She climbed a short flight of stairs and stood knocking at his weathered front door. A voice from above sang out. Lena looked up to see a middle-aged woman peering down from an upper balcony.

'That'll do you no good, luv. Konrad packed up and left last night.'

'I don't understand?' stammered Lena.

'Said he'd come into some money and wanted to visit his daughter in London. Didn't even leave a forwarding address, and me and him've been friends for years. You never can tell about people, can you?'

'No,' sighed Lena. 'You never can tell.'

CHAPTER THIRTY-SIX

The day of Mark's funeral dawned hot and humid with an ominous sky. Beth gazed out the window at heavy grey clouds sliding eastwards against the backdrop of mountains. Too often lately there'd been the promise of relief from the drought, only for the storm clouds to pass without dropping their gift of rain.

A European wasp landed on the windowsill. It was large, with vivid colours – a queen. One of Zenandra's royal daughters perhaps; one who'd somehow escaped the carnage. Would Beth be exterminating this new queen's nest next summer? She shuddered. The sadness of the world threatened to overwhelm her.

'Mum, I can't do up the button on these trousers.'

Beth finished supervising her children as they dressed. Rick's mood was good, almost upbeat, as she coaxed him into black pants and a shirt with a button-down collar. The reality of his dad's death hadn't yet sunk in. Accustomed to not seeing Mark every week, the day-to-day rhythms of her son's life remained largely unaffected by his father's passing. Beth feared that when the truth hit home, Rick would take it very badly.

By contrast, Sarah was only too aware of the finality of her loss. She'd been teary and quiet since the news, missing not only her father but Lena and Chance as well. She hated the idea of going to the funeral and had asked to stay home. 'Sorry, darling,' Beth said. 'This is something we all have to do.' Then Sarah asked if she'd still be able to see her baby brother, but Beth couldn't promise that either. 'I hope so, but it all depends on Lena,' she'd said, giving her sobbing daughter a long hug.

Beth had phoned Lena on the day after Mark's death and found the young woman unexpectedly open to the call. The tragic news seemed to have changed her. No longer absorbed in the games she usually played, Lena was almost reflective about her life. She talked of her fears around raising a child alone and asked Beth about her experience as a single parent. Did this mean that Lena's handsome young lover was out of the picture? Or perhaps not committed to Lena and her son.

Beth checked the time. Karen would be here soon to drive them to Melbourne for the funeral. She examined herself in the mirror. A simple black suit, teamed with a black pillbox hat and a little veil. It would do.

The phone rang. Karen's raised voice sounded at the end of the line. 'The car won't start!' she wailed. 'Paul's tried everything and unfortunately my Land Rover is in the shop again. We're waiting on the auto club mechanic.'

'That could take ages,' said Beth, worrying whether she was up to making the long, sad trip herself.

'You can't drive when you're upset,' said Karen, reading her friend's mind. 'I'll pay for you to take a taxi and we'll meet you at the church as soon as we can.'

'A taxi all that way? It will cost the earth, and you know they're hard to find around here. Actually, Noah said he'd take us. I'll see if his offer still stands.'

Vanessa and Robert York were also preparing for Mark's funeral. Vanessa was elegant in an Yves Saint Laurent ensemble, bought especially for the occasion.

Robert wasn't dressed, though. He was standing out on the balcony, staring at the ocean. A tall, imposing figure, still handsome despite greying hair and advancing years.

He stood with slumped shoulders and an uncharacteristically bowed head. Since Mark's death, he'd sunk into a deep malaise. Guilt as much as grief had brought him low. For most of his life he'd let his son down, and now Mark was dead. No chance of redemption.

Robert scrubbed his hands over his eyes and looked through the French doors to where Vanessa was rehearsing her eulogy in front of the mirror. He lacked courage – that was the problem. Oh, he loved his wife well enough, but he'd always lacked a spine where she was concerned. Especially when it came to their son.

Vanessa had been tyrannical when it came to Mark. Robert had known that, but had given up trying to assert himself early on in the marriage, content to take the easy option of letting his wife have her way.

Their only child had become his mother's project. Vanessa rode roughshod over Mark's aspirations, insisting that he complied in every way with her expectations. Robert's tentative attempts to stand up for his son had been ruthlessly crushed. Abandoning Mark to his mother's not-so-tender mercies, Robert had buried himself in his work, becoming a distant and uninvolved dad. He knew now that it was unforgivable.

'Bobby, do come in, dear. It's time to dress.' Robert remained unmoved.

Making little tut-tut sounds beneath her breath, Vanessa came out and physically guided him back inside the house. She laid his clothes out on the bed, all the while making soothing, encouraging noises, as one might for a child.

Robert turned to Vanessa with a desperate look, as if beseeching her to make everything alright.

Taking his large head tenderly in her hands, she kissed him. 'Please get dressed, Bobby. The driver will be here precisely at twelve. You want everything to go smoothly, don't you, dear?'

He nodded, and with an enormous intake of breath began to dress.

Vanessa frowned. Robert's depression since Mark's death worried her. She hadn't seen him like this before. He and Mark had never been close, not since their son was a child. It was she who'd guided and formed Mark's character, insisting that he study at the top university in the state and organising for him to be inducted into one of the finest accounting firms in the country.

Robert, on the other hand, had never been properly focused on Mark's future. He'd even encouraged his son's brief interest in unsuitable pursuits such as music and architecture. If it wasn't for her, Mark would never have achieved the success and respect that he had.

Touching as it was to see Robert show his sentimental side, it was time for him to pull himself together. It had not been easy to organise the funeral and reception without him. Although, even if she did say so herself, she'd done a sterling job of it. The London Yorks were flying in, and a who's who of the uptown financial sector were attending. A High Court judge would even be there. Mark had discreetly managed His Honour's personal tax affairs for years. Well done, Mark!

Yes, the last thing they could do for their only child was to give him a fitting send-off, and that meant keeping a stiff upper lip. Thank goodness Robert was finally getting ready. Vanessa hurried downstairs to phone the church, praying that the liliums and lisianthus had arrived on time. They were hard to come by at this time of year. The florist had suggested substituting roses, but they were so passé.

A suburb away, Lena was dressing a sleepy Chance in his new outfit: little black gabardine overalls, a tiny white linen shirt and matching black jacket. How grateful she was for the excellent advice of the lady at the department store. He looked so cute. As the piece de resistance, she fitted a little elasticised bow tie around his neck and tried to fasten tiny black, patent leather booties onto his pudgy baby feet. This was not a great success. Chance managed to remove first the left, and then the right shoe, triumphantly bringing them to his mouth and using them as teething rings.

In exasperation, Lena gave up. Leaving Chance happily chewing on his shoes, she went to get dressed. She suddenly wished that she'd asked the shop lady's advice for herself as well. Having never actually been to a funeral, she was unsure what to wear. She'd seen enough on television to know that everyone always dressed in a very drab way. But black was not exactly her style.

It was a testament to her new philosophy on life that she hadn't rushed out to buy a new outfit. No, it was important now to be financially responsible, so she would make do. As she suspected, an inspection of her wardrobe revealed nothing in black. But she did have a sleeveless dress in a rather deep shade of purple. It was almost black really, and it wasn't tarty, being satin-lined and not too short.

She teamed the dress with a soft grey wrap and black stilettos. A ribboned clasp held her luxuriant blonde hair up in a deft French twist. Looking in the mirror, she was pleased with the effect.

Her bruised and swollen face had subsided substantially in the last few days. A quick trip to the emergency room revealed on X-ray that her cheekbone was indeed fractured, but would require no treatment other than rest and analgesics for the pain. As long as she plastered on the make-up, her injuries would go unnoticed.

Despite their recent problems, Lena's grief for Mark was very real. His death represented every abandonment that she'd suffered by the men in her life. What was different this time was her reaction to it. This time, she had a child to consider.

What if she didn't depend on someone else? What if she depended on herself? She could go to Sydney and stay with her mother. The two of them had a few issues, but compared to Vanessa, Mum was an angel. She was also potty over her first grandchild.

Things would be tight financially. The house was mortgaged to the hilt, thanks to her own stupidity in trusting Konrad. When it sold, she'd receive next to nothing. A quick conference with her newly hired lawyer informed her that since she wasn't married to Mark, the estate and life insurance went directly to Beth. She could contest, of course, but it would take time. There was an action in restitution available to her against Konrad, but she'd have to find him first. Once again, she was looking a long way down the track before she saw any money. In the meantime, she'd get a job.

The more she thought about moving to Sydney and standing on her own two feet, the more she liked the idea. Melbourne had been a disaster for her. Mark was dead. For all she knew, Jason and Konrad had conspired together to rip her off. After all, they'd both disappeared at the same time. She could expect short shrift from Vanessa, and Lena's gambling had lost her most of her other so-called friends.

There really was nothing for her in this town. Except for Beth, of course, who'd been the only one to support her over this terrible week. And Beth would thoroughly approve of this whole independence thing. Feeling in a more positive frame of mind, she picked up Chance and left for the church.

Mark inspected Jason's wardrobe. What did one wear to one's own funeral? The previous morning he'd visited a local costume shop and purchased a blond wig and matching false beard. He'd then spent most of the day practising how to wear them and perfecting his look.

He was quite pleased with the result. Now he needed to choose clothes. Mark decided against going formal. Selecting a pair of track pants, a T-shirt, and a hooded jumper, he tried them on. Good, they fitted him well enough. He tried on a pair of Jason's joggers. A little big, but not too bad with two pairs of socks. It felt rather creepy to be walking around in a dead man's shoes. He tried, rather unsuccessfully, not to think about it.

Mark knew the church. It was a large one, practically a cathedral. Trust his mother to make an event out of his death. Its main doorway was on the street. He planned to casually jog up to the doors and stand within the entrance area at the back of the church. Not far enough in to attract attention, but close enough to hear the service and observe the guests. His disguise and the hood of his sweater should hide his identity.

Mark raised the window shutters a fraction and saw gathering storm clouds. Good. Rain would give him an excuse for wearing a jumper on a warm day. He traded his Rolex for a sports watch he found in the bedroom. A bumbag, a water bottle filled with whisky, dark sunglasses, and an iPod with headphones completed the picture.

Looking in the mirror, Mark barely recognised himself. Protected by the guise of the anonymous jogger, he finally felt ready to leave. He took Jason's Holden and drove to the church, full of nervous anticipation, parking a few streets away so that Lena wouldn't see the car. How wonderful it would be to see Beth and his children again, even though he couldn't yet reveal himself to them. Mark was beginning to enjoy himself. After all, how many people got to attend their own funeral?

CHAPTER THIRTY-SEVEN

Festoons of flowers decorated the interior of the chapel. As the mourners filed in, they added their own floral tributes, placing them on a raised dais before the pulpit. A pipe organ played the Twenty-Third Psalm as sombre-faced men in black suits guided people to their seats.

It was a full house. Dozens of relatives were in attendance. An impressive turnout. Colleagues from Blue Sky were there, along with various other members of the legal and accounting professions. How soon we forget, thought Mark bitterly, as he peered at the crowd from the church door. Only a few short days ago, these same colleagues were ready to throw him to the wolves.

People were still streaming in, so Mark decided to go for a jog around the block until the service began. Perhaps he'd be able to spot Beth arriving. The prospect of seeing her sent a jolt of joy right through him.

A blue four-wheel drive pulled into the kerb further down the street. As he jogged towards it, a tall man exited the driver's seat, then went around to open the door for the front passenger. Mark stumbled to a halt as Beth got out of the car, dressed in mourning black. Mark was struck by her style and beauty. How he longed to be with her.

Rick and Sarah climbed out of the back seat. Beth seemed to gulp back tears, and the driver laid a familiar arm across her shoulders. Mark's nostrils flared with anger. Who was that man, and why was he with Beth?

But he couldn't stand there gaping. It was a busy footpath, and pedestrians were jostling him from behind. There was nothing for it but to resume jogging and hope he remained unnoticed. He passed within a few feet of his family, glancing back over his shoulder when he thought it was safe. Rick had turned to stare at him.

'Come on, Rick,' said Beth, 'This way.'

The boy trailed after his mother, still turning occasionally to watch the retreating jogger. Sarah was crying softly.

Noah walked with them for a few paces. 'I could come in with you.'

Beth shook her head. 'The church will be filled with Mark's friends and relatives. I don't want to make any awkward explanations.'

'Shall I wait?'

'No, you go home. Karen's on her way. I can catch a lift back with her.'

'I'll pop round tonight then,' he said. 'Check on how you and the kids are doing.'

'Noah, I need some time alone to process everything that's happened.' Beth took his hand and squeezed it gently. 'Come tomorrow. And thank you. Thank you for everything.'

Noah's face lit up with pleasure. 'Call me when you're ready,' he said, before returning to his car.

As they neared the church, they saw Lena and Chance approaching from the opposite direction. Sarah ran to meet them. Lena gave her a big hug and let her cuddle a willing Chance. Beth smiled. How very welcome the young woman always made her children feel. Rick ran over too, starting a rather noisy game of peekaboo with the delighted baby. Side by side, the two women entered the church.

A succession of people offered their condolences. It was amusing, really. Some offered their sympathies to Lena, many more to Beth. Some hedged their bets and commiserated first with one, then with the other, just to be on the safe side.

When Mark's parents arrived, Beth excused herself and went to meet them. Robert hardly acknowledged her, his expression pained and confused. Vanessa, on the other hand, was bearing up well. She regaled Beth with a list of all the problems she'd encountered organising the service, and then with an equally long list of the ingenious solutions she'd found to solve them. She began to point out various guests, name-dropping shamelessly. Beth, who had no idea – and even less interest – in who all these important people might be, was unimpressed. Vanessa soon moved off to seek a more receptive audience.

The service was about to begin. A large photo of Mark appeared, projected on the wall behind the chaplain. It had been taken ten years ago, early in Mark's marriage to Beth. Thick, dark hair framed his handsome, boyish features, and his eyes twinkled in a slightly roguish way. He was the epitome of debonair charm. Beth was surprised to feel a tightening in her chest. This was the Mark she'd loved before his cutthroat career stole him from her. A flood of long-buried feelings surfaced, threatening to overwhelm her. It required all of her resolve to compose herself.

The formal part of the ceremony commenced. The mourners sang a hymn and listened to a prayer with bowed heads. Mark was again standing at the back of the church. The funeral wasn't fun for him after all. It was an emotional roller-coaster ride, difficult to endure. To add to his misery, he couldn't stop thinking about the driver of the blue car, and the casual arm draped over Beth's shoulder. Who was he, and why was he with Mark's family? Beth had never mentioned a new man. Had she been deceiving him? The possibility made his jaw clench in a painful spasm. He took a swig of Dutch courage from the whisky-filled water bottle.

A Presbyterian minister recounted faintly amusing tales of Mark's younger years. Mention was made of his academic achievements and career highlights. Chance began to grizzle. People turned to look. Chance cried louder. Why didn't Lena take him outside? The child's cries made it hard for Mark to hear. Trust her to spoil things for him.

Frustrated, he was tempted to move forward. Yet that was too risky in a church full of people who knew him. Clearly, his mother had picked the music; it didn't speak to him at all. The minister droned on. Chance howled louder.

Someone started to sob. Who was it? Craning his neck around a stone pillar, Mark finally spotted the crier. To his delight, it was Beth. There was no sign of the man who'd driven her to the church. Sarah joined in with her mother's weeping. Mark drew in a sweet breath as tension drained from his body. Any lingering doubts about his wife vanished. Beth still loved him – that much was obvious.

His father also began to cry. Not soft sobbing like Beth and Sarah, but deep, pent-up wailing that vied with Chance's cries in volume. Mark could imagine his mother digging her husband in the ribs. She'd be mortified at this embarrassing display of emotion. He silently thanked his dad.

The sermon was almost over. A large group of men seated towards the front of the church began to sing. Ah, the Welsh National Male Choir. Nice touch, Mum. The rich tones and harmonies of the choristers served to soothe the congregation. Even little Chance stopped crying.

Mark edged forward for a better look at the coffin, an immense oak sarcophagus, ornately carved and richly inlaid with bronze. It was a closed casket. Were Jason's remains inside, or had there been next to nothing left of him? Mark's mind went back to that fateful afternoon when he'd confronted Jason at the flat. The bastard had almost killed him, and now he was dead. Served him right. Well, at least he was getting a decent send-off.

A few hymns and prayers later, and the huge coffin was hoisted onto the shoulders of six pallbearers. To the sound of solemn organ music, they slow-marched it outside, destined for a private cremation.

The mourners now began to leave, with the immediate family

moving off first. As the Yorks filed out, Robert's large frame was still racked with sobs. Mark felt irresistibly compelled to put a comforting hand on his father's shoulder as he passed by, despite the risk of blowing his cover. Robert stopped in his tracks.

'Don't worry, mate. He knows how much you love him,' Mark said in a low tone, attempting to disguise his voice and kicking himself for his careless use of the present tense.

Robert looked at him, intently. 'Did you know my son?'

'I did. He said you were a great dad.'

Robert stepped forward to hug him, and he instinctively returned the embrace. When they drew apart Mark was horrified to see recognition in his father's eyes. In a panic he pulled away, hurried from the church and jogged off down the street. Daring a glance over his shoulder, he saw Robert staring after him. Fool, he thought. Whatever had possessed him? Reaching the car, he jumped in and drove back to the flat. He needed time to think.

Back at the church, Vanessa was pleased to see that Robert seemed more like his old self. He stood in the vestibule, graciously receiving the sympathies of the guests, engaging them with great dignity. But her relief was short-lived. When the time came for them to proceed to the crematorium, Robert refused to get into the car.

'Go if you wish, my darling,' he told her. 'You've worked so hard to arrange all this, but I'm afraid I won't be joining you.'

'Why ever not?' asked an astonished Vanessa.

'Because our son is not dead.' With that he kissed his wife and walked away.

CHAPTER THIRTY-EIGHT

For Beth, the cremation ceremony passed in a blur. She felt out of place at the reception afterwards. Lena had decided not to attend. The only other person she might consider to be a friend was Mark's father, Robert, but he wasn't there either. Beth assumed he'd been overwhelmed by his sorrow.

After ten minutes, Karen arrived. 'Sorry I'm so late.' She launched into a long explanation.

'Never mind that,' said Beth. 'Just rescue me, will you? I can't take any more of this.'

She made her apologies to Vanessa, then escaped out the door with Karen and the children. Sarah was crying again. Although Beth was concerned by her daughter's distress, she was equally concerned about Rick's lack of reaction. He was clearly in denial. She'd done some reading about grief and loss in children, so she knew how the process was meant to go. It was important to encourage them to express their feelings. She'd try to get Rick to open about his father's death in the car on the way home.

Her opportunity came when her son told his sister to shut up and stop blubbering.

'Sarah's crying because she feels sad and misses her dad. How do you feel, Rick?'

'I'm fine. Can we get pizza?'

Things were worse than Beth thought. 'There's nothing wrong with crying when you lose someone you love, honey. It's natural.'

'But I haven't lost anyone,' said Rick with a hint of exasperation.

'Yes, darling, you have. You need to accept it.'

Karen slammed on the brakes as a truck cut in front of her. Beth suddenly regretted starting such an important conversation while they were driving through city traffic. 'We'll talk about this when we get home.'

'Can't I tell you about my dream? It's about Dad. I thought you wanted me to talk about Dad?'

'Of course, I want to hear.'

'Well, I dreamt that Dad's not really dead. He made a clone of himself. It was the clone that died in the car crash. Then Dad disguised himself and went around watching us to see if we were sad. You know, to see if we loved him or not. But he let me in on the secret. I bet he's really happy with Sarah. She's cried more than anyone. But I know he's not dead, so I'm not sad.'

Beth didn't know what to say. A minute passed in silence, while Rick went back to playing his Nintendo Switch.

'That was just a dream,' she offered, lamely.

'That's what I thought too,' said Rick. 'Until I saw Dad at the funeral today. He was in disguise, like he said he'd be. But when you looked at his eyes, you could tell it was him. Dad was there the whole time, at the back of the church.'

'Shut up, Rick. You're just making up stories!' yelled Sarah.

'Am not!'

'That's enough!' said Beth. 'You're both upset. I don't want you to say another word to each other till we get home.' There was sullen silence in the back seat. Beth could have kicked herself. Now she'd closed down the very discussion that Rick needed to have.

They arrived back at Benbullen in the late afternoon to find a car Beth didn't recognise parked in the driveway. Karen's children piled out of it, followed by her husband, Paul. He offered Beth his condolences, then gestured to the car. 'Borrowed it from a mate. Thought your kids might like to see their friends when they got home.'

Bec ran over and gave Sarah a big hug. So very sweet, and for the first time that day Sarah was smiling. Seeing Bec seemed to be just the tonic she needed. Rick was laughing and showing Simon his new game. Such an ordinary, familiar scene. Beth could almost believe that the horror of the past few days was a dream.

Her legs went weak as a tide of dizziness swamped her. Beth steadied herself against the car door, feeling physically and emotionally wasted.

'Are you okay?' Karen took her arm. 'What can we do to help?'

'Take my kids for the night,' said Beth. 'They could really use some normality.'

'Cool,' said Rick, while Sarah started telling a wide-eyed Bec about the funeral.

'Done.' Karen helped Beth into the house with a guiding arm.

'I'll go pack the children's overnight bags.' Beth could hear the tremor in her own voice.

Karen held up her hand. 'You'll do no such thing. It's just one night. I can find anything they need at my house.' She gave Beth a searching look. 'Please come home with us. Or maybe ask Noah over?'

Beth squeezed her friend's hand. 'I want some alone time.'

'Well, if you're sure …' Karen looked doubtful. 'I'll bring them home tomorrow at lunchtime so you can sleep in. Call me if you need anything – anything at all.'

'Don't worry about me. There's nothing I need more right now than time to myself; time to adjust.'

Beth kissed her kids goodbye and watched the cars drive away.

CHAPTER THIRTY-NINE

Beth went back into the house. She turned off her phone. Curling up on the couch, she replayed the events of the last few days over and over again in her mind. Before she knew it, she'd drifted off to sleep.

It was early evening when she awoke, feeling more refreshed than she had for weeks. What a rare luxury – to let the fears and sorrow of the past few days fade from focus. Beth fed the dogs, but left them in their run. She'd walk them in the morning. She took a long, lazy shower and slipped into a cool cotton nightgown. Things seemed far less daunting now she was rested.

What a mess, she thought when she went back downstairs. No housework had been done for days. Clutter filled the lounge room and dishes mounted high in the kitchen sink. Beth packed the dishwasher and turned it on, but left the lounge room as it was. There was something familiar and comforting about its lived-in look. The rest of the house was eerily quiet.

She was ready to go upstairs to bed when the dogs began to bark. A knock came at the front door. Beth was almost pleased that Karen had returned for some reason, despite all her protests about wanting to be left alone. She remembered that she'd turned off her phone, and felt a little guilty, hoping that she hadn't worried her friend.

Beth switched on the outside lights and opened the door. The globe had blown in the lamp by the entrance, making it hard to see. A man stood to one side, swathed in shadows. Beth blinked and peered into the gloom. 'Noah, is that you?'

The silence yawned between them. Then the man spoke, barely a whisper, but the sound thundered in Beth's ears. 'Who's Noah?'

That voice, so familiar. The figure stepped into the light and a wave of confusion engulfed her. It couldn't be. Her dead husband loomed in the doorway. Beth stood, open-mouthed, unable to process the evidence of her own eyes.

'Can I come in?' he asked, softly.

Beth stood stock still, unable to speak. He reached out, took her shoulders and gently moved her aside. She was too astonished to resist. His hands felt real enough and his breath smelt strongly of whisky. Beth's veins turned to ice.

Mark entered the house and closed the front door. Staying as close to the doorway as she could, she turned to face him.

'Surprised to see me?'

'How?' she stammered. 'How can you be alive?'

Beth flinched as Mark put a forefinger to her lips. 'Shh,' he said. 'It's our little secret. Nobody else can know.'

He sounded quite mad. Beth's mind desperately ran through possible explanations for the impossible. She was still asleep, and this was a dream. She was deluded and hallucinating. She was seeing a ghost.

His hand stroked her cheek and she remembered Rick's silly story. What had he said? He'd seen his father at the funeral. She examined Mark more closely. He wore a cheap polyester tracksuit and was growing a beard. Not his style at all. What else had Rick said? A disguise. He'd said that his father was wearing a disguise.

As the reality of Mark's existence sank in, Beth felt an explosion of fear in the pit of her stomach. Her chest hurt and she could feel her heart racing. Every instinct screamed at her to flee.

Beth reached behind her and felt for the door handle. Slowly, imperceptibly, she turned it until she felt an opening click. For an instant she was too terrified to move, but suddenly she found the courage to spring backwards. Beth burst through the door and make a mad dash away from the house.

Several seconds passed before Mark realised what had happened. This wasn't how he'd imagined it at all. His wife was supposed to be overcome with joy at his survival.

Beth had looked so young when she opened the door, with her tousled hair, fresh-scrubbed face and wide eyes. So lovely. The heavy outline of her breasts had showed through her thin nightgown, making him burn with desire. They were supposed to make passionate love. They were supposed to celebrate their new beginning, their new life together. It had to happen that way.

Disappointment gave way to anger. Mark charged into the night, fury mounting with each stride. Beth had a small head start, but he was faster. By the time she reached the end of the garden, Mark had her. As she tried to slip through the paddock rails, he grabbed her and hurled her to the ground. In an instant he was upon her, kissing her lips and biting her neck, pushing her nightgown up around her waist.

Beth felt so soft and vulnerable beneath him that his anger began to wane. She'd reacted from shock and astonishment, that was all. Once she accepted the truth, she'd come round. The moon was not yet risen, but he could see the pale porch light reflected in her eyes. It was too dark to read her expression.

Beth lay quietly, not daring to move. Mark no longer held the element of surprise. He was no dream, no hallucination, no ghost. He was flesh and blood and intent on raping her or worse. Her fear was replaced with a steely resolve to defend herself.

He spoke her name several times, but she didn't respond. Straddling her, he slipped her nightgown straps from her shoulders. With one final tug, he exposed her breasts then fumbled with his trackpants but couldn't pull them down. Beth seemed compliant enough now. He stood up and tugged them off.

As he lowered his body over her, she seized her chance. With all her might, she slammed a knee into his groin. The blow was well placed. Mark howled with pain and lost his balance. Beth shoved him off her and in an instant was away, diving through the rails of the fence and sprinting barefoot into the darkness.

Mark scrambled to his feet, cursing and pulling up his pants. He peered into the night and could see nothing. Rage mixed with fear and pain made him shiver, despite the warm breeze. All his future plans depended on Beth. They were going to start a new life together, far from here. He had no plan B. Mark turned to face the blackness, roaring out her name.

Beth crawled behind a big banksia bush, lungs burning and gasping for air. Her hiding place was a long way from the house and the night was profoundly dark. She felt protected, as if the bush meant to shelter her. Beth's knowledge of the land was excellent, while Mark's was poor. The valley was crisscrossed with timbered gullies, all leading down to Dingo Creek. She planned to make her way along the tree line, ford the creek to the road beyond, reach a neighbour's house and call the police.

But for now, she was content to crouch out of sight in the undergrowth, recover her breath and try to calm her hammering heart. It was pounding so loudly she was convinced Mark would hear it.

Mark returned to the house, muttering to himself and growing increasingly desperate. His wife had rejected him. It made no sense. She loved him, he was sure of it. He paced the kitchen, racking his brain for answers – praying that at any moment Beth would burst through the door, full of remorse.

Time passed. Ten minutes. Fifteen minutes, and still no sign. Rushing blood throbbed in his ears, drowning out the ticking wall clock. That man who'd driven Beth to the church – he must be to blame. She'd been expecting somebody when she answered the door, somebody called Noah. And she'd been dressed in nothing but a flimsy nightie.

Mark cracked his knuckles and hurled a vase of flowers against the wall. His fists clenched as the ugly truth hit home. Beth had deceived him and she'd have to pay. In the meantime, he needed a drink to help him think. As he walked over to the bar, he noticed the miner's lamp that he'd given Rick for Christmas lying on the floor beside the couch. It gave him an idea.

He picked it up and turned it on. Good – it worked. In the laundry he found a length of rope and shoved it into the pocket of his track-pants. Then he went out the back door to the dog run. Dell and Scrap had been locked up all day and were eager for some exercise. They greeted Mark excitedly, tails wagging, full of pent up energy.

'Let's find Beth,' Mark said, as he opened the gate.

He put on the headlamp and walked with the dogs to where he'd last seen his wife, calling them through the fence and into the paddock.

'Find Beth, find Beth,' he urged.

Dell barked her approval and the little one yelped in anticipation.

Beth's blood ran cold when she heard the dogs. They'd lead Mark straight to her. With no time to lose, she made her way down the dark gully, cutting her bare feet on the rough and broken ground and scratching her thinly clad body again and again on sticks and branches. Her progress was painfully slow, impeded by tea-tree thickets, bracken and the occasional wombat hole.

For half an hour or more she battled on blindly through the bush.

Then, exhausted and bleeding from cuts all over her legs, she slumped down on a stump to rest.

Looking back over her shoulder, she was horrified to see a beam of light. Mark. He was wearing a headlamp and coming quickly down the grassy hill adjoining the gully. With the advantage of a torch and the help of the dogs, he would catch her soon. The gully wouldn't hide her if the dogs betrayed her.

Feeling around for some sort of weapon, Beth managed to tug a lump of wood from the ground. She emerged from her cover and moved into the next paddock. She might have a better chance of defending herself out in the open.

By now, Mark was just on the other side of the gully. His torch danced like a wicked firefly through the trees, coming ever nearer. Beth backed away, swinging the heavy lump of wood, hoping for a miracle.

Suddenly the light went out. Why would Mark turn it off? Then it struck her. Mark must be wearing Rick's headlamp. She gave quiet thanks for that faulty connection. Of course, the temperamental torch could click back on at any moment, but at least it had bought her some time.

Beth edged her way towards the next gully, afraid to turn her back on her pursuer. She tripped over a fallen tree and fell, hitting her head. An odd buzzing noise rang in her ears as she scrambled to her feet. Beth prayed she hadn't suffered a concussion. She needed all her wits about her.

A rustling sound came from the darkness. Before she had time to run, Scrap and Dell appeared from nowhere, licking her toes and whining with excitement. Beth exhaled and laughed out loud with relief. Without his torch, Mark had been unable to keep up with his canine guides. He'd never find her in the dark now. But Beth's reprieve was short-lived. Behind her, the great silver orb of a full moon rose above the trees, lighting the night.

Surrendering to her fear, Beth fled blindly across the paddock, followed by the dogs. Mark's lamp was still off. She reached the cover of the trees and crouched down, trying to keep the dogs quiet as her lungs tore at the air for breath. Looking back across the open ground, she saw Mark's dark figure emerge from the moon shadow cast by the gully. Beth stood and ran, praying that if the dogs stayed with her, she might still elude him.

CHAPTER FORTY

Mark spotted Beth running, with the shadows of the dogs at her heels. Sensing victory he raced after her, covering the ground in swift, confident strides. He jumped a fallen tree lying in his path, but in the moonlight he misjudged the distance. Mark tripped, and fell heavily to the ground. The impact of the fall made his head-lamp flicker back on. What a stroke of luck. He now had a definite advantage.

As he scrambled to his feet, he heard a soft background hum that became a distinct buzzing sound. Dusting himself off, he saw insects flying towards the beam of his lamp. Moths or something. He swatted them away from his face with the coil of rope. But the buzzing grew louder and louder. Then he felt an intense burning sensation on his hand.

Mark lost his balance and crashed awkwardly back to the ground. He screamed as a river of fire ran up his arm. Stay calm, he told himself, shining the beam of his torch about, trying to identify the source of his pain.

Wasps. European wasps were erupting from the ground, crawling over his body and exposed limbs. A shriek of pure terror escaped his lips. Desperately he tried to ignore the pain and climb to his feet, but they were swarming so thickly now, attracted by the lamp and flying directly at his face.

Wasp stings hurt, but they are more painful than poisonous. If Mark had, despite the agonising stings, dragged himself away from the nest, he might have escaped. But this ignored the psychological effect, the almost uncontrollable panic caused by such a mass attack. Mark was so terrified that he lost the ability to reason. Instead, he desperately tried to defend himself.

Mark shared the characteristic attitude of most people towards insects – ignorance about them, fear and dislike of them, and a desire to kill them on sight. He also vastly underestimated the extent of the danger.

Mark didn't know that in Australia's mild climate, some European wasp nests did not decline and die in the autumn – they continued to grow. His luck had run out. He'd stumbled upon such a super-nest.

Unchecked by the previous winter, it had kept producing royals month after month, and not all the young queens had sought out new territories. Many remained within the nest, cooperatively reproducing and contributing to a vast population of wasps. This one perennial nest alone contained a staggering 120,000 workers, more than two hundred queens, and measured two metres wide.

Mark's violent swatting merely antagonised the insects, and the bright torchlight drew them to his head. Maddened by pain, he threw himself forward onto the ground in a vain attempt to shield his face and protect his mouth and eyes.

By now, the mass envenomation was harming his muscles, damaging his blood vessels and attacking his nervous system. Mark's veins and arteries began to leak, dropping his blood pressure, making him dizzy and faint. His skin ballooned with ugly swellings. His lungs filled with fluid until he was struggling to breathe.

Mark's entire body felt like it was being pierced by razor-sharp, red-hot skewers, and the more he writhed around, the more he exposed himself to the assault. Convulsing in pain, he forgot to protect his face and let out a series of anguished screams. Instantly, the wasps advanced.

As Beth fled across the paddock, Mark's first ear-shattering shriek rang out. She dived for the shelter of some tea-trees, too frightened even to turn around. More bloodcurdling screams tore through the night. The dogs lay whimpering at her feet as clouds obscured the moon.

Plucking up her courage, Beth peered behind her in the direction of the noise. She saw the faint glow of a torch near the fallen log that had tripped her earlier on. But it was static, unmoving. Was all the screaming a ploy to trap her? Surely not. Such frightful cries could only be made by someone in genuine agony.

What on earth was happening to Mark? Dell licked Beth's hand and trembled as the tortured screeching continued. Beth curled up on the ground with the dogs, covering her ears, trying to block out the nightmarish sounds. After what seemed like an eternity, the cries disintegrated into anguished, choking gurgles that were almost more disturbing.

The wasps climbed into Mark's open mouth and stung his tongue before clambering down his throat and attacking his tonsils. He frothed at the mouth and the tormented screaming stopped. His body went limp as shock set in.

He couldn't breathe as his throat swelled, blocking his airways. His face turned blue and he lapsed into unconsciousness. Mark had already been stung hundreds of times, and more wasps kept pouring from the nest. His body spasmed one more time, and his heart failed.

This time, Mark really was dead.

Blessed silence. Beth remained on the ground in the foetal position for what seemed like an eternity, afraid to move. When she finally unfolded herself and dared to look back, the faint glow of the torch was still there. It illuminated an odd golden mist that was hovering halo-like around the fallen log.

After a few more minutes, Beth stood up. The dogs cowered on the ground at her feet, reluctant to move. Clouds scudded sullenly across the sky, revealing the round, bright moon and a slice of stars. Taking a deep breath, Beth stretched her aching limbs and crept from her hiding place in the tea-trees. Cautiously, she inched her way towards the torchlight. As she drew closer, she could hear a familiar, low buzzing drone and she was hit by a sickening realisation – there was a second nest.

Now she stood directly in front of the fallen log. Mark's lifeless form lay on the other side. Thousands of European wasps swarmed about his body. Attracted by the torchlight, they crawled thickly over his swollen face and up his nose, pheromone-driven to sting even after their victim was dead.

'Beth!'

Someone was shouting her name. She looked up to see a figure with a bright light running down the hill towards her.

'Beth, I'm here.'

Noah's voice. Thank God. She'd asked him to stay away until morning. How grateful she was that he'd ignored her request. Beth stumbled up the hill to meet him, with the dogs at her heels. She sagged into his arms.

'I had to know if you were okay.' He stroked her tangled hair. 'Then I saw a strange car and found the door wide open. There was a smashed vase in the kitchen …' He ran the torch over her bruised and bloodied body. 'Beth, what on earth has happened to you?'

'Turn off your torch.' She took Noah's hand and led him to the body. Mark's lifeless eyes bulged grotesquely. His mouth, wide open as if still gasping for air, was filled with a crawling mass of angry wasps.

The pair of them stood in shock as still more insects streamed from the colony entrance beneath the log. Soon Mark's corpse had disappeared beneath the seething swarm.

Beth could not grieve for Mark. She'd already grieved. He'd somehow cheated death, but not for long. Her exhausted emotions struggled to rise to the occasion. Horror, sorrow, astonishment – they were all there. But in the end, simple relief won out.

The full moon sailed high in a sky free of clouds. It flooded the bush with its friendly light – the bush that had offered her its comfort and protection. Noah lifted Beth, cradling her in strong, protective arms. She whispered a prayer of thanks to the sacred night as they began their long trek home.

ACKNOWLEDGEMENTS

Thanks go again to the team at Pilyara Press. You are all magnificent!

Special thanks to Desney King for her eagle-eyed copyediting and terrific suggestions.

Thanks to Janine for proofreading and to Robyn Grundmann for her editorial help and putting up with my passion for amateur entomology.

Thanks to my chief beta reader, Marcia Ray, for her skill, support and enthusiasm.

Thanks to my lovely agent, Clare Forster of Curtis Brown Australia.

Lastly, I am indebted to Robert Frost whose wonderful poem, *A Considerable Speck*, provided the inspiration for this novel.

ABOUT THE AUTHOR

Bestselling Aussie author Jennifer Scoullar writes page-turning fiction about the land, people and wildlife that she loves.

Scoullar is a lapsed lawyer who harbours a deep appreciation and respect for the natural world. She lives on a farm in Australia's southern Victorian ranges, and has ridden and bred horses all her life. Her passion for animals and the bush is the inspiration behind her best-selling books.

Visit Jennifer's website to receive a free book, and also enter the monthly prize draw! If you enjoyed this novel and have a moment or two, please leave an online rating or review. Reviews are of great help to authors.

www.jenniferscoullar.com